# Jennifer Chapman

# JEREMY'S BABY

BRANDON

A Brandon Original Paperback

First published in 2001 by
Brandon
an imprint of Mount Eagle Publications
Dingle, Co. Kerry, Ireland

10 9 8 7 6 5 4 3 2 1

This book is published with the assistance of
the Arts Council/An Chomhairle Ealaíonn

The author has asserted her moral rights.

ISBN 0 86322 277 3

Cover design: id communications, Tralee
Typesetting by Red Barn Publishing, Skeagh, Skibbereen
Printed by ColourBooks, Dublin

Most of the things that really matter in our lives tend to happen in a trice: birth, death, conception, each more poignant, painful, pleasurable when they are the result of a sudden accident. Chapman's story deals with all three of these big ones in quick, quirky writing reminiscent of her earlier novels published a decade ago.

Now she is dealing with a new aspect of our lives, the work-obsessed generation which has moved on, or tried to. Values have changed, but is that enough; are we equipped to deal with the sudden accident that forces real change?

Two couples who have been the greatest of friends and whose lives, hitherto, have followed the relatively smooth path of upward mobility are stopped in their tracks as a result of a single moment of madness.

What follows provides us with a chilling exposé of raw human nature, stripped of the posturing pleasantries, the kissy-kissy greetings, the safe urbanity.

We will all recognise parts of ourselves in here, the parts that frighten us most.

*Jeremy Holden is a literary editor. His own novel,* The Best of Friends, *is published next year.*

# PROLOGUE

'It's me,' Angel told Marsha's recorded voice, not thinking to leave her name or even for a moment considering that there must be dozens of 'me's' in Marsha's life, let alone Paul, but he was more 'the Big I Am'. Marsha was the sort of woman who made you feel like the only 'me', which was of course the trick, and why you didn't consider it.

'And sorry I've missed you,' Angel added. 'It's been longer than I thought.'

Weeks rather than months, but it was a friendship blessed with delight, and Angel needed a bit of that at the moment. She was at a stage where nights seemed very long but were too short to mend the day. She found it difficult to sleep because the caseload in her life added up to more than enough, keeping her in a semi-conscious state of anxiety over what could be resolved and what could not. And in the morning there would be the slightly jet-lagged feeling, a little removed from reality, floaty, yet it didn't seem to affect her work. She would not allow it to. Other things, perhaps, but not the obsessional drive that made weeks fly by and put old friendship on hold.

The message was an invitation. 'Come for the weekend. Love to Paul.' Both bits wholehearted, although it was Marsha she loved more now, and there would always be that

7

splinter of awkwardness with Paul, an old wound of the sort you had to pretend did not hurt any more because there was no other help for it. Everyone had inflicted or taken wounds like that at some time or other, but either way you never really forgot.

'Yes. Invite them if you like. Sorry, another call,' Jeremy had said when she phoned him with the idea, as if it could not wait until the evening. It was not really so much that it couldn't wait, more that this was how they communicated, marriage by telephony, even though they lay side by side in the same bed most nights, smiled at one another in passing, planted auto-pilot kisses and tacitly carried on as if the real thing would still be there when they had time for it.

There must have been all manner of things they had talked about over the past weeks at home, in the evenings and at weekends, but pinpointing a single memorable exchange or decision, impossible. Until this moment it had even occurred to Angel that absolutely nothing was going on between them.

'So, we're reduced to this,' she thought, before an in-coming call pushed aside further bleak reflection. Later in the day it caught up with her again, but only long enough to hope that the weekend would happen and somehow mark a change.

'It's me.' Marsha listened. Angel's voice was one she liked to hear but was prepared to resist tonight. The nineth of ten voices on the machine, eight of them demanding answers from her, answers and commitment. A weekend in the country with Angel and Jeremy would be a couple of days to draw breath, to hide away from the now constant recognition that dogged her every move in London. Because she never watched it herself, she never really believed that anyone else saw daytime telly, but over the past few weeks it seemed as if the whole world had nothing better to do than watch her toss pancakes and roll pastry. There'd been a man in a pinstriped suit who'd cornered her by the flower stall on the traffic island by South Ken. tube, fished out a shopping list from his briefcase and insisted she sign it. Someone lurking outside the studio had given her a pancake to sign, even had a felt tip he said he'd already tested on batter.

Such madness. Paul loved to hear these stories, but always steered them, however devious the route, into episodes that had frustrated his own day. Perhaps a weekend in the country would do him good, although it was when they were with Jeremy and Angel that she liked him the least. He'd drink too much and get a bit bumptious, silly boy, so that she would want to say to Jeremy and Angel, 'He's not really like this, you know,' and, of course, they did know. And, of course, she wouldn't say it because she'd never do or say anything to hurt Paul, nothing she could imagine, anyway.

However, she hadn't done anything about wiping the messages before he came home and started to run through them himself. The only call for him was from a woman with a Silk Cut whine who'd been trying to sell him a pension for the past six months, and whom he could not bring himself to turn away with the simple truth that he was stony broke but actually didn't need a pension because his wife was Marsha Miller. End of story.

So the only call to talk about was Angel's.

'D'you suppose they mean this weekend?' he said, coming into the kitchen and peering over Marsha's shoulder, sniffing the aroma of something Marks & Spencer exotic on the stove. Marsha was less energetic than her success implied. She also got very tired these days and had settled for a life of compliance at home if she was to survive all the rest.

'Probably.' She knew he would want to go.

'We'll say yes, then.'

'If you like.'

'I'll call them, shall I?' He was already at the phone.

Angel answered. He would have preferred Jeremy. Every time it was Angel he experienced the split second that ripped away a layer of flesh.

'It's me,' he said. 'It's me, Paul.'

# CHAPTER ONE

'Right. We've done spin doctors, Camilla and the Booker Prize. What next?' Paul paused for suggestions, holding out his glass as Jeremy approached with the wine bottle. They had started off with something rather good, a chilled red Loire that Jeremy and Angel had found during a recent weekend in Saumur; but by now they were on to whatever was left in the rack from the last time there had been a party.

Paul, loquacious, well-oiled, began again, spluttering a little as he gulped down a swig of whatever it was Jeremy had just poured.

'The thing is. . .' Paul often preambled with 'the thing is'. 'The thing is, why do we do it?'

'Do what?' Marsha said, stretching her long legs up and on to the sofa, effectively robbing Jeremy of the seat he had occupied for most of the evening.

'Work so bloody hard.'

Jeremy had returned to the sofa and, after a brief moment of staring at Marsha's legs, lifted her feet and sat down, now placing them on his lap. Neither looked at the other. This sort of behaviour was just a thoughtless piece of nonsense, old friends relaxing in safe intimacy.

Across the room Angel, Jeremy's wife of fifteen years,

11

surreptiously took a glance at her watch. A quarter past midnight. She did not want to be the one to break up the evening, but she felt bone-weary tired and wished they could stop now, just leave everything, the dirty plates and glasses, Paul's overflowing ashtray, just rise above it to the bliss of bed on a Saturday night with a long, late Sunday morning to follow.

'I suppose it's because that's what we choose,' Jeremy answered Paul's bloody question.

'That's right. That's right. I mean, what else is there in life?' Paul said. Did smoking and drinking together make you more drunk, wondered Angel.

'Oh, we're not going to get on to the meaning of life, are we?' Marsha said.

'Could be,' murmured Jeremy, settling back into the evening, just beginning to catch a whiff of old times: the three of them, Paul, Angel and him, drinking Scotch till three, four in the morning at the flat in Shepherd's Bush; talking, talking, talking; the discovery of new and astounding thoughts when it was still possible to find new and astounding thoughts.

The idea of Scotch took hold, and when Angel got up and said 'Coffee?' he said, 'How about some of the hard stuff?' And as it was at that moment Angel passed through the sleepy tiredness of the past hour and into late night wakefulness, she set to and obliged. Perhaps she, too, had glimpsed a suggestion of the past, a sensation he, Jeremy had not come across for years, even though they had never stopped seeing Paul, regular weekends for more than a decade, ever since he and Angel had moved out here to the sticks. Paul with Susan. Paul with Karen. Paul with Penelope. And, for the past, what? . . . six years, Paul with Marsha. Thank God, Paul with Marsha. None of the others had quite made up the quartet, and if Paul had married one of them perhaps the weekends would have diminished, which would have left a void. Paul and Marsha, Angel and Jeremy, like a fine painting, a favourite book, a friendship that had become precious. God, I must be drunk, thought Jeremy.

Absentmindedly he stroked Marsha's feet. Paul was batting on about Hillary Clinton of all people.

'D'you think they still do it?' he heard himself enquire, as if the thought had not really meant to come out.

Marsha moved a little and let out a small piece of laughter. 'Course not.'

'How d'you know?' Paul said this in a way men sometimes speak to their wives, with that edge. It would sound rude said this way to anyone else.

'I just know,' Marsha said, ignoring her husband's tone. Jeremy and Angel had, when alone, talked about this one and only glitch in the perfect friendship the four of them enjoyed.

'D'you suppose they row about it afterwards, when they're alone?' Angel had said. She and Jeremy, with nine years advantage, had long ago agreed never to pick up on what either had said in company. They had begun to do so, in the early days, but neither wanted the strain of lifelong caution, the marital policing of social intercourse.

'How? How do you know?' Paul was not going to let this one go.

Marsha, ten years older than the other three, tended to show a mature tolerance when such moments arose, a gentle smile, perhaps a little sigh. A sign to Paul to let it be. But tonight she seemed less willing to back off.

'Why should they be any different from the rest of us?' she said.

The ghost of a cold, wet flannel passed over the room.

'Well, you're the one who's always tired,' Paul broke through the divide, suddenly pushing the evening into a new dimension of awkward truth. 'What is it, six months since we did it?'

'Paul.' This was Angel, trying to put a halt to things.

'Seven,' said Marsha.

'Nine,' said Jeremy.

'Christ,' said Paul, cheering up.

'What's wrong with us?' asked Marsha, looking round at the other three.

'Like Paul said, we all work hard. That's all,' said Angel, who was avoiding looking at her husband. This sort of talk might ensure they didn't go to ten months, but she was damned if she was going to play ball tonight, not after what he'd just said. It was like blackmail. She could feel his gaze hovering in her direction, waiting to catch her eye. The way she felt was contrary, she knew that, but the longer you put off making love the more difficult it was to restart. It was almost as if you became shy of one another. She had begun to worry a bit. Perhaps they would never make love again. Perhaps Jeremy would find someone else. Maybe he already had. No. He just didn't have the time. Just as she didn't. Travelling to London each day, that was knackering enough, and his job on the paper, he couldn't risk letting up for a moment because there were God knows how many others just waiting to take his place. Literary editor of a national newspaper. How many jobs were there like that? You could count them on the fingers of a stab in the back. She was glad she didn't have to do the London bit, but her job in Cambridge was hardly nine-to-five.

'So, what are we going to do about it?' Paul's tone had altered, almost sober, almost purposeful, but he was looking at Angel, not Marsha.

'It's an idea,' said Jeremy.

Angel looked at him now. What was he saying? What were the pair of them cooking up, he and Paul? They couldn't be serious. Her gaze slipped to her husband's lap where again he was caressing Marsha's feet, her bare brown calves. Marsha's eyes were closed, as if she had abdicated the decision to the other three, as if it really hardly mattered.

'Why not?' she murmured.

A surge of anger rushed hot into Angel's face, then fell away into sudden enervation. 'Why not?' she heard herself say. 'Why bloody not?'

Of course, there were plenty of reasons why not. Breakfast the following morning. The awful possibility that one of them

14

might, however obliquely, allude to what had happened. But none of them did.

Sitting in their dressing gowns round the kitchen table, Paul in a ghastly silk affair, Marsha in white towelling, Jeremy too, Angel in her old orange candelwick, the one she'd meant to take to Barnardos but had left hanging in the spare room. Sitting there, reading the Sunday papers, eating their way through a whole loaf of toast, the moment of dread slipped by, faded into the aberration of the previous night to be closed off, put behind them like a binge in a broken diet. They had got away with it. There was a little, intoxicating guilt that added to their sense of well-being rather than spoiling it. They had all kissed one another this morning, straight off, as if of one mind. Nothing had changed. Everything had changed.

# CHAPTER TWO

Paul and Jeremy had met their first day at Stoop. They were among the handful of day boys allowed to attend the two-hundred-and-fifty-year-old school with its noble history of fagging, flogging and febrile academic pursuit. But day boys were not quite the thing, with the suggestion of family impoverishment rather than the convenience of living close by. Day boys were sidelined and therefore stuck together. Paul and Jeremy, who might otherwise have looked elsewhere for close friendship, set about making the best of what, for years to come, would seem more like a practical arrangement rather than a chosen alliance.

Paul was good at games, an all-rounder, cricket, rugby, hockey, squash. Jeremy, slow in physical coordination, excelled in the classroom. Where they coincided was in being taken over by testosterone, the simultaneous discovery of 'women', as they always referred to girls. So, while their boarding classmates were busy buggering around with each other, Paul and Jeremy joined forces for visits to the pub, hanging around the rec after dark for groping sessions with girls who called then 'Nob' and mimicked their public school pronunciation.

It was Paul who attracted the women. He looked a bit like Paul McCartney, who, while no longer a heartthrob for that generation, had moved into popular immortality. Jeremy, big and heavy, pleasant but not in the least good-looking, would come into his own in later years, because it was Jeremy who became a girl's friend before he became anything else.

'Oh, Jez,' girls would cry on his teenage shoulder, telling him all about themselves and the awful time they were having with their parents and other boys, quite often Paul. And Jeremy would put a brotherly arm around the trembling shoulders and somehow manage to hold back.

They went to different universities and saw little of one another during those three years away; then the practical arrangement reasserted itself when both needed to find somewhere to live in London. The flat in Shepherd's Bush was on the fifth floor of an Edwardian tower, next to the BBC. It had three bedrooms, and on the wage Paul was earning in advertising and with Jeremy scraping along with the intermittent freelance commission, they could not afford to leave the third room empty, which was how Paul's girlfriend, Angel, came to move in, except, of course, the third bedroom remained empty.

'Paul Lewis
Jeremy Holden
Angela Williams'

. . . read the list of names beneath the bellpush for No. 7.

Angel, Jeremy could see from the day he met her, would never call him 'Jez', but it was just a matter of time before she'd need his shoulder. Paul had found her in a cupboard at a surprise birthday party organised for one of his colleagues at the advertising agency. She'd gone in there for a little nap but might have remained inside, huddled in a corner all night, if it hadn't been for Paul.

'Finder's keepers,' he said, because he tended to say that sort of thing in those days.

Berkinstein, she thought, but nice looking.

'D'you need somewhere to kip down?' he asked.

'I thought I'd found somewhere,' she answered, curling into the back of the cupboard.

'Fine,' he said, closing the door.

'Has anyone left anything in the cupboard?' she heard him call out.

They went back to his new flat in Shepherd's Bush, except he said it was Kensington. They took a taxi he couldn't really afford; Angel could see he had an eye on the meter the entire journey, but he gave the driver a tip. Maybe he didn't have the balls not to; maybe he was generous. She was sufficiently interested to find out which. She'd told him she lived in a student hostel and that it would be too late to get back in tonight. This wasn't actually true, the too late bit, but not a lot had happened to her since she'd come to London and she was beginning to feel vaguely desperate, as if all the studying and swotting and A levels had been a con.

The flat was nice: high ceilings, lots of space, made to seem more so because there was so little furniture. She waited to be offered coffee, but Paul yawned and said did she mind if they went straight to bed? He'd got an important meeting first thing.

She wasn't about to make it this easy, but before she could think what to say he was fetching blankets and pillows for the sofa.

'Goodnight, then,' he said, lightly kissing her cheek, and he was gone, leaving her with directions to the bathroom and an entire sofa to herself.

In the morning she found Jeremy in the kitchen. A big chap, nothing special to look at.

'Hello,' he said, mildly surprised, but friendly. 'Would you like some of this toast? I'm Jeremy.'

'Angel. Where's Paul?'

'Had to leave early. He asked me to make sure you left your number.'

'Why not?' said Angel, thinking aloud.

Paul didn't phone her for three weeks, so that when he said his name she couldn't, for a moment, think which Paul it was.

'I've been away in New York,' he said, but she wasn't sure she believed him. Big-time bullshit? It was possible.

He took her to a Polish restaurant close by South Ken. tube station. He steered her away from starters, but the rest of the evening was generous, and, although he was a touch boastful, she decided he had been to New York and that he really was very good-looking yet not all that confident. There was something even a bit vulnerable about him, the wanting to impress when he didn't actually need to. Just being three years older than her and not fresh out of school was enough.

They went back to the flat, but this time he offered coffee, and as he was making it she began to feel slightly concerned that he might not make a move. She liked the back of his neck where the dark hair went into a ragged point. She like the powerful, muscular look of him, combined with the delicate facial features.

They took the coffee through to the drawing room and sat down on the sofa where she had slept the first visit. He talked about his job. And he talked about his job. The room smelled sort of male, changing-roomish. She sipped at the milky Maxwell House. He hadn't even asked her what she was studying. She didn't mind. Talking about herself was not the way she had been brought up.

The sofa creaked. The coffee mugs stood abandoned on the floor.

Paul's bed contained a concentration of the sitting room smell, but Angel liked it and shivered with desire. She moved in the following week and remained Paul's girlfriend for the next three years. Jeremy, of course, was there too, the nicest friend she could possibly have and, of the two men, the one she saw most. Paul was always working late, which was probably why the relationship lasted as long as it did. Although at the time Angel didn't see it, she was sleeping with the one man and thinking with the other.

Weekends would have been bleak, too, without Jeremy gliding about in the flat, cooking strange vegetables in his wok, tapping away on his typewriter, playing Vivaldi and the Rolling Stones by turns. Then the Electric Light Orchestra full blast, making Angel feel impossibly alive, fit to burst. Paul was either working or playing some game or other, hockey, rugby, squash, the sweat of those muscles returning to her in the small hours associated with away matches. She never went to watch. It was a closed world to her, sport, one she didn't want to open. Perhaps she was just nervous of seeing another side to Paul, one she wouldn't want to recognise and find unattractive. Heartiness. This potential for revulsion was part of her own immaturity, but there was nothing she could do about it other than wait to grow up. She still liked Paul enough or, rather, liked the couple they made, not to want to risk seeing him in a setting that might make her go off him.

If Jeremy saw the tenuous nature of Paul and Angel, he was careful not to do or say anything that might tip the balance. He had fallen in love with Angel in year two. They were easy together. Fond, physical and jokey.

It took Angel another year to realise that it was Jeremy she wanted to be with, whom she was with in every way other than sex. She told Paul first. Then he told Jeremy.

'I'd better move out,' said Jeremy.

'Yes, you better had,' said Paul, feeling an urge to punch.

'No, it ought to be me that goes,' said Angel, coming into the kitchen.

'Don't be ridiculous. You've got your finals in less than a month,' said Jeremy.

'Don't call me ridiculous,' she glared at him, angry, not just with him, but with herself, too, for bringing to an end what had happened to her in London, this lovely three-way living together, so completely satisfying, she realised now, if not entirely while it was happening. But it was over and could never be reinstated, and, of course, she wanted to move on to the new phase in her life, to begin an adult relationship with Jeremy wherein Paul could no longer be an integral part.

'Huh,' scoffed Paul, bitterly. 'If you two are going to fight, I'd prefer to be the one that moves out.'

'Supposing Angel moves into the spare room, just until she's finished her exams?' said Jeremy. 'None of us is going to be able to find somewhere else straightaway.'

Paul looked at the two of them, perhaps thinking he might yet regain ground. 'Just until she's finished her exams.'

# CHAPTER THREE

Marsha was preparing a Roquefort soup in front of two and three quarter million people when she felt the first wave of nausea.

'Ummm,' she said to camera, sucking the finger she had just dipped into the mixture. It tasted like the mould that it was.

When her piece was over she made a hasty exit, leaving the soup to boil over.

In the loo she went through last night's menu in her mind, knowing that when she hit on the bad bit her stomach would tell her what it was that had been poisonous. Trout? Caesar salad? Crème brûlée? Couldn't be the coffee, she hadn't had any. Couldn't be the coffee anyway. She hovered between the fish and the crème brûlée, undecided. That restaurant had never upset her digestion before. It was Paul's favourite at the moment, the place where he liked to show her off. Six years and he still got a kick out of introducing a black woman as his wife. The telly fame was just a bonus.

The sickness engulfed her again. Perhaps it was nerves, although she thought she'd got over that; she'd lost count of the number of dishes she'd cooked in front of the cameras.

'Marsha? Are you OK?' Sally, the production assistant, was outside the cubicle.

'Upset stomach.'

'Would you like me to wait?'

'No. I'll be all right in a minute. Sorry I had to do a runner.'

Today of all days. She was due to meet Angel at twelve thirty. A quick lunch at Kensington Place. Angel was in town for a case, something impossible to understand, commercial law. It wasn't often the two of them had a chance to chat alone, without the men. Angel and Jeremy were the bonus Paul had brought to her, Angel in particular. They had not spoken properly since that last weekend together when things had got a bit out of hand. She wanted to see Angel, to sit and talk, although not about that, but just to make sure it had not spoiled anything, that they were still the same.

She really hadn't thought much about what had happened, not all that much. She had been so busy during the intervening weeks with the cookery school, even though she had found someone very good to run it now that so much of her time was taken up by television. And there was the new book due to be delivered to the publisher by the end of the month. There were days, especially mornings and evening, when she began to feel her age. Forty-six. As far as Paul and the rest of the world were concerned it was forty-two; she'd lied at the beginning when she had met and fallen in love with Paul, and there had never been a subsequent right moment to put the record straight. Maybe she hadn't looked for one.

Younger men. Sometimes, in her dreams, she came across her first husband, at the age he was when they had married, but she was always forty-six. She'd find him sitting in a hitherto undiscovered room in a huge house they had viewed but not bought. There were more and more things wrong with it each time she went back there, involuntarily, usually just before dawn. Douglas never seemed to recognise her. It was as if she had become invisible. Perhaps she was just picturing his indifference, the last few months when they'd hardly spoken. Then, once or twice, Paul had been there, too, and they'd be trying to find somewhere hidden, somewhere to lie down together, but there was always interruption, sometimes her own waking.

The sick feeling had begun to ease. She splashed water on her face, wriggled out the creases in the tight black sleeve of her dress, painted her lips and left the studios, hailing a cab to get across to the West End.

Angel was already there, sitting in a dimly lit corner of the basement restaurant, flipping through *The Guardian*. They kissed one another and settled into the first few moments of delight. No shadows, thought Marsha, with relief.

'How's Jeremy?' she asked, testing the water a little further.

'Fine, as far as I know. He's so busy we hardly have a chance to talk these days. Share a bed and a kitchen.' She didn't make this sound loaded, just factual.

'I know what you mean.'

'Paul's all right?'

'Oh yes.' Sometimes when Angel asked about Paul, Marsha remembered that there had been ownership there once.

'It is nice to see you,' Angel said.

'Yes,' said Marsha, smiling, relaxing.

The first time she met Angel she had wondered why Paul had ever let her go. He'd told her that she had been his girl-friend before she'd married Jeremy. For a start there was her appearance, the long red hair (recently cut short), handsome, almost beautiful face, green, green eyes. Then the slightly quirky way of speaking, the odd turn of phrase that indicated a view on life that was very much her own. And she was kind, tolerant. She rarely spoke ill of others. It wasn't until some time after they were married that Paul said something, she couldn't remember exactly what, but suddenly she'd realised that Angel had left Paul. It was then that she had seen Angel in another light. No longer the victim. For a short while she had felt less inclined to continue the friendship. No woman, however nice, could possibly fail to take some pleasure in having rejected another woman's husband. But Angel really was not like that, and Marsha began to feel rather pathetic and narrow. It was pride, she supposed. She loved Paul so much she couldn't imagine any woman not wanting him. But the revelation had coincided with the end of that first, over-intense phase of love. It had come as they were going through the transition that takes a marriage on or leaves it floundering. So it was with something like triumph that she came out the other side, loving Paul in a slightly different but less exhausting way; loving Angel because she was Angel and the past was the past.

'Tell me about this case you are working on,' she said now.

'Really?'

'Really. I'd like to hear about it.' But Angel was only into the preamble, her doubts about the barrister, when Marsha felt the sickness again.

'Sorry,' she muttered, leaping up and rushing to the stairs.

The lunch was abandoned. Angel insisted on going with her in the taxi home. There was no effort to chat now. The immediacy of Marsha being unwell precluded the need.

Angel took her into the flat just off Onslow Square, Marsha's home, the better of the two when she and Paul had set up home together. Very white walls, almost hurting the eyes, sparse, spiky bits and pieces bought in the Fulham Road. Not a home at all, but a setting.

'Something I ate last night,' said Marsha. 'Sorry.'

'Please. Don't be. Is there anything I can get you?'

'I'm not sure I could keep anything down.'

'There's nothing worse, is there?'

'Worse?'

'Than food poisoning.'

Marsha was standing by the bare marble mantelpiece, holding on, staring without seeing at an ornamental twig in the grate.

'I don't like to leave you like this.' Angel, hovering between sitting down and standing up, had fixed a worried gaze on Marsha's bent head.

'It'll pass. Do go, Angel, dear. You haven't had any lunch.'

'Can I at least see you into bed? I'm worried you might faint or something. You are looking very thin, you know.'

'Television adds a good stone. I have to be careful. I don't want people thinking my recipes will make them fat.' She let out a little laugh. 'There. I'm feeling better now.'

'Shall I make some tea?'

'No, darling, really. I think a quiet, darkened room is the answer.'

'Don't kiss me,' she said in the hallway as Angel moved towards her. 'Just in case it's a bug.'

Marsha went back into the drawing room to wave to Angel as she headed off down the street. A hungry walk, Marsha thought, another wave sweeping through her, lingering, with unpleasant precision, in her throat.

She went through to the bedroom, equally white and stark, drew the curtains and slipped under the duvet, hardly making a hump. Perhaps she was too thin; the bed was not hard but her hip bone felt painful against the mattress.

She went into one of those daytime dozes that get crowded with mutations of real life. Douglas appeared again, distant but with a grudge. It was the old argument. Children. She'd lied about that, too, just like her age. Douglas wanted children. She didn't, not at first. Then, when she'd stopped taking the pill and nothing had happened, there'd been this stupid, irrational sort of pride: it was better for Douglas to go on thinking that she didn't want children than to know she couldn't have them. And it all went too far, slipping beyond her control, as these things do, before she'd realised it, so that Douglas had found someone else. Said he had; Marsha'd never met her. Douglas left a note, on the bare marble mantelpiece: 'Gone back to Jamaica.'

Marsha had packed up in the flat everything with Douglas associations, which didn't leave a lot; but the clean-slate feel gave her a perverse kind of comfort, a light, airy sensation. Freedom. She had not realised just how oppressive Douglas had been. But she was not cut out for the single life, and once the novelty of her freedom had worn transparent, she'd been oppressed again, but now by a horrible, empty loneliness.

'Bloody hot in here,' Paul had said to her at the book launch. 'D'you think anyone would mind if we shoved off for a cool drink elsewhere?'

'No, I don't suppose so,' she had said, allowing him to take her hand and lead her out of the heat.

'What's your connection with this thrash?' he'd asked when the cold white wine was set before them in a bar round the corner.

'I'm the author,' she said.

The following weekend Paul took her with him to New York. He was working much of the time, coming back to the hotel every now and then to join her in bed. She didn't mind being alone the rest of the time; she no longer felt lonely. From the beginning she saw through all the big-timing, saw through it to a man who wanted the same as her, not to be lonely.

'Marsha!' Paul was standing by the bed, the same expression on his face she had seen in Angel earlier in the day.

'Paul?' Bleary, blurred speech, the taste of iron filings in her mouth.

'Marsha. What's wrong?'

'Nothing. Nothing. Something I ate.'

'Marsha, we've got the account.' He sat down on the side of the bed.

'Darling, I'm so pleased.'

'God, I can hardly believe it. Touch and go, you know. All those late nights have paid off.' He twisted round and lay down beside her so she could cradle his head.

'You sure you're all right?'

'Umm. Tell me about the account.'

'It's Bracken's new range of baby food. Big stuff. International. Worth six figures.' She could feel his heart beating. She knew all about the Bracken account, the big pitch of the year, and how badly Paul had needed it. The agency had been up against it for months. The last six Paul had drawn no salary at all, and modern as they liked to think themselves she knew how he'd felt about living on her money, even though there was plenty of it. He wouldn't refer to her own part in the pitch, how he had used her name, Marsha Miller, the dusky Delia Smith. She was glad to have been able to help, for once proud in an otherwise modest nature. The last thing she wanted now was to take any of the credit. Paul's triumph. Paul, like a boy, with his head against her puny breast.

He began to move against her, a prelude to sex. Getting the Bracken account would break the duck, bring him back to her, but she couldn't, not today. And this thought led on to the other, recurring one.

# CHAPTER FOUR

Angel, the day she had planned now a vacant slot, considered turning up at Jeremy's office. Then caution got the better of her; should she ring him first? If, just if, Jeremy were messing about with some other woman, Angel wasn't sure she really wanted to know. Of course, she didn't truly believe there was anything going on, but she allowed herself to play with the idea every now and then, when she wasn't too preoccupied with her own work.

In a way she was quite relieved Marsha had been ill. She had approached the lunch date with part pleasure, part dread, part curiosity. Would they say anything? Was it really possible not to? She had found it difficult to concentrate during the morning, to take all the right notes. The barrister she had engaged for her client was not on good form. At one point he appeared to muddle the case notes, saying something that evidently sprang from some other brief. He'd employed a coughing fit in an attempt to mask the mistake, but nobody could have been fooled, and the judge had perked up at the sniff of incompetence. The incident had jolted Angel, made her realise that she, too, was not fully on the ball. A big ball, too. If they lost the case the client could say goodbye to more than half a million. Had Marsha really been ill?

Had Marsha felt the same dread? Of course she must have. Angel wondered whether they had talked about it, Marsha and Paul. With Jeremy there had not been a word said. Tacit agreement to silence. She had been terrified he might throw in a line, 'just like old times', or something similar, the way he did, finding one of those short little phrases of his, a headline, summing it all up.

Only once, long ago, had he asked her, 'What's the matter? Not as good as Paul?' They had been going through a mildly bad patch, sex drives out of sync.

'I'm sorry. I'm sorry,' he'd countered quickly, urgently, as if he didn't want her to stop and think about it.

She'd reached her stop on the tube. She earned enough for taxis these days, but they took too long in the London traffic at this time of day. She remained seated as the doors opened, still undecided about going on further east, then she leapt up and made a dash for it. She would not be particularly pleased if Jeremy were to turn up at her office in Cambridge unexpectedly in the middle of the working day. Angel had been careful all her life to be in a wanted position, never a nuisance or a drag.

On the train back to Cambridge she made an attempt at going through her notes but her mind was still off track. She began to ponder how the four of them could plan another weekend without the underlying expectation of a repeat of what had happened the last time. She wanted it to be as it had been before. Surely all four of them wanted it that way, but you could never be entirely sure about these things. She couldn't even be certain about Jeremy, what he might expect. Perhaps they really had spoiled it all for good and there might never be another weekend. It was a bleak thought.

When she reached Cambridge she decided to drive straight home from the station instead of going back to the office. It seemed odd seeing the house in daylight midweek, making her realise again the silly hours she and Jeremy were working. She let herself in by the back door and, standing in the kitchen, suddenly wondered how she would occupy herself for the next few hours until Jeremy came in and they ate supper.

The kitchen, like the rest of the old house, was perfectly neat and tidy, too neat and tidy; they were there too little to mess it up. It smelt strongly of lavender wax because Sylvia had been in earlier in the day doing the cleaning.

Angel put the kettle on to make herself some tea and sat down at the table, what-to-have-for-supper thoughts lining up to fill the gap. Then the back door opened, making her jump, and there was Sylvia.

'Hi there. Didn't expect to find you home.'

Angel smiled, genuinely pleased to see Sylvia, even ready for a chat. Normally she would do just about anything to avoid dear, kind Sylvia, her mother's age, blessed with the conversational aids of varicose veins, a faulty damp course and a two-month-old grandson.

'Let me do that,' Sylvia said, taking charge of the kettle. 'You look worn out, if you don't mind my saying so. I just popped back to finish the ironing. Didn't have enough time this morning, what with the builders in again and the doctor's, and I promised to have Chaucer for an hour while Denise nipped down the supermarket.'

Angel settled into the flow of Sylvia, allowing it to wash over her like background music, a sort of displacement inactivity. Jeremy intruded after a short while. They still had not made love. Perhaps there was someone else. Perhaps he didn't want her now, not after Marsha . . . Silly. Stop it. Nothing had changed.

'I'm glad to have caught you,' Sylvia was saying. 'I told Denise that she ought to be the one to ask, but seeing as you're here. What I wanted to say was, would you be Chaucer's godmother?'

'Sylvia. I'd be delighted.'

'Oh, that's a relief. We couldn't think of anyone else who goes to church, and we thought his godmother ought to be a churchgoer.'

'Yes,' said Angel, slightly flummoxed.

'And Jeremy too, for his godfather.'

'Ah. You know that Jeremy is not a churchgoer?'

'Yes, but you are. One's enough, isn't it?'

Angel was glad that Sylvia had not asked about belief. Going to the village church every now and then was no more than a link with her past, a hanging on to happy childhood, the singing of hymns with gusto, a wonderful mindless compliance with tradition. And she liked the smell of stone and pew: dusty, musty, everlasting. Jeremy saw it as an aberration, but Jeremy, thank God, had never shown intolerance or disdain; this was a very lovable aspect. To her it indicated more than anything else that he loved her as much as she loved him.

'I said to Denise, Angel will do it, and she's the right sort, upright,' Sylvia was saying. 'And she said you might think it was a bit of a cheek, you hardly knowing her really; but I said I was sure you'd agree and . . .' Angel sipped at her tea, no longer listening at all. She hoped Jeremy would not be too late tonight.

At half past eleven she opened the oven and inspected the plate of drying food. Pity they didn't have a dog. She felt wide awake now, having dozed through 'Question Time'. She decided to do some work and went through to the small room she and Jeremy shared as a study. She badly wanted to win this case. It was a complex matter and could easily go either way, but if she lost she knew it would be a serious blot on her career and that she would not be trusted with anything as big for years, if ever. She couldn't bear the thought of being black-marked, considered not quite up to it. There were others in the firm who'd met their various Waterloos in the shape of similar cases. She'd seen the way things had gone for them afterwards, not exactly a downward spiral, but a static presence. They were stuck, some thankful they still had a job, knowing it would be difficult to make a move other than in the direction of something in a high street. The law could be the most interesting occupation possible, but it could also be the most tedious and dispiriting.

She was only twenty minutes into the case notes when she heard Jeremy come in. He found her straightaway, looping his arms round her neck from behind and kissing her ear. He'd not done that for a long time.

'Sorry,' he said, the smell of train brushing across her face.

'Busy day?'

'Horrendous.'

'Your supper's all dried up.'

'I grabbed a bagette at King's Cross.'

'Ah.'

'Sorry I didn't phone you.'

'Would you like me to make you an omelette or something?'

'No, thanks. Bed, I think.' He yawned and stretched. 'Anyone call?'

'No. Were you expecting them to?'

'Nope.'

'I got back early today. I very nearly called you to see if we could do something in town.'

'That would have been nice, but just as well you didn't. I haven't stopped all day.'

'You know I was having lunch with Marsha today?'

'Ah. Yes. I'd forgotten.' Had he?

'Anyway, I didn't. She was ill.'

'Nothing serious, I hope.'

'Something she ate last night, poor thing.'

'So you didn't see her at all, then?'

'Yes. I went back to the flat with her, to make sure she was all right.'

'And she was?'

'I think so. Perhaps I'll call her tomorrow.' She thought she probably wouldn't.

'Yes.' He yawned again.

In bed he said, 'We must fix up another weekend.'

'Weekend?'

'With Paul and Marsha.'

Angel didn't reply.

'Angel?'

She switched out the bedside light.

'Are we going to talk about it?' he said, into the darkness.

'Nope,' she said.

She lay awake, thinking he had gone straight to sleep, but of course he hadn't. Then, at some point in the night, when time no longer seemed to have any measure, they turned to one another.

# CHAPTER FIVE

'I can arrange a termination for you,' the doctor said. Marsha had not fully taken in the fact of her pregnancy, let alone the need to make such a decision. The doctor seemed to assume only one course, no decision at all. He was already lifting the receiver.

'I'll be able to book you into the clinic next week. Thursday suit you?'

Marsha left the surgery feeling a different sort of sick. She was due at the television studios by ten thirty. Bread and butter pudding.

She forgot the sultanas but otherwise managed a rather good performance, her head as light as the mouthwatering pudding which she tasted and actually enjoyed.

'Sorry about the soup last week,' she said to one of the studio hands. 'Was it an awful mess?'

'Blue Peter's dog didn't think so.'

They laughed. Marsha felt deliciously trapped inside the brief time capsule of her extraordinary condition. Extraordinary to her. She was not yet ready to think about the next bit. Nature had got the better of her.

'Shall we finish this up?' she said, indicating the pudding.

'It's all right for you,' said the girl. 'I have to watch what I eat or I get to be the size of a house.'

Jennifer Chapman

Marsha imagined being such a size, all porch. What a thought. But it would not get that far.

The lightheadedness began to fade, replaced by the beginning of a deadly weight. It needn't be. She could be through it all by next Thursday. Paul didn't even have to know, and she certainly wasn't going to tell Jeremy. For God's sake, what had they been doing? Crazy. But she'd never thought, not for a moment, such a thing could happen. And at her age. Besides, she'd thought she couldn't have children. Douglas.

Somehow she managed to float along on this plane of prideful joy for the entire week, not properly stopping to consider what she was about to do on Thursday, or rather, what she was willingly going to allow to be done to her, her and it. The entity had begun.

It probably helped that Paul was away in the States. They'd been very close again just before he'd left, and he might have guessed there was something if he had been at home over these days. He would have sensed the difference in her. Seen her glow.

Thursday was not a good day for her. She'd planned cranberry scones. She decided to do the programme first then go straight on to the clinic. It would be all right as long as she didn't eat anything, nothing at all from midnight on Wednesday.

She took a small bag with her to the studios and managed to keep her mind in neutral as she rolled the pastry. But her palms were sweating and she worried about the scones. The shapes were a bit uneven when she brought them out of the oven on camera, but the show's hosts, Gerald and Pauline, said they were delicious, and Gerald did the whole of the following item with a crumb at the corner of his mouth.

The time had come. Marsha collected her bag and went out into the daylight, checked the address of the clinic and hailed a cab.

'I forgot to tell you. You're going to be a godfather,' Angel told Jeremy on Sunday morning. 'Sylvia's grandson. She asked me last week. Said they didn't know anyone else who went to church.'

'So how do I qualify?'

'Because you're married to me. Aren't you fortunate?'

Jeremy looked across the breakfast table at her and smiled. 'Very,' he said.

They'd been a bit like this the past ten days, since they'd rediscovered one another as lovers. The drought in the marriage had given way to a monsoon. They were both shagged out, which was why Angel was still sitting over breakfast and not dashing about getting ready for church. She had thought to go this morning, top up the credits for godmother status.

The past week had been like the beginning when they first fancied one another, or rather when Angel had realised it was Jeremy she wanted. It had been such an intoxication, the switch from Jeremy, her good friend, always that, to Jeremy, a being she could hardly keep her hands off. She got up now and went round to his side of the table, standing behind him, wrapping her arms around his rather over-solid torso, pressing her cheek against his. He put a hand up to her shoulder. 'Mercy,' he said.

'No chance.' But she went back to her side of the table and, pushing the Sunday papers on to the floor, said, 'What shall we do today? I don't want to spend hours reading this lot, do you?'

'How about Aldeburgh? We could be there for lunch.'

In the bathroom he said from under his towel, 'Perhaps we should ring Paul and Marsha, see whether they'd like to join us at Mabey's or the Wentworth.'

He pulled the towel away from his face when she didn't answer.

'Angel,' he said, looking at her, 'it was nothing. You know that, don't you?'

'I'll give them a ring,' she said.

39

Paul answered the phone.

'Angel. Yes, we'd love to. If we leave now we can be there by, say, one thirty.'

'Right. Get your bucket and spade out. I'm taking you to the seaside,' he told Marsha, who was still in bed.

'Oh, Paul,' Marsha groaned, turning into her pillow.

'Come on, Marsha. We're meeting Jeremy and Angel in Aldeburgh for lunch. That was Angel on the phone just now.'

'Do we have to?' Marsha murmured.

'I think we do.'

Marsha turned and sat up. Paul was looking at her.

'They're good friends,' he said. 'And it's a good opportunity. Neutral ground.'

'But you've only just got back from the States,' she protested, lamely, knowing he would get his own way because he always did and she never normally minded. To dig her heels in now would lead to the discussion she didn't want to have.

They set off half an hour later in the new Mercedes they called hers but which she had never driven. This was the way she bought things for Paul, the way he was able to feel comfortable with them. Without her he would have had next to nothing these past two or three years. The recession had just about finished him, but the Bracken account might be the start of better times again. She fervently hoped so. Paul had shown the beginnings of bitterness, resentment towards her because she was closest to hand. There had been several occasions when he'd said something in front of other people, with an unnecessary tone. Nasty, embarrassing. She'd wanted to take him to task when they were back at the flat, just the two of them, but she somehow wasn't able to, and when they were alone he was always so nice. Sometimes too nice, so that she knew he was trying to make up for the nastiness.

The roads were clear and they reached Aldeburgh before Jeremy and Angel. Marsha did not share the passion the other three had for this gritty, windblown place, perhaps partly because the three of them had discovered it long before she had come on the scene. It was full of recapturing potential for them, a clinging on to days that in memory were probably more magical than they could possibly have been at the time. Hours had been spent throwing stones at the sea, trying to get them to bounce across the brown waves like the dam-busting bomb. Jeremy and Paul shed twenty years when they were on the beach at Aldeburgh.

Then there was the ritual of buying fresh fish from the black huts at the top of the beach and smelling it all the way home in the car. There was the waiter with the harelip at the Wentworth Hotel; if they weren't served by him the day was spoiled.

'Remember the time we came here and Peter Pears was sitting at the next table?'

'Remember the time . . .?'

'Remember the time . . .?'

Marsha indulged them, wondering at the beginning, before she knew Angel better, if there weren't something not quite nice in the accelerating airing of these exclusive memories. Remember, remember, the time when it was just us three.

'Sorry we're late,' said Jeremy. 'Angel wasn't feeling too good.'

'A touch of what you had?' Angel said to Marsha. 'Are you better?'

Marsha nodded. The two women kissed one another and then each other's men. The first hurdle had been jumped.

'We'd better order or there won't be much left,' said Paul. They had agreed on Mabey's, their new place, the one they had started going to since Marsha, and always her preferred choice, even if the menu was written up on a blackboard and she had to put on her glasses to read it. They had only just got their drinks when a couple sitting at a nearby table started nudging one another and looking in their direction. Marsha was never quite sure whether she enjoyed having a famous face.

Paul, aware that his wife had been noticed, was now telling the others about the Bracken account. He was back on form, thought Marsha, thought Angel, thought Jeremy. Nice to see him ebullient again even if they'd all be stifling yawns by the end of the day.

Are you sure you're all right?' said Marsha to Angel when Paul paused as the waiter came to their table. An incredible thought had come to her.

'Fine. Really. Just a bit, you know.' Marsha wondered whether she did.

'Read any good books lately?' Paul asked Jeremy.

'We've just bought the serial rights for John Prescott's book.'

'How much?'

'A lot, but we beat *The Sunday Times*.'

'Ah, but they had Camilla,' said Paul. He couldn't resist it, thought Marsha, thought Angel. From time to time both women had puzzled as to whether Paul was aware of the way he tended to counter Jeremy's triumphs.

Lunch was delicious, although Marsha noticed that Angel barely picked at her goat's cheese salad. Her own appetite, such as it was, had returned, surprisingly.

The sun had come out as they left the brasserie and began a gentle stroll down the High Street. They continued, turning down a narrow passageway to reach the seafront. The whole place was just made for nostalgia, thought Marsha, the Victorian cottages, pinks, creams, pastel greens washed over the pebbledash, sash windows flung up to let in the sun and sea smell. It was a lovely place, but she wondered whether this might be the last time she would come here.

Paul and Jeremy had gone on ahead, talking cars now. Angel linked her arm through Marsha's.

'God, I hope they don't want to buy fish,' she said.

'I know how you feel,' said Marsha, convinced for no very good reason other than instinct that Angel was pregnant.

They walked on in companionable silence, as if an unspoken understanding had brought them close.

A few yards further along the front there was a patch of grass and on it a Punch and Judy show in progress. The two women paused behind a group of children sitting cross-legged on the grass, right in there with the puppets, shouting and screaming at Mr Punch. Then Judy came out to be clobbered.

'Not very PC, is it?' said Angel.

'That's the way to do it! That's the way to do it!' said Mr Punch in his strangled voice.

Paul and Jeremy were over by the lifeboat house. Marsha and Angel moved on to join them.

'Angel,' Marsha began, hoping the men were still out of earshot. 'You're not pregnant, are you?'

Angel smiled. 'Good heavens, no.'

Marsha's expression collapsed. What a stupid piece of wishful thinking; and she hadn't even got as far as taking into account that it might have been Paul's.

'I am,' she said, before she could stop herself.

# CHAPTER SIX

'That's the way to do it!' Mr Punch gurgled on behind them. A silly, mocking voice.

'Marsha. Oh, congratulations. How marvellous. Paul must be so pleased.' Angel was hugging Marsha. Paul and Jeremy, watching them approach, looked quizzical.

'Hey, what's all this?' Jeremy said.

'Marsha's expecting a baby,' said Angel, moving forward to embrace Paul, congratulations dying on her lips as she saw his expression.

The sound of the sea pressed in on Marsha. A freakish gust of wind suddenly swirled round the four of them. Marsha had astounded herself almost as much as she had the other three, blurting it out like that, safety in numbers; there'd be no talking her out of it now. Had she been so sure that was what Paul would have done?

Her eyes beseeched him not to say anything, and he didn't, just glared at her.

A similar intensity of gaze had taken root in Jeremy, leaving only Angel in a floundering position, disbelieving what the others were telling her by their silence.

'Look, I'm sorry,' Marsha began. 'I never dreamt this could happen.'

'Oh, no,' moaned Angel, tilting her head up to the sky.

'I'm sorry,' repeated Marsha.

45

'You'll have to get rid of it,' Paul said that evening at the flat. The journey back to London had been a series of surges, the way Paul always drove when he was agitated. He had remained tight-lipped the whole way, speaking only when absolutely necessary and then as if he hated her.

'I was going to last Thursday but I'd have missed the programme,' she said, lamely.

'For God's sake,' Paul shouted, beginning to pace about. 'Couldn't you have missed the bloody programme for once?'

'Paul, I just couldn't do it. I mean, this could be my last chance.'

'What are we talking about now, the programme or the state you're in?'

'I can't have an abortion, Paul. I won't do it. It's a baby. A person.'

'Spare me the goo.'

'Can't we pretend it's . . .'

'No,' he cut her off. 'Absolutely no.'

'Where are you going?' she called after him as he strode towards the front door.

He didn't reply. The door slammed.

'Can't we pretend?' she repeated to herself with scoffing self-mockery.

'How could we have been so stupid?' Angel murmured.

'We don't know anything for certain,' Jeremy said. 'Do we?'

They had stopped off on the way home at one of those local country pubs where everyone turns and stares when strangers walk in. They had chosen a corner table, as far away from the bar as possible. The white wine they ordered was sweet and tepid.

Angel wanted to say something along the line of surely Marsha would not go ahead, but she couldn't. She felt oddly distanced from Jeremy, as if this huge thing they were discussing did not actually involve her, even if it was going to change both their lives for ever. Desperate ideas jumped about in her head. She could have a baby, too. Yes, that was the answer. Marsha had already seen that possibility. There wasn't any other course to take, yet she knew she couldn't do it, that to plan such a pregnancy, as an expedient . . . She fell to wondering how it was that other people managed to have babies by accident all the time and simply got on with it. Denise for one. Seventeen years old, Sylvia's youngest. Denise would probably be a grandmother herself by the time she reached Angel's age.

'We've really fucked up, haven't we?' Jeremy said. He didn't normally use such language.

'You could put it like that.'

'Don't be prim, Angel. Don't be clever.'

'I can assure you that I don't feel particularly *clever* right now. I don't think any of us has been very *clever*.' She heard herself lay sarcastic emphasis on 'clever'.

'We shouldn't fight. There's no point,' she said, resuming a more equitable tone. 'I mean, there's no saying what might happen. I really can't see Marsha going through with it.' There, she'd said it. It was obvious that Marsha would not go ahead when she'd thought about it more.

Angel felt a touch of sanity creeping back, but then she saw the expression on Jeremy's face.

> *Daniel Presley's wanderings, his innate sense of displacement, are rooted in his childhood. He does not know who his real father is, and this void blights his life. Everything he does is about the search for true identity.*
>
> *From an early age he feels out of step with the rest of his family. A cuckoo. The home environment is intellectually cramped, and always he senses an inexplicable resentment between his parents. Like many children, he assumes himself to be the cause of their disharmony, and, of course, he is, but not, as he has always thought,*

*because he was difficult and badly behaved; and
by the time he discovers that Arthur Presley is not
his real father, the psychological damage is
already irreparable.*

Angel read this section of the review again and wondered
how much of it was in the book and how much Jeremy's own
interpretation. The past few weeks had been unreal, a night-
mare, made endurable only by the extra hours both spent
working. They were drifting further and further apart, never
mentioning the subject that engrossed them both. There had
not been a word from Paul and Marsha: a real pregnant
silence. At least, Angel had not heard from them. It occurred
to her that perhaps Jeremy had been in touch with Marsha;
he certainly wouldn't tell her if he had.

She waited, expecting something to happen, even beginning to wish it would. Anything had to be better than this
weird limbo, a future seemingly dictated by someone who
wasn't even born.

At one moment she would choose to assume and even
believe that Marsha must have dealt with the problem and
in time it would all be forgotten, although she no longer kid-
ded herself that the four of them could remain friends. Then
she would see with absolute clarity that Marsha was keeping the baby, that she would never have mentioned the pregnancy at all if she had not already made the decision to go
ahead. This notion would lead on to one of secret meetings
between Jeremy and Marsha. Plans. Plans for a future that
did not include her. She felt awfully sorry for herself. Wet
and weedy, as her brother used to say when they were children daring one another to do silly, often dangerous things
down by the railway line, or in the derelict house at the end
of their road.

Robert had five children, which had kept the heat off her
to provide grandchildren. Jeremy's mother turned up the tem-
perature every so often. A widow, left well provided for, she

sometimes threw out a vaguely despairing arm indicating the sweep of riches there for the inheriting.

By chance, a long-standing invitation, Grace was with them this weekend, and this afternoon was the christening. Angel folded up the books section of the paper and got up to fetch more coffee.

'Yes, please, dear.' Her mother-in-law held out her cup and saucer.

Grace had sensed an atmosphere although she was not a particularly sensitive woman. Always inclined to be self-centred, she was becoming more so with age, but she would have to be gaga not to have noticed the lack of communication in the house. What made it worse was that Angel could see she was taking a degree of pleasure from the disharmony. Whenever she said anything, she'd then defer to each of them in turn, watching with eagle intensity for the rift to take shape in anything to hand. It was like Daniel Presley and his parents in reverse, only Grace would never hold herself accountable. And there was no reason why she should. Angel knew she was being unfair, but generosity of spirit tended to be the first casualty for ordinary mortals when unhappiness struck.

'How's Paul and . . . Marsha, is that his wife's name?' Grace was asking, as if sixth sense had come into play.

Fortunately, or unfortunately, Jeremy was in the lavatory, otherwise Angel might not have said what she did.

Baths were taken in turn. Jeremy and Angel had never managed to share theirs when his mother was around, but then they hadn't shared a bath now for weeks, not since Aldeburgh.

Angel lay in the third bath and felt horribly unloved; the feeling sorry for herself was getting out of hand. A sudden rashness galvanised her out of the water, through the steam and into the bedroom where Jeremy was getting dressed.

'Please. Please! Let's be like us again.' She flung her wet arms around him and pressed her cheek into his back.

He turned within her hug and put his own arms about her slippery back. They clung to one another for quite a long moment.

'Angel,' he whispered against her ear, 'I want to ask you something.'

# CHAPTER SEVEN

'I name this child Chaucer Kevin. In the name of the Father . . .'

Angel took hold of the huge baby, gripping him tightly as he wriggled and screamed, the trickle of water running down on to his button nose. She wondered where the child got its size. Denise was like a stick insect, and the boy who stood beside her, who, with Denise and the baby, now occupied the spare room in Sylvia's house, had that pinched, undernourished look about him. Sylvia had said he was an unrewarding soul to cook for, and the way to his heart would never be via his stomach, which was just as well considering Denise's showing in home economics. Angel smiled at the sound of Sylvia's voice in her head.

Sylvia was smiling, too, as proud as could be of her latest grandchild. It was just the five of them round the font, plus the vicar and the baby: Sylvia, Denise and Kevin, her and Jeremy.

'I want to ask you something,' he had said.

She gazed down at the struggling baby and tried to imagine a maternal thought. Chaucer's nose was running.

'We could share the looking-after. I'd do my bit, more than my bit.' Jeremy had been at his most wistful, a ploy he rarely used. He was not normally a man to ask much for himself.

51

'You're assuming rather a lot, aren't you?' she'd said.

'We both know Paul.'

'But do we know Marsha that well?'

'She's in her forties. She's rich and famous. She doesn't want her life changed. I've really thought about this, Angel. It's the only answer.'

She'd forgotten how persuasive he could be, how he could make her believe just about anything.

'You haven't said anything to her?'

'Of course not. I had to discuss it with you first.'

'I can't decide just like that. I mean, it's such a big thing.'

'All I'm asking is that you think about it.'

'So Paul's wife is going to have a baby,' Grace said.

Angel glanced at Jeremy, who in turn gave her a questioning look. Grace was looking from one to the other, her own expression asking a different question.

'Isn't it about time, dears? Oh, tell me to mind my own business.'

'Mind your own business,' said Jeremy.

'Such a rude boy,' murmured Grace, lighting a cigarette, casting an eye about in the expectation of being given an ashtray. Neither Jeremy nor Angel smoked.

'Paul's going to have to cut down,' Jeremy commented in an abstracted tone as he set down the cut-glass wedding present Grace had given them fifteen years ago.

'Naughty man. Does he still smoke?'

'You've got no room to talk.'

'Darling, I'm past the watershed.'

'All the same, if we were to have a child you'd have to stop doing it here.'

'So you are thinking about it.' Grace exhibited an exaggerated perking up. Angel, who had said nothing in this exchange, fixated on the dark pink impression of lipstick Grace had now stamped around her filter tip. Horrid colour.

'Possibly, but it is none of your business so shut up about it, will you?' Funny how Jeremy had this semi-beastly relationship with his mother, thought Angel, a layer of concentration still darting about in search of anything other than the big issue to hand. Jeremy wanted them to adopt Marsha's baby.

'I'm pretty sure we wouldn't even have to go through official channels,' he had said, sparing her the spelling out.

'Well, you'll both be making an old woman very happy,' Grace said, and Angel now wanted to tell her to shut up. Her mother-in-law had arranged herself on the sofa, in the same place where Jeremy had sat stroking Marsha's feet. Her cigarette, a beacon of defiance sending out a thin blue reed of smoke, filled the room with the aroma of that evening when Paul had filled the ashtray and all night she'd smelt it on his hair, the acrid, mousey stench. They hadn't done it. What was the point? Paul wanted Marsha and she wanted Jeremy and, besides, Paul had asked her why she'd had her hair cut and told her it looked like a cowpat, as if he had some kind of licence to say that sort of thing to her. They'd ended up sulking with one another, without the passion and desire to transform the little spat into a bedroom scene.

'Fuck you,' she'd said to him.

'I'd rather not.'

Contrary to appearances, Paul had never been particularly interested in sex; she should have remembered that from the first meeting, the night she'd spent alone under his blankets on the sofa at the flat. Then there was all that exhausting sport. Throughout the entire relationship when supposedly they had been lovers there hadn't been much love at all. Oh, it had been all right when it happened, even good, but by contrast Jeremy, who appeared anything but the great lover, had awakened her to undreamt-of excursions via bodily fluids.

'Would you like something to drink, Mother?'

'Is it too early for a Scotch?' Grace answered.

'Yes, but have one all the same.'

'I don't think I shall be drinking another cup of tea for at least a week,' Grace added, darkly. 'Really, you'd think they might have laid on the odd glass of champagne.'

'They haven't got any money.'

'Beer, though. At a christening!'

'It's what they like. And don't be such a snob.'

'Huge child. D'you think that boy can really be the father?'

'Does it matter?'

'No. No, not at all. I don't want any ice.'

Angel could see they were in for an evening of sparring and for once felt a sense of relief rather than tension at the prospect. These were sessions where she did not have to take part. She even wondered whether it might be possible to escape to the study for an hour or so and immerse herself in some work. The big case had been won. Her star was in the ascendant at the office, high streets fading fast, a positive motorway ahead of her. But the pleasure, of course, was spoiled.

From beyond the study she could hear Jeremy and Grace laughing. He might have suggested their own baby, probably would once they had Marsha's installed. Jeremy had always dealt with the here and now, tackling life as it was rather than how it might be. There was a baby coming and it was as much his as any baby they might have together. It was natural that he should feel as he did about it. The question seemed to be, did she love him enough to love it, too, even though the other half of it would be Marsha and not her? It was quite logical, but didn't help.

'You shouldn't have told her,' Jeremy said in the bedroom when they were getting undressed.

'Well, I didn't tell her that you're the father.'

Jeremy stepped out of his trousers and scratched his balls. Angel had a sudden desire to kick them, mentally if not physically.

'You're full of secret glee, aren't you? It's all macho stuff. I bet you hope it's a boy.'

He sat down heavily on the side of the bed, shirt-tails dangling, looking a touch comical in his socks.

'Please, Angel. Please.' He sounded as if forbearance was wearing thin.

'Sorry,' she said, going over to him, placing her hand on his shoulder. 'This is new to me, feeling such a bitch.'

He put his arm around her waist. 'I know it's not easy.'

'It's bloody difficult.'

'But not impossible?' He glanced up at her. 'I love you, Angel. I'm just trying to do the right thing.'

'Are you?'

'You don't doubt that, do you?'

'I don't doubt your motives; at least, I don't think I do. No, of course I don't.' She hugged him again, another attempt at convincing herself they were still close while in truth they were speeding apart at a rate of knots. She could not bring herself to tell him tonight that there was no way she could see herself bringing up Marsha's baby.

# CHAPTER EIGHT

'BRACKEN FOODS'. The sign was enormous, as was the logo, a chubby baby in a diaper, a single quiff of hair curling up from its big round head.

Paul parked the hire car in the visitors' bay outside the factory, straightened his tie like someone out of a cliché, checked he had everything he needed in his bag, and then proceeded towards the main entrance and his first proper meeting with Sasha Parrish since she'd told him he'd won the account. God, why couldn't they have made dog food? A nice bowl of Chum. Just right for chummy, chummy Sasha, a bit of a dog herself. The tie felt too tight, strangling. The first proper meeting last night at the hotel had been more improper.

'Has anyone ever told you you look a whole lot like Paul McCartney?' she'd asked, moving in on him. 'I once met John, you know. John Lennon. When he was living in New York, not long before that Chapman guy shot him.'

Sasha, big red slash mouth, that American jaw. Snap, snap, snapping at him. The poor bitch didn't know his balls had already been bitten off back home. Paul thought in Americanese when he was in the States. Couldn't help it, wasn't even particularly aware.

He'd always been impressionable, even tried to be like Jeremy, fancy that. Good old, dear old Jez. He'd always admired him and at the same time resented this unwilling admiration. Jez had depth; he didn't. Jez got the woman in the end. Jez didn't look like Paul McCartney, nor even Ringo Starr. Jez looked a bit like a younger Roy Hattersley. Well, a bit. Jez was one of those brainy buggers who looked like his face had been cast in blancmange and who ended up, even when he was losing his hair, appearing on sit-down programmes on the box pontificating about the Booker Prize, interviewing Arthur Miller, taking part in droll, clever, clever quiz shows. Jez, his best buddy, who probably thought he was a prick – and always had. God, he felt sorry for himself, he really did.

And he'd blown it with Sasha, that big red gob eventually narrowing, collapsing at the edges. He'd bored her rigid, frigid; he hadn't even tried to get his leg over. She'd wanted that, he'd clocked on to that straightaway. Facial flashing, the eyes, that mouth. He wasn't even interested. Women with balls turned him off, turned him into a wimp. They'd sat in the hotel bar till midnight and he'd told her the story, the whole lot. She loved it at first – who wouldn't? – but when she'd realised it wasn't going anywhere and she wouldn't get a part, and didn't even want one by ten, ten thirty, he'd gone into overdrive and couldn't stop. 'It's getting late.' 'I really oughta go.' 'Say, is that the time?' Said at roughly fifteen minute intervals until, 'Hey, Paul, I'm outa here. Goodnight.'

As the glass doors slid apart and he walked up to the reception desk, Paul wondered how Sasha would get rid of him now that there was no potential for an interesting sideline to the account. He saw Bracken Foods dripping away through his fingers, a bland little mess. He was on self-destruct.

'Paul.' Glacial eyes. Ice. 'You OK this morning?'

'Yes. Look, I'm sorry about last night. Unforgivable giving you all that lumber.'

She smiled. 'S'OK.' For a moment he thought she meant it, that she had a bit of softness after all. He might make an effort. Perhaps all was not lost this side of the Atlantic.

Jeremy was waiting by the studio door. They were having a heatwave, the high noon sun blazing down through windless air. He was sweating, but not with the heat.

He'd tried to get into the studio, but the usual tactics had failed him. Perhaps they'd sensed his nervousness, misconstrued its source. He felt furtive hanging about in the street, like some sort of foodie groupie. The studio people probably thought he was a nutter.

He'd lost count of the number of times he'd tried to telephone Marsha. Always the answerphone, but he couldn't leave a message, not about this. He'd thought of going to the flat off Onslow Square, but he wanted to speak to Marsha alone. Paul alone, too. It seemed the only way.

His great fear was that Marsha could already have acted, under duress from Paul, and that maybe he was already too late. This was the thought that kept nagging at him, that had eventually brought him to this side street at midday on a Thursday, with the build-up to press day at its height.

He began to pace back and forth, once again rearranging the words he might say to Marsha. He disliked the huge power he prayed she still contained: his child, in her. He felt remarkably ambivalent about Marsha herself. A small residue of the old fondness remained, but it wasn't enough for him to really care, not about her, only the part that was a vehicle for what was his. If anyone had told him, only weeks ago, what it would feel like, this lavish desire to ensure the survival of his child, he simply would not have believed it possible, at least, not for him.

He had never given much thought to becoming a father; he and Angel, astonishingly it now seemed, had never once even talked about having children. It wasn't that he or rather they, because he had come to assume joint thought, had ruled it out, nothing so positive, after all; they really had not talked about it, considered the hugeness of it. Perhaps that was it, too big to contemplate. The change of lifestyle so utter. The only person who said anything was his mother, but he'd never taken much notice, another status quo he couldn't envisage changing.

He loved Grace, but in the context of their particular relationship he had always felt it his filial role to thwart her whenever the opportunity arose. Of course, it was childish of him to include providing her with grandchildren in such a pettish campaign, but these things were difficult to alter. In every other respect he had long felt like the grown-up in his dealings with her, as long ago as his early teens when he thought he had stopped allowing her to upset him. She was a childlike woman, the sort who had been spoiled rotten by adoring elderly parents, then indulged by an equally elderly husband. 'My little girl,' he remembered his father issuing softly in the direction of his mother, across the big mahogany dining table when she said something pert and quirky and pretty silly. But whatever it was about her that had attracted the otherwise sombre figure that was his father had a similar effect on him. He could forgive her just about anything, and she knew it, but there was still plenty of room for the thwarting, and life would have been quite untenable during his teens, until he went away to university, if there hadn't been this element in their relationship, because Grace could be, if allowed, a tyrant.

She'd tried it on a bit when he and Angel were first married, the old possessive stuff, mother and son, almost overt attempts to exclude Angel when the three of them were together. But Angel was more than a match. For a start she had twice the brains, although that didn't always count for much in such situations. Angel, being Angel, had decided to make Grace a friend, a novel experience for a woman who all her life had eschewed any sort of friendship with women. Grace was, until Angel, exclusively a man's woman, unable as well as unwilling to make the effort where her own sex was concerned. Angel, quietly, almost with stealth, had worked on Grace and won her round, never presuming too far, allowing space for the mother-and-son bit. Jeremy watched it happen, with admiration and renewed surges of love. Angel's secret was that she was not a possessive woman, which gave him hope for what was to come.

He had not thought of himself as possessive until now; after all, he'd had plenty of practice in years gone by, taking the supporting role, watching Paul get off with the girls he'd fancied first. Then the ultimate restraint, when the three of them had shared the flat in Shepherd's Bush and he'd fallen in love with Angel, a good two years before she'd begun to love him.

It ought to have been unbearable, all those nights when she had been in bed with Paul and he'd been alone in the room next door, praying they wouldn't be noisy. They'd never discussed her bedroom life with Paul, before or after the miraculous moment when she'd chosen him. He'd been careful not to make it seem like a miracle, to effect the transition from friend to lover in a manner that was almost casual, and this had set the tenor for their whole relationship, a restrained passion, a hidden, unspoken core set to last the distance.

The strangest part now was how divorced he felt his marriage to Angel was from the business in hand. He had utter faith in Angel's acceptance of his plan, her ability to adapt to having another person in their home to manage it with all the pragmatic skill she had employed with Grace; and if she wanted they could have a child of their own. He didn't want this first child, Marsha's, to grow up alone the way he had.

The studio door swung open and Marsha emerged, shading her eyes against the emerging brightness.

'Jeremy? What are you doing here?'

'Marsha.' He didn't kiss her. 'Is there somewhere we can talk?'

'Is this a good idea, Jeremy?' She didn't attempt to hide her wariness.

'Is Paul at home?'

'No. He's in the States.'

'Can we go to the flat then,' he said, making it sound like a decision.

Jennifer Chapman

They didn't speak in the taxi. The driver did this for them, a twanging monologue about nothing in particular, sprinkled with extreme right-wing politics.

'I'd hang the lot of 'em,' he continued, even as Jeremy was handing him the fare.

The traffic was heavy with buses, and Jeremy took Marsha's arm as they crossed the road.

'The white mausoleum' was how he always thought of Paul and Marsha's home, cold even on a day like this. Marsha ushered him into the drawing room and followed, not asking him if he wanted a drink or anything, seemingly not even wanting him to sit down. He felt a sudden chill in his heart, momentarily convinced he was too late.

'You've had an abortion,' he accused her.

'No.' She turned from him with a weary sigh. 'No.'

He sat down, uninvited. The relief was overwhelming.

'Paul wants me to.'

'I assumed so.'

'Don't. I feel as if I've stuck a knife in him.'

'He's not left you?'

'I really don't know.'

'Marsha, I'm sorry.'

'Oh.' She covered her face with her hands and began to sob.

Jeremy waited a moment and then he went to her. For quite some while they remained by the fireplace, Marsha's deep sobs reverberating down through his shoulder. Neither heard the front door nor saw Paul as he came into the room.

# CHAPTER NINE

He had come home in conciliatory mood. Just enough distance and time had elapsed for him to have compromised with his pride, although his thoughts were trapped in the situation like a record stuck in a groove.

He had tried to watch the film on the plane, but if anyone had asked him about it he could not have been sure whether there were cowboys and Indians or crooks and cops. He had been here before, all those years ago in Shepherd's Bush when Jeremy had taken Angel from him. He had not seen it coming then either. He had never seen it coming with Jeremy.

Jeremy, the fat boy at school: he had felt sorry for him. Circumstances had thrown them together, and Paul had discovered a surprising sense of loyalty, of the lame-dog sort. Sharp words and fists at the ready when the unkind taunts floated across the playing field. 'Leave him alone.' 'Bugger off.'

The alliance had robbed him of the wider circle of friends he might otherwise have enjoyed; not that he'd thought about it like that, not at the age he was then. The odd part was, Jeremy hadn't even seemed particularly bothered by his unpopularity or whether Paul remained his friend. Paul did all the running, chasing after something he didn't understand. From the outset Jeremy controlled the relationship, but it took years before Paul realised Jeremy always got his own way and that if he was seen as vulnerable he used this to advantage.

The only time Jeremy was actually vulnerable Paul did not see it, only registered in a superficial schoolboy way that his friend was somehow different when he was at home. Visits to Jeremy's house were very few, and in memory wrapped up into just one occasion. They must have been thirteen or fourteen. It was the first time Paul met Mrs Holden and he was quite smitten by her. She was much younger than his own mother, than the mothers of any other boys he knew. She was pretty, too, and she flirted with him, actually flirted with him. He liked it, but at the same time could see what this behaviour was doing to Jeremy, who became sulky, something he never did at school.

It was the first time Paul remembered feeling awkward, and not because of Mrs Holden. Well, indirectly it was because of her, but really because for once he felt that he and Jeremy were on different sides.

Mrs Holden said things to him that, although to begin with they appeared straightforward and flattering, were perhaps more to do with Jeremy than with him. They were remarks that hinted at unfavourable comparison: she had heard about how good he was at games, and with his physique she could see why. She liked a boy with a healthy appetite, and he was lucky not to have to worry about getting fat. No chance of that, not for him.

The entire visit had been like that. He had become aware that Jeremy wanted them to go somewhere else, out for a walk, anywhere, but Mrs Holden managed to counter her son's restive attempts at escape, as if she had planned the afternoon and had an arsenal of enticements at the ready: a cricket match on the new colour television (they still had black and white at his house); a bottle of beer, just for him, 'Jeremy has not yet acquired the taste'; even the offer of a cigarette; and a wonderful calorific tea which Jeremy was enjoined not to 'stuff in his usual way'. He'd felt sorry for Jeremy, even more so than he did at school.

He'd thought no more about it, not for years and years, not until the thing had happened with Angel and he'd tried to puzzle out why she had chosen Jeremy, and in a brief and uncharacteristic piece of mean-thinking it had come into mind that perhaps she, too, had felt sorry for him.

He had chosen to be dignified about what had happened, finding some comfort, if there could be any in such a situation, in this very dignity, in having the strength of mind not to display his bitterness and sense of betrayal. The truth, if he could have found it then, was that he did not want to lose either of them and would have been hard pushed to make a choice. He had not felt ready for marriage himself, had not even given it much thought, other than as a natural progression for some time fairly far distant. It was only when faced with the fait accompli that was Jeremy and Angel that he took any account of his own shortcomings. Somehow it was easier to blame himself, for being careless, rather than to accept that however he might have behaved Angel would still have chosen Jeremy.

He thought he had managed it all rather well, and the magnanimity he felt had helped him through the miserable spasms of jealousy and loneliness when he had seen that there was no longer any room for him between the other two. He knew that really he was a fool, but he could not imagine the rest of his life without Jeremy and Angel remaining some part of it.

'Don't be too kind to us,' Angel had said, mystifyingly, on a rare occasion when it had been just the two of them in the flat. 'We've treated you shamefully. You ought to hate us and I think we need that for a bit.'

To his own shame he seized on the 'for a bit', hearing it as some kind of promise for the future. It had damaged him, Jeremy and Angel. Perhaps he had never really felt the same about himself since, even after he had found Marsha, but he had thought the friendship had come through it, bloody fool that he was.

*Jennifer Chapman*

The image of Marsha and Jeremy in the hallway was now so hot in his mind he could barely concentrate on the traffic. He had already surged through one set of red lights. Horns had blared, the sound making him feel even more murderous. It seemed that at last the hatred Angel had asked for all those years ago was something he could really feel. He wanted to do harm, real harm, a sensation he had never experienced before. He sped along the A10, exceeding 100mph when the road dualled. It might have been better if he had been stopped by the police, but if they had asked him where he was going he could not have said, even though it was a blind, headlong rush to the only place he could go.

# CHAPTER TEN

'She's all grains and pulses and big buckle sandals,' muttered Cliff, his gaze not shifting from the huge television screen that dominated Sylvia's sitting room.

Sylvia laughed. So did Angel. The social worker, she of the sandals, had just left, a cup of Sylvia's extra strong tea inside her, plus a bourbon biscuit.

Cliff, his vast stomach hanging over the settee, his slippered feet resting on one of Sylvia's macramé cushions, spent his entire time in this relaxed pose while the rest of the household got on with life around him. Angel was not sure whether he and Sylvia were married, or whether he was the father of all her children. He was simply Cliff, 'The Immovable Object', as Sylvia referred to him.

Denise called him 'Dad' although there was no likeness. She and the baby were on the floor. Kevin, who had chain-smoked throughout the social worker's visit, was in one of the armchairs. He looked even more diminutive sitting there, his feet not quite reaching the carpet.

This, it seemed, was how they spent their days, with Sylvia running around after them, providing endless mugs of tea. The vacuum cleaner, a highly complicated-looking piece of machinery, seemingly brand new, stood abandoned next to the telly, its tubes and flex in listless disarray. A row of wayward busy Lizzies lined up on the windowsill, tumourish-looking shoots rucking up the net curtain. The room was square and small, a strange mixture of smells: Shake and Vac (an innovation Angel had been forced to ban Sylvia using in her house – the awful smell), Kev's cigarettes, the sugar-sweet, mallowy pong of baby. It was a room with no space for style, just the random additions of necessity, extra chairs, a strange shelving arrangement within Cliff's reach and upon which stood a complete survival kit of electric kettle, thermos flask, tea bags, biscuit barrel, a couple of four-packs of lager, a box of tissues, Alka Seltzer.

The colours had all merged into a general mauvey greyness, as if full value had long ago been had from every piece of hard and soft furnishing. But for all this the room had a warmth that made it feel more pleasant, easy and inviting than dingy and depressing. It was the sort of room where you felt like sitting down for a bit – if you could find a spare seat – and letting it all ebb and flow around you. Angel, who had called round to deliver Chaucer's christening present, an antique silver tankard she'd had engraved with his name, took a bite from the biscuit Sylvia had placed on the side of the saucer when she'd handed her tea.

'No, you stay there,' Sylvia had insisted when the social worker turned up. 'After all, you're Chaucer's godmum.'

Angel wasn't quite certain who the social worker was visiting; perhaps it was the whole family, although she couldn't imagine Sylvia had ever needed such outside interference in the management of her family. Capability incarnate was Sylvia.

'Egg boxes and toilet roll inners, that's what you'll be needing, girl, from now on,' Cliff declared, his eyes still glued to the screen as children's television began.

'He's not even crawling yet, Dad.'

'Even so.'

Mid-afternoon on a Thursday and here she was paying a social visit. Angel took another nibble at the biscuit. It was

years since she'd been near anything more biscuity than a
Ryvita. It seemed years since she'd had time to breathe, but
all of a sudden she had reached some kind of plateau at work.
The struggling, the climbing, she'd never thought about it
coming to an end this way, albeit probably temporarily,
although that didn't stop its being quite terrifying, the clear
desk.

Her tea drunk and nowhere apart from the floor to put her
cup and saucer, she got up and took it out to the kitchen
where Sylvia was stirring a pan of mince.

'Everything all right?' Sylvia asked, banging the wooden
spoon on the side of the pan to knock off the residue of meat.
'If you don't mind my saying so, you haven't been looking
quite yourself lately.'

'I'm fine,' Angel said, prickling a little.

'I didn't mean to pry.'

'No, of course not.'

'It was nice of you to call by. Jeremy all right, is he?'

'As far as I know.' Damn. Why had she said that?

'I'm always here if you want me,' Sylvia said in a slightly
martyred voice designed to stave off any further suggestion
that she was minding other than her own business.

'Yes.' Angel hovered for a moment, dangerously close to
sudden confession. Jeremy came and went, came and went.
So did she. She hadn't actually told him that she wouldn't be
able to adopt Marsha's baby, but he knew. He'd stopped any
mention of the situation, but she knew it consumed him every
moment of the day and night and that he was working to his
own agenda now, no longer even inviting her to the meetings.

'I'd better go,' she said to Sylvia.

'All right, dear. Take it easy, though.'

She had to pass through the living room to leave.

'Even so,' Cliff was saying. 'Oh, bye.' He waved to her
from his settee.

'Bye, and thanks for Chaucer's present,' trilled Denise.
'Wave "bye, bye",' she said, lifting the baby's chubby arm.

'See yer,' muttered Kev.

Outside, Angel walked slowly down to the end of the road, past all the council houses that looked exactly like Sylvia's, same colour front doors, scrubby bits of garden going brown with the summer drought, children's bikes abandoned on the pavement. She turned into the road that ran through the centre of the village, past the church and then into the lane. She saw no one. It was that time of day when nobody was about and it seemed hard to believe that anyone lived in the silent cottages and bungalows clustered close to the church. The ghost of an afternoon. She felt peculiarly alone.

Turning the last bend in the lane before she reached the farmhouse, she saw Paul's Mercedes parked just beyond their gate. She quickened her step, convinced that it had to be bad news. Possibilities shot into her head. Marsha had lost the baby. Marsha had left Paul. Paul had left Marsha. Marsha had lost the baby. Oh, please, Marsha had lost the baby.

Paul was in the garden, sitting, smoking a cigarette, on the surreal rustic seat she and Jeremy had paid a ridiculously huge amount for and then suffered pangs of decadence withdrawal so that they eventually moved it out of sight from the house.

He stood up when he saw her, although she hadn't called to him.

'Has something happened?' she said. No greeting. No pretence now.

Paul threw down the cigarette.

'Careful,' she said, automatic words, 'the garden is tinder dry.'

'For God's sake,' Paul said, unpleasantly, but grinding his heel into the grass.

'Well, it is,' Angel protested, but weakly. She could see in his face that there was something she probably wouldn't want to hear.

It was nearly nine o'clock. Jeremy felt cold despite the oppressive heat that persisted outside. The air-conditioning must have been turned up to maximum, trapping him in this false atmosphere for which he had come ill-prepared. Others were still working, but it had thinned out, quietened down, random clacking of keyboards rather than the daytime full orchestra.

He was attempting to write a piece about a new biography of Kenneth Grahame, comparing the life to that of other children's writers of the era: the common thread of peculiarity, the persistence of childish cruelty throughout adult life; a sort of monstrous mutation. The piece was getting out of hand. He could see Toad with the makings of a serial killer.

'Fancy a glass?' Sybil Greenford, avant-garde gardening writer. She'd done a few reviews for him. 'Come on. You look as if you could do with one.'

Sybil looked about fourteen. Short-cropped hair dyed a vibrant sherbet. Small, boyish body wrapped in a powerful piece of plastic, lime green and potentially sweaty had it not been for the refrigeration.

'No thanks, Jail.'

Despite this she came and perched on the corner of his desk, the plastic squeaking on the melamine.

'Don't call me that. It's my birthday.'

'Really?'

'Well, nearly. December, actually.'

'Celebrating already?'

'No. It's a big one. With an '0' at the end.'

'Wait till you get to your teens.'

'Shut up.'

He was typing again now. Sometimes it was easier this way, just keep the words coming with his mind partly engaged elsewhere. For a moment the brief badinage had deflected the overwhelming preoccupation that had nothing to do with *The Wind in the Willows*.

Sybil remained perched, swinging a long bare leg back and forth.

'Come on, then,' he said, powering down the machine, pushing back his chair.

He felt oddly light-headed, hugely relieved that the baby was still intact, that Marsha was evidently as fixated on its survival as he had been from the start. He almost felt like celebrating.

Marsha, alone at the flat, switched on the 'Nine O'Clock News' but couldn't concentrate on the stories, so far removed from the drama that was her own life right now.

Paul's sudden appearance and equally sudden departure replayed itself again and again. He'd got the wrong idea, of course he had, of course he had. She'd asked Jeremy to leave straightaway; she couldn't bear him near her a moment longer. The smell of him, the feel of him, so close, so wrong. She ached for Paul.

She'd tried ringing him on the car phone, but that automaton of a female voice had kept repeating, 'The Vodafone number you are calling is switched off.'

'Where are you?' she said out loud into the emptiness of the flat.

The weather was on when Marsha felt the first flutter from inside. 'No let up for some time to come,' the weatherlady said. 'Have a good evening.'

It was quite dark now but Angel did not switch on the light. She had never been frightened of Paul before, not in all the years she had known him. At the beginning when he had been a gentle, almost lazy lover, never frantic, never out of control, she had enjoyed him as a lover, his casualness about bed, as if it really didn't matter all that much to him whether they did it or not. The boy before him, and boy he was, had tended towards clamminess, limbs sticky with desire, awkward, uncoordinated jerkings, her own body waiting to respond then subsiding in a frustration she had not understood until

72

Paul and his brilliant hands. But this was not how she was thinking of him now.

He had been so angry, as if all of it were her fault, but she could accept no more than a quarter of the blame. Jointly and severally, all four of them. She must have used these words at some point.

'Don't give me your bloody legal tosh,' he barked at her.

'Don't shout at me, please.'

'Who's going to hear, then?' This had been the moment when fear had switched on, perhaps for both of them.

'Let's have some coffee or something. Would you like a drink?' she said, trying to sound calming. 'We ought to sit down and talk.'

'About what? My wife and Jeremy caught in a clinch? What more is there to say?'

They were in the kitchen, by the table where the four of them had sat scoffing breakfast, feeling little more than naughty, thinking they'd cheated on the rules and there wasn't even anyone to catch them out.

Paul sat down heavily, a jarring scrape from the chair. Angel twitched.

'Coffee then?'

'Scotch.'

'Here,' she said when she had returned from the drawing room, and handed him the glass.

He took a gulp and coughed, lit a cigarette and seemed marginally less agitated.

'It is your bloody fault, you know.'

'Oh, Paul, what's the point in blaming?' She sighed and sat down opposite him. There was a huge part of her mind blocked up by what he had told her, the so-called 'clinch', the realisation that even as they sat here Jeremy and Marsha were probably planning the most obvious and perhaps only route they could take.

'It all started with you,' Paul continued, sullen, still accusing.

'That's unfair, and I don't think it was my idea; in fact I know it wasn't. I didn't want it to happen, but I was angry because you and Jeremy . . . oh, this is ridiculous. It happened.'

'I don't mean the weekend. I'm talking about at the flat. You and me and then you and Jeremy.'

'But that was years ago. Surely you haven't been blaming me all this time?'

'Why did you leave me, Angel? You never explained. What was wrong with us?'

'Nothing was wrong, it just . . . oh, I can't remember.'

'So I'm not even memorable?'

'Paul, I'm sorry. Really. Of course I remember, but I just can't think about that now, not after what you've told me.'

'Who'd have thought it, hey?' he laughed, a nasty, harsh, mirthless laugh. 'Old Jez. Not content to take one woman off me, he had to have two.'

'You don't think you might have been mistaken? I mean, when you saw them together.'

'For God's sake, woman. I think the term is "red-handed".'

She poured herself a whisky and passed the bottle across to him.

'Can I have one?' she said as he lit another cigarette.

'Angel. Angel. What are we going to do?' he said, suddenly altering his tone, staring at her hard.

'God, I don't know. Nothing, I suppose. What can we do? It's not up to us, is it?'

'It could be.' He offered her a wistful look.

'No.'

'Why not?'

'You know why not. It doesn't work like that, and you don't really want me. You love Marsha.'

'I don't love her. I hate her.'

'What's the difference? You loved her yesterday, you hate her today; you're all Marsha. There's no room right now for anything else, anyone else, and why should it be me?'

'Why not?'

'Don't keep saying that.'

He stood up, came round to her side of the table and in a sudden movement pulled her up to him and kissed her hard on the mouth. Her chair fell over but he took no notice, holding on to her with a great force. She began to struggle, pushing at his chest, but he tried to kiss her again.

'Come on. Come on,' he demanded. 'Let's just see.'

Now that she had started to struggle it was difficult not to, although the cool-headed Angel registered that passivity was known to be the best course in such a situation. But cool-headedness was no more than a theory as Paul yanked up her skirt.

'Careful,' she pleaded, a seam screaming as the stitching gave way.

'For God's sake!'

'Sorry,' she said, as if apologising for being unromantic. Then, 'For God's sake yourself! Stop it! Stop it!'

'That's better. I need you to be angry, Angel,' he said, breathily, still controlling her with his overwhelming strength, pushing her down to the floor then trapping her beneath his weight.

'Come on! Be angry! Aren't you angry?' And suddenly she was, but not with him. She managed to release an arm and hit him hard across the back.

'I feel I want to kill you, to harm you, but I can't, can I, not really?' He was losing it.

Angel kept hitting him, like pummelling a punch bag, while another, detached part of her thought, 'No, he can't, it's Jeremy who harms me.' Pulling his hair now, the tempo changing; he had penetrated her and she was aroused, damn it, she was aroused.

It did not last much longer, and when he rolled off her his whole being seemed to shrivel, like a caterpillar curling into itself. He started to cry.

'I'm sorry,' he sobbed. 'Angel, I'm so sorry.' He had his back to her.

They both lay very still for a while. Angel could feel her body beginning to stiffen and ache from the earlier resistance. The light had gone from the room and they were in a murky twilight.

'Can you ever forgive me?' he murmured, at last breaking the silence.

'Oh,' she moaned. She might have touched him then, made it somehow all right, but she could not quite allow herself to do so.

He rolled over to face her. 'What a mess. Neither of us needed this.' His expression was pained, as if he had just witnessed a horrible accident.

'I had the impression you did,' she said.

'Angel.'

'Don't. It's all too much.'

'I am sorry, really. I feel bloody awful.'

'I can see that.' She eased herself up off the floor and stumbled out into the hallway, then on through to the drawing room.

'What are you going to do? Will you tell Jeremy?' He had followed her, anxious now.

'Do you think I will have the opportunity?'

'Oh, for . . .' He went over to the window. She heard him zipping up his fly.

'Well, do you?'

'Of course you bloody will. Jeremy will hang on to both of you.'

'And you think I'll let him!' She almost choked out the accusation.

'Yes, I do. Why did you leave me, Angel, why? We were all right together, weren't we? Sex. Friends too. It was nice and easy.'

'That's probably it. Nice and easy isn't always the answer.'

'Well, it should be,' he said quietly. 'It should be.'

'I don't know whether that means you expect too much or not enough,' she said.

76

'Neither do I, but then I'm not as clever as Jeremy, am I? If I was I don't suppose I'd be standing here now.'

'Let's leave Jeremy out of this.'

'I wish we could.'

'You wish. You wish.'

'Angel?'

'No.'

'I suppose I'd better leave.'

'Yes, you'd better.'

'Are you sure you're all right?'

'Of course I'm not all right.'

He had moved away from the window and come towards her. 'Is there anything I should do? I mean, you're not hurt, are you?'

'Don't flatter yourself.'

'Christ, Angel, you're so, so . . .'

'Unsatisfactory? I know that.'

'Don't be silly. I didn't mean that.'

'What then?'

'Oh, I'm not into these word games. You never used to be like this, you know.'

'What was I like, then?' She felt very weary and sounded it, too. She was also beginning to feel that the lack of light was turning melodramatic.

'You weren't cynical and sarcastic for a start. You were,' he hesitated, 'untroubled.'

'Ah.'

'There you go again. Angel, you should have married me.'

'You didn't ask me.'

'I thought it was understood.'

'Understood?'

'Well, you always understood.'

In another corner of her mind Angel heard Jeremy's voice: 'You just don't understand.'

She wasn't ready to 'understand' anything, and long after Paul had gone and an even deeper confusion set in she remained, dishevelled and inert, in the dark, enveloped now in a victim status she felt powerless to shake off. She could have got up, had a bath, gone to bed, but a side of her she hardly recognised kept her where she was.

She had lost all sense of time and no longer expected Jeremy to return. At one point it had crossed her mind that Paul had perhaps hoped Jeremy would come home tonight, that he would find them, just as Paul had found him with Marsha; but it was such a sad, pathetic thought and quickly moved over as she allowed anger to resurface, only to be replaced by a whimpering self-pity and longing for discovery. Like Paul, she could no longer determine the right direction for anger and in her own confusion was almost able to understand why he had come to her as he had. She remembered, with inconsequential clarity, a terrible crime that had taken place in her home town when she was a teenager. A man, crazed with jealousy, had raped and murdered the wife of his own wife's lover. She even remembered his name, Sothcott, unusual, Keith Sothcott. He'd worked all hours to satisfy his wife's obsession for domestic appliances. Day shifts. Night shifts. And while he was at work his best friend was at his house screwing his wife. When the affair had come to light the lover's wife had gone round to see Sothcott and he'd ended up knifing her. There were three different types of washing machine in the kitchen. Hardly room for anything else. She'd read the story in the local evening newspaper, followed the reports of the trial. She'd already decided she wanted to do law. Sothcott was the one who had her sympathy.

Shortly after midnight she heard Jeremy come home, heard him briefly in the hallway, then going upstairs. Soon he might start to search the house, or perhaps he wouldn't. She began to feel panicky at the thought of being found, equally, not being found. She wished she had stirred, had the bath, prepared herself for a dignified confrontation. This sitting in the dark, the wounded animal, she and Jeremy had never played it like this, victim and aggressor. She had nothing she wanted to gain by being found like this.

Her mind began to race, her heart pound. She considered and decided on what seemed like the most minor course of deception, to stay where she was and make it appear she had fallen asleep waiting for him to come home. There was the awful possibility that he might not look for her, that he would work it out Paul had been. He might think she had already left. He'd sleep and begin the sorting out in the morning. But she didn't have to wait that long. He switched on the main light straightaway, revealing her on the sofa, and by his expression she must have looked a mess.

He hurried across the room, anxiety swishing.

'Angel! What happened? Have we been burgled? Are you all right?'

'Burgled?'

'There's a chair knocked over in the kitchen. I'll call the police.'

'No!'

He stared at her, uncomprehending.

'Paul's been.'

He still looked puzzled.

'Jeremy, he practically raped me.' She hadn't meant to say it.

Dumbfounded now.

'He came to tell me about you and Marsha.'

'Oh God, I never thought.'

'You're going to be with her. You are, aren't you? It's the obvious solution.'

'What are you talking about? Just because Paul came home and found us together? He got it all wrong, but I never thought he'd come here, that he'd tell you.'

'What did you think, if you did at all?'

'I went to see Marsha to make sure she was all right, that's all.'

'To make sure she hadn't got rid of the baby, you mean.'

He sat down in one of the armchairs and covered his face with his hands.

'Yes,' he said quietly.

'Have you been with her all evening?'

'No. I left straight after Paul. I've been working.'

'Working! You smell like a brewery.' A huge sense of relief had flooded through her and now she was having a go at him.

'I was working till nine, ten, I don't know. I went for a drink with a colleague. You didn't expect me to ring, did you? To ask your permission? I didn't think we were like that, Angel. We never have been.'

'I'm not sure what we're "like" any more. And did you hear what I said a moment ago, that Paul practically raped me?' She was going to use it now, as a weapon, and she hated herself for the compulsion to do so.

'You're not serious.'

'I am.' She could hear herself sounding petulant.

'He couldn't have known what he was doing.'

She stared at him in disbelief.

'Don't you mind that Paul came here and forced me, forced me to . . . I could have him arrested, you know.'

'Don't do that. We don't want to make things any more difficult than they already are.'

'What are you saying? Jeremy?'

'I'm sorry, Angel. He didn't really hurt you, did he, not Paul?'

'You wouldn't do anything about it even if he had, would you?' She was verging on incredulity, but a clear, cold reed of truth had finally got through. 'You don't want to rock the boat, only the bloody cradle.'

# CHAPTER ELEVEN

'No shirts to iron?' Sylvia had knocked on the study door but come straight in anyway.

'No shirts,' said Angel, without looking up from the file of papers she was studying. Jeremy had been gone a week, back to his mother's, of all places. Angel could hear their conversations in her mind's ear. Grace reassuring him with all the bad points peculiar to a mother-in-law's eye. Jeremy probably telling her to 'shut up' but building up the dossier of faults that would free him of guilt. A sense of loss? How quickly you sped apart when you had been so close; lost the sense of what it had been like, being together.

'Nothing wrong, is there?' Sylvia remained in the doorway, her head, Angel now saw, tilted a little to one side, inviting confidences.

Remaining silent just a little too long, Angel realised she had confirmed Sylvia's suspicions; more horrifying, perhaps she had wanted to.

Sylvia sighed.

'Shall I get you a nice cup of tea?'

As opposed to a nasty one, thought Angel, hearing the silly response Jeremy gave to such offers. She couldn't concentrate while she waited for Sylvia to return with the tea. She had the awful certainty she would tell Sylvia that Jeremy had gone home to his mother.

Grace had seemed less pleased than expected when Jeremy rang her to say he'd like to spend a few days at the house in Amersham. It was the place his father had bought when he'd retired, a return to family roots, except all trace of the Holden relatives had long disappeared, and there was little remaining in the sprawl of new housing and out-of-town shopping to trigger nostalgic reverie for a rural boyhood. Grace had protested at being taken away from her locale, the friends she had made at the tennis club, the amateur dramatics society, but in this one thing Harold had been insistent, and Jeremy, hearing his mother's plaintive whinge, had suspected it was largely because of the tennis club and the am drams, neither of which included Harold, that his father had decided on the move. He wanted Grace to himself for his retirement years, taken later than most, when he was already well into his seventies.

He'd lasted eighteen months, that was all. He wasn't, after all, a man who could live without work, and even the full-time presence of Grace could not keep him going.

Unexpectedly, Grace had remained at the house in Amersham, more affected by Harold's death than anyone might have guessed. She'd aged very quickly, putting on what looked like about fifteen years in the space of a few months, so it was quite a shock to remember she was only in her mid-fifties, the same generation as Joan Collins, Joan Bakewell, vintage birds Jeremy and a host of other men really rather fancied in a silver-screen-distancing sort of way.

Jeremy had taken a single bag of clothes from the farmhouse the morning he left. He'd gone straight to work, stowing the bag under his desk amid the nest of computer cables. At the end of the day he'd taken the train to Amersham, then a taxi to the house which was outside the town.

It was a large house, solidly built – in the same year as his father's birth. It was much too big for Grace, had been too large for two people. Jeremy had considered suggesting a move to somewhere smaller, but he would have felt obliged to urge such a move to be in the direction of Cambridge, and he was not ready for the final confirmation of this role reversal, even though for years he had felt more like the parent than the child.

He let himself into the house. Grace had given him a key soon after his father had died, just in case. Both knew this was a small piece of melodrama, but Jeremy had seen the truth of her bereavement and taken the key without comment.

'Is that you, Jeremy darling?' he heard her call from the dining room.

He flung down the bag in the hall and pushed open the dining room door which was already a little ajar.

'Darling, how nice.' The briefest pause, then: 'This is Wilfred. Wilfred, Jeremy, my son.'

Jeremy stared, he realised, a little rudely, at the man sitting adjacent to his mother at the big mahogany dining table. Wilfred was a man of indeterminate age, but probably younger rather than older. Jeremy's immediate impression was of a certain shiftiness, as if Wilfred anticipated the demand for some sort of explanation.

'Wilfred is my PG' Grace announced, standing up to fetch a plate for Jeremy, who noted straightaway that she had affected a subtle change in her appearance. Her hair was shorter, a different colour, more brown, and the clothes she wore, they were not the style he had become used to on her, more flowing, the absence of beige. He kissed her lightly on the cheek she proffered as she passed him to fetch the food.

'We didn't wait. You see, you didn't tell us what time you'd be home.'

Jeremy sat down in the place that had always been his father's and felt vaguely cheated. He had not looked forward to the inevitable need to explain to Grace what had happened between him and Angel, but now that any discussion of the subject was ruled out by the presence of this Wilfred person, he felt a little piqued.

Grace set down a steaming plate of spaghetti bolognese in front of him.

'Your mother's pièce de résistance,' said Wilfred with an awkward little laugh.

'Yes,' said Jeremy, managing to stop himself adding, 'I know.'

Wilfred is an actor,' said Grace, airily. 'I expect you've seen him on television.'

'I'm sorry, I can't say I have,' Jeremy answered, twirling the spaghetti on his fork.

'Blink and you'd miss me,' Wilfred laughed. 'Of course, I know what you do, Jeremy. I've read many of your reviews. Just as well it's not theatre, hey.' He repeated the awful, grating little laugh.

'I'm sorry?' Jeremy knew what he meant but chose not to give him the satisfaction.

'My son is a nasty, cruel boy, Wilfred. Don't take any notice of him,' Grace said, avoiding Jeremy's eye.

'It's nice for Grace to have you home for a few days,' Wilfred persisted. 'She's always talking about you. A proud mother I would say, and with good cause.'

Jeremy wondered whether he would be able to finish the spaghetti without being sick, but the next several mouthfuls were accomplished through a hovering silence that gave added volume to every extraneous sound.

'I know Angel's not a pudding-maker, so I thought I'd give you a treat,' Grace said, beginning to sound flustered, and now avoiding looking at either Wilfred or Jeremy as she brought forth a baked jam roll too perfect in shape to have come from anywhere other than Marks & Spencer.

The word 'Angel' had been said.

There was even custard.

Jeremy prayed that Grace would not start criticising his wife, however obliquely; he really wouldn't be able to stand it. Being in the wrong was a new experience for him, quite alien to his nature; he had never played life that way, not until now. Even taking Angel off Paul had not seemed wrong.

He allowed Wilfred and Grace to dissuade him from

helping with stacking the dishwasher and went upstairs to the room Grace had prepared for him, the one at the far end of the landing, not the one where he and Angel had occasionally slept. Perhaps this had been given over to Wilfred.

He sat down on the single divan and pulled out his mobile phone. The number rang three times, then he heard his own voice on the answering machine. If he'd been a different sort of person, his conscience might have been eased a little by this action, but because Angel's failure to answer engendered a superficial sense of relief, he felt worse on the deeper level of culpability. He pressed the button for the other number he had programmed into the phone and waited for Marsha to answer. Paul, Angel had told him, would already be back in the States. Marsha wasn't replying either.

Downstairs in the drawing room his sensibilities were still sufficiently intact to be assaulted by Wilfred's white socks, hitherto not exposed but now revealed above the grey-moccasined foot resting across Wilfred's knee as he lounged in Jeremy's father's chair, a cigarette pincered between his fingers.

Is this some sort of statement I'd rather not know about? thought Jeremy, suddenly seeing that the subtle change in his mother was edging towards the two Joans. He glanced at Grace, who for a very brief moment met his gaze then looked away and started to chatter.

Jeremy was grateful when Wilfred got up and turned on the television, although the manner of his doing so added further to what he was beginning to see as a proprietorial edge. He even held on to the remote control, flicking through the channels, settling without consultation on ITV.

When they all went to bed Jeremy waited for a while, expecting a knock on the door, Grace coming to find out what was going on with Angel, but she didn't come, and at last he fell asleep.

He had not anticipated the sense of displacement that grew as the first week wore on. He began to realise his own stupidity and selfishness to have assumed there would be a place for him at the house in Amersham, but any such sensitivity was largely dulled by the increasing anxiety caused through the unanswered phone at the flat off Onslow Square. By Thursday he was beginning to fear for Marsha's safety, remembering what Angel had told him about Paul's manic state of mind, but then he saw her across the office, standing in a studio kitchen. He got up and went over to the television.

'Didn't know you were into pastry,' a female colleague observed.

'You'd be surprised.'

'And then you make separate little parcels,' Marsha was saying.

'If you don't mind my saying so, what you two need is a baby,' concluded Sylvia, picking up Angel's untouched and now cold cup of tea.

Angel had not told her the whole story, just enough to explain the lack of shirts to iron and the likelihood that there wouldn't be any for some time to come, if ever again.

'You two would make wonderful parents, and with such a lovely home, I mean, what's to stop you? I'd always help, you know, with the looking after and that, although I expect you'd want a proper nanny. Oh, I'm sorry, this isn't like me, interfering, but I don't like to see two people unnecessarily, well, miserable, 'cause I bet your Jeremy's just as unhappy as you . . . sorry, I'll mind my own business. Shut up, Sylvia, and look after your own interference.' She left the study, closing the door very gently behind her.

Angel was furious, but with herself – and Jeremy, and Paul, and Marsha (Marsha least of all, actually), Sylvia only for being the messenger. There was nothing worse than being told the truth when it hurt so much. There should be a baby and it ought to be hers and Jeremy's; it ought to be, it ought to be. She'd call him and tell him, straightaway.

She rang the newspaper but he wasn't there. The abject sense of capitulation and desire to give more than forgive had diluted a little by the third unsuccessful call at six thirty. She'd tried the mobile but it was switched off, which usually meant he was at his desk. She tried again at seven thirty; still no joy. In desperation, before she lost the resolve altogether, she rang Grace's number. A man who said his name was Wilfred answered. Jeremy, he informed her, had just called to say he would not be home tonight and that he was staying at his friend Paul's.

# CHAPTER TWELVE

Jeremy was quite glad it had been the odious Wilfred who'd answered the phone. Grace would have known straightaway that he was a little drunk. He didn't actually know where he was going to spend the night. He'd been to an early evening book launch at the Groucho and tipped rather too much champagne down his throat. He'd come back to the office to write up the piece, but his head ached, that astringent champagne ache, and he felt a bit sick when he looked at the computer screen.

He got up, swayed a little, then headed for the coffee machine. Jail Bait beat him to it; she'd got the lurid green on again.

'Ghastly, ghastly, awful,' she said to him, the most appalling-smelling drink steaming up through her fingers.

'Yes,' he said, glumly, trying not to see or sniff the drink. 'What is it, chocolate?'

'The launch, ducky. The launch. Didn't you see me there?'

Jeremy marvelled at how he could have missed her.

'Are you going to review it?'

'I suppose so.'

'You shouldn't, you know. It's an Aga Saga in thin disguise.'

'How do you know?'

'I pinched your review copy when it first came in two months ago.'

'For God's sake.'

'Well, you didn't even notice.'

'How many other books have you taken?'

'None. Well, just a few, the ones I know you'll savage anyway.'

'How would you like it if I nicked your gardening manuals?'

'You wouldn't, though, would you? Real booksey bods like you don't.'

He didn't miss the flattery. 'Don't do what? Half-inch books or tend to their gardens?'

'Both,' she laughed. 'Jez?'

'Yup.'

'D'you want some help with it? The review?' She had an evil glint in her eye. 'I'm in the mood for a bit of savagery.'

They went back to his desk where she took control of the keyboard. 'Aga Saga Revisited,' she keyed in at the top of the screen.

> *Does anyone admit to writing an Aga Saga these days? Does anyone admit to owning an Aga, bastion of the once upwardly mobile, sub-text to a way of life we all thought we wanted and then found wanting?*
>
> *Agas and sagas were all about huge families . . .*

'What about the book? Any chance of a mention?' Jeremy sipped at his black coffee and realised he was wondering what it would be like to make love to Jail. He had already been through the shoulder-crying stage with her, heard all about the bastard boyfriend. He'd twigged some weeks ago that she'd become passable, that it wouldn't take much to start an affair; but in the fifteen years he'd been married to Angel, only twice had he strayed, on both occasions regretting it, ruing the risk.

'Right,' said Jail, beginning to type again.

> *This saga is an Aga that's run out of heat, out of time, out of place. It doesn't work any more. It*

> *used to be quite efficient, in the eighties, when*
> *writers first started cooking up this Spanish*
> *omelette of prose . . .*

Omlette, Jeremy remembered. When he'd first started this job, he and Angel had challenged one another to include certain unlikely words in what each was writing: his reviews, her reports. 'Bet you can't get *"Zeitgeist"* in,' she'd come up with after 'omelette' got on to the page, but he had, and the wretched word had caught on like a virus.

'That's enough,' he said, leaning across and switching off the monitor. 'Let's go and have something to eat.'

He did not feel particularly hungry but thought a bit of food might help shift the stabbing pain between his eyes. Jail picked up her huge, heart-shaped bag and slung it on her arm.

'I thought you'd never ask,' she said, looking at him as if famished. 'How about a takeaway back at my place?'

'Sorry,' he said, brushing a grain of egg-fried rice from her cropped hair.

'Oh, don't say that. I can't bear it when men apologise.'

'That's your trouble.'

'And don't start explaining me. I don't want that tonight. I want you to fuck me.'

'I know.'

Sybil's flat was as weird as her clothes, horrible clashing colours that had done nothing for Jeremy's head. They were sitting in a huge room that appeared to serve all parts of the day and night. There were three beds, two of them double, a long narrow dining table that looked as if it belonged in a monastery, a bench either side, then the cavernous sofa in which the pair of them were now sitting amidst the debris of chicken chow mein. The lighting was glimmer-level apart from a praying mantis table lamp on the floor close by them and one of those hideous lava lamps reincarnated from the seventies, with a great blob of goo slowly rising and falling inside a tube of turquoise liquid.

Jeremy could feel Sybil's restless frustration and wondered whether he could concentrate enough to make an effort. He doubted it. His heart was full of Angel, more than it had been for weeks, Marsha and her condition suddenly relegated to a proper proportion. Staying with Grace, if nothing else, had brought him to his senses, the horrible uprootedness of travelling back to the house in Amersham rather than the farmhouse which contained Angel and everything they had put together to build a home, the familiar comfort of it all, even the bloody Aga. All poor Sybil had was a small impersonal microwave in which they'd heated up the takeaway.

Grace, of course, had a straightforward electric cooker which she avoided as much as possible. Travelling back to Amersham on Friday night, Jeremy tried to work out what he was going to say to Angel. He had every intention of collecting his things from his mother's house and by whatever means, even if it meant a taxi, returning to his own home for the weekend. Uppermost in his mind was the urgent need to effect a reconciliation with Angel, but there was also the rider that he couldn't face another weekend of Wilfred.

'Hello there, stranger,' Wilfred greeted him gaily. He was wearing one of Grace's floral aprons and a pair of pink rubber gloves. 'I've made a nice turbot mornay for tonight. Oh, by the way, your wife was trying to get hold of you last night. I told her where you were. Did she reach you OK?'

'Darling boy!' Grace exclaimed, appearing at the top of the stairs like a sepia film star. 'We didn't expect to see you, did we, Wilfred?'

'Really, Mother?' Jeremy said, drily.

'We thought perhaps Angel had forgiven you and you'd be back there tonight.'

'My stuff is here, remember?'

'There's no need to be like that, dear.'

'Like what?'

'Grumpy, darling. Cheer up and let me pour you a drink while Wilfred's putting the finishing touches to his fish pie.'

'Turbot mornay,' sang out Wilfred, retreating to the kitchen, 'as you well know.'

'That man is insufferable,' Jeremy said, following his mother.

'No, dear. You are.'

'Thank you very much.'

'So, are you going to tell me what's going on? I think I've been very good this past week. I haven't said a word, but neither have you. Are we to have the pleasure of your company indefinitely or do you have other plans?'

'Meaning, when am I leaving?' He sat down heavily in the chair that had been his father's. It was true he felt grumpy, although the word was hardly adequate. He had got out of the habit of coping with disappointment, of being, oh, so patient. Perhaps everything had been going his way for too long, not that he was really the sort of person to believe in uncontrollable fate.

'Darling, it's lovely having you, even like this,' Grace said. Jeremy waited for the 'but'. 'But I can see you're unhappy . . .,' she floundered. 'A mother knows,' she added, a little mawkishly.

'Bit late for all that, isn't it?'

'Don't be cutting, Jeremy. It doesn't suit you. I always did the best I could.'

'Sorry. Sorry.' He meant it. Grace had always been true to herself, not a particularly good mother, not especially bad, just selfish, as she was being now, with her mind fixed on the cosy little set-up she had with Mr Fish Pie and in which there was no room for a third party. He knew that he had inherited a large degree of this selfishness himself, but he was generally more subtle about it, a dogged undertow most people didn't see but which invariably got him what and where he wanted.

'I don't want to interfere,' she began again. Jeremy took this to mean she was about to. 'But is all this anything to do with having children, because if it is you have to let Angel have a baby. It's simply not fair to deny a woman that right. No, hear me out. I saw the way she looked at that fat child, Churchill, what's his name, and if you leave it much longer . . . I know I was terribly young when I had you . . . the thing is, leave it too late and you could regret it. I mean, where would I be without my boy?'

'Happily eating fish pie with Wilfred.'

'Stop it, Jeremy. Don't turn everything I say into your slick little critiques.'

'Nice one, Mum.'

'You're being very silly.'

'I'm afraid I am.'

'I just don't understand why you don't want children.'

'Who said it was me?'

Grace looked momentarily thrown.

'Oh, darling boy. But I was on the right track.'

Jeremy said nothing.

'I suppose it's made worse by Paul and his wife starting a family. I expect Paul's full of it, isn't he?'

'You could say that.'

'There you go again. Surely you're pleased for him. Your best friend.'

Of course, he could have said 'yes' and left if at that, but he knew Grace would not leave it alone, and now that Wilfred had told Angel last night's lie he could see the whole thing was utterly hopeless. She knew that Paul was supposed to be back in the States, and if he told her where he'd really been on Thursday night . . . he wasn't sure she would let him tell her anything anyway.

'Do they know if it's a boy or a girl?' Grace was asking. 'You can find out these days, can't you? But I think it spoils the surprise . . .'

'Mother, it's mine.'

'Turbot mornay on the table,' trilled Wilfred.

# CHAPTER THIRTEEN

Awhole month and not a word, not from any of them; but then what could they say? Jeremy and Marsha no doubt were too absorbed in one another and their new life together, and Paul, head down in America, getting on with another sort of new life. Angel felt very left behind, stuck in the place where it had all begun, alone and too miserable to do anything about it.

During the first week she had kept expecting Jeremy to ring, if only to see if she was all right, but by the end of the second week she'd almost accepted that he'd decided on a clean break. She felt that he probably still loved her; – it seemed impossible he could stop, she'd relied on that love so long. He would make contact in due course, but not until time had distanced them even further. The house would have to be sold, everything split up, although she wasn't sure how much of it she wanted. Perhaps he felt the same. Pity it couldn't just be sold as a complete house, like they did in America, ruthless and pragmatic.

Pragmatism was her course now. 'Don't think about things too deeply,' Jeremy had said to her when she was fretting over a case. 'Just get on with what has to be done and the thing will work its way through.' How was she going to survive the rest of her life without Jeremy?

She didn't think she could face another weekend alone, and it wasn't just the missing Jeremy. She had become nervous since Paul's visit, a silly irrational sort of terror creeping up on her and sending her into an uncontrollable shiver. She tried not to think about what had happened that night, not to over-dramatise it. The whole situation was bad enough without allowing herself to dwell on Paul's attack as a criminal offence. Besides, it wasn't Paul that frightened her, but Jeremy, his not being there. It might be easier if she wasn't alone, but she couldn't imagine inflicting herself on any of her friends, and the thought of her family was out of the question. She had told them, a week ago, that Jeremy had left. They were less shocked than she might have expected, as if they'd always seen the possibility, which had rattled her. Her mother had said she'd be welcome any weekend, and her sister-in-law had issued a fey invitation, shrieking mid-sentence, 'Mummy's on the phone. Go away!' But she didn't want to have to tell any of them about Marsha and the baby and had more or less decided that they need never know. There was no reason why they should ever see Jeremy again. The awful notion then leapt into mind that she might never see him again herself.

The phone rang on Friday evening and her heart missed a beat. She knew it would be Jeremy, and the need to hear his voice hit her like the craving for a drug.

'Angel? Sorry to ring you like this. I told Denise she should ring you herself. The thing is, could you possibly have Chaucer tomorrow night? I know it's short notice . . .' The excuses ran on, 'a difficult situation', they wouldn't be asking otherwise, and they'd tried everyone else . . .

'Yes. Yes, of course, Sylvia.' Angel put down the phone.

On Saturday morning she drove into Cambridge. She bought some food for the week, most of which she couldn't imagine eating. She managed to go to Mothercare and buy a toy for Chaucer, then she went to one of the estate agents.

'It's bungalows that people really want at the moment,' the man who took the details said.

'I don't,' said Angel.

'Ah,' said the man, young and too self-assured, 'that's just as well because we don't have any.'

What did she want, he asked. They'd just been offered a nice semi, three beds, on the Arbury Estate. Full central heating, garage and nice low-maintenance garden. On the bus route for the local schools, he added, glancing at the Mothercare bag.

'I'd like a one-bedroom flat in the city centre,' she said, giving him a hard look that told him to mind his own business.

'At a premium, I'm afraid. Get snapped up before they even come on the market.'

'I thought that was bungalows,' she said, drily.

He smirked at her. A difficult customer.

Despite the lack of takers for fully renovated, centrally heated, characterful farmhouses, he pressed her to make an appointment so he could 'measure up'.

'As it happens, I might have a punter for you, but it would have to be a quick sale and at a keen price. Will you be at home tomorrow?'

'Sunday?'

'Our business is seven days a week.'

'Yes,' she said. 'Tomorrow is fine.' At least it would occupy part of the day.

She didn't hang around in Cambridge, didn't go for a coffee in Belinda's the way she and Jeremy so often had after shopping, soaking up the cosmopolitan atmosphere of the place, enjoying the brief lull in their week. 'Perhaps we should try somewhere else,' he'd said, not so many weeks ago, but she hadn't wanted to break the pattern; she liked things the way they were.

Sylvia and Denise brought Chaucer round at six thirty, asleep and balanced precariously in a Moses basket that was far too small for him. Denise left all the talking to her mother: instructions for the next feed if he woke up, which he probably wouldn't, a quick lesson in nappy-changing. A bottle of gripe water and a dummy if all else failed. They'd be back by eleven thirty. As soon as they'd gone, Chaucer opened his mouth and started to yell. Angel, her hands flapping like useless flippers, hovered over the basket as if trying to work out how to seize a wild animal. Chaucer, sniffing the anxiety, yelled harder.

Bracing herself, Angel lifted him up and clasped him tightly to her chest, then moved him up to her shoulder, gently rubbing his back. The crying subsided, and after a while he let out a huge burp followed by a milky dribble that trickled down her bare arm. She took him out into the garden and began talking to him. She showed him all the flowers and shrubs, the hideous rustic seat at the far end of the lawn. She talked on, telling him about Jeremy and what had happened, but they both got a bit upset, so she changed the subject and started on the hapless estate agent, saying the unkind, noticing sort of things she would have said about him to Jeremy: the out-of-date hairstyle, long at the back, the vulgar mohair sheen to his suit, the horrid judgemental things she could say to Jeremy and no one else. Chaucer had fallen asleep on her shoulder. A quiet satisfaction lay over her sadness as she watched the sun drop into a blaze of pink on the vast East Anglian horizon.

She knew she had forgotten to do something on Saturday, and when the Sunday papers arrived she remembered what it was. She'd meant to cancel them, at least one of them, but Jeremy's pages were the first she opened, like ripping open a letter you knew you couldn't really bear to read.

> *Once upon a time . . . is by no means the worst way to start a novel, promising, as it does, a beginning, a middle and an end. After all the twitchy, quirky, time-out novels we've seen in recent years – you know the ones, where plot is a four-letter word – maybe it's now time for the return of the big story, the solid satisfaction of unselfconscious writing, the*

*resurgence of what we've come to dismiss as middle-list.*

*In the first part of this big serial novel Daniel Presley, dreamer, would-be wanderer, but small-town businessman, was faced with losing every-thing, his wife and children, his home, his business, his self-esteem. He is an ordinary bloke who, like most ordinary blokes, has taken it all for granted, but he can't even cook an omelette.*

'Are you all right? I mean, would you like me to come back later, only the thing is, I've got this couple in the car who are rather keen . . .' The estate agent, one hand in his trouser pocket, the other dangling car keys, looked embarrassed, torn between the hot scent of a sale without the expense and bother of putting together particulars, and the awkwardness of having to deal with a woman who'd obviously been crying.


'It's the onions,' said Marsha. 'No, it really is.' She sniffed and smiled and shook the pan.

'You didn't have to give me supper,' Jeremy said, his gaze dropping to the pan of sizzling onions, then in a short horizontal switch to the slight swell of Marsha's belly.

'It's nice to have someone else to cook for,' she sighed. 'It is my thing, isn't it, cooking?' She glanced at him, the first time she had looked at his face since he'd arrived at the flat.

A wave of fondness ran through him, and he had an urge to touch her, just to make contact.

'You haven't heard from Paul?'

'Not a word. It's nearly two months now.'

'I don't like to think of you being here alone.'

'Don't be protective, Jeremy. I'm all right, really.'

'Do you think he will come back?'

'No.'

'You seem very certain.'

'You think you know him better than I do?'

'I didn't mean . . .'

'No. I'm sorry. Look, if you want to make yourself useful you can toss the salad.'

Jeremy, who had come round in the hope of making himself useful in other ways, set about the lettuce and allowed his thoughts to slip into Angel. She had sold the farmhouse, so quickly and finally it had taken his breath away. A large part of him had gone on assuming that none of what was happening would ultimately mean the end of being married to Angel. He didn't know how it was going to come about, but somehow he had believed that everything would fall into place once Marsha had had the baby; but he'd been living in a twilight zone of improbability where wish-fulfilment had to be a possibility even if it made no sense.

'How have you been?' Marsha enquired, tentatively, her concentration still on the pan.

'Oh, fine,' he answered.

'Really?'

'Of course not. For the first time in my life I've been behaving rather badly. You know, I've always seen other people doing the sort of things I'm doing now and, well, kind of envied them, not exactly what they got up to, but the amoral element that allows them the licence.'

'You mean you're having an affair?'

'No,' Jeremy paused. He really hadn't thought of Sybil as 'an affair'. Anyway, the idea seemed somewhat archaic. No, the behaving badly he associated with the way he was treating his mother and poor old Wilfred. He was being as sharp and cruel as an adolescent, as if this phase of behaviour, having been denied him at its proper time, was now his right.

'What do you mean, then?'

'I hear myself saying things I'd never had said even a few weeks ago.'

'You mean the hurtful truth.'

'Certainly the hurtful bit.'

100

'That's because you're angry. You and Paul are more alike than you think. He gets angry when things are beyond his control. I think most men do.'

He didn't bother to say any more, knowing she had hit upon the hurtful truth herself. He disliked her intensely for a moment, but in the next he was saying what he'd come here to say.

'Marsha, I want to make some sort of financial commitment. I know you don't need it, but I'd feel a lot better if you'd let me contribute. There'll be things you'll have to buy and then, I suppose, a nanny.'

'There is no need.'

'It seems only fair. And I want to do it.'

'Fair to whom?' she said.

# CHAPTER FOURTEEN

'I'm sorry, dear, but you've no one to blame but your-self,' Grace said. 'A man has a right to a child.'

Angel felt sick with fury. She had rung to speak to Jeremy, what she had told herself was a necessity call. Who was to have the rustic seat? There had been several such calls over the past couple of weeks, polite, to the point, but it was something to hear his voice.

Today he wasn't there. 'He's with Marsha,' Grace had informed her, as if there had never been even the pretence of friendship.

Angel picked up the cut glass ashtray that was beside the phone and hurled it into the hearth. Amazingly it didn't break. For a moment she was tempted to lift the receiver again and dial Marsha's number. The doorbell saved her.

'Hi there,' chorused Jane and Gregory, who had bought the farmhouse and were now hovering in the doorway with two bottles of champagne and Terry the estate agent, who was Jane's brother.

'Thought we'd give you a hand,' said Gregory, 'seeing as how you're on your ownsome.'

Sylvia had already offered to help with the packing up but Angel had refused. She couldn't bear the idea of anyone else going through the things she and Jeremy had chosen together, but these three were not the sort of people you could refuse. They had bombarded their way into buying the place and now they wanted her out as quickly as possible, the cosmetic coating of champagne a poor disguise.

'Hi,' said Terry, following the other two past her and into the house. He gave her a look that implied knowing her better than was the case. She'd sensed that he fancied his chances when he'd taken her to see the flat in Cambridge. She'd agreed to buy the first and only place she'd seen, unable to face further viewing. Terry had insisted on taking her through the patter, the awful property-speak that turned every disadvantage into a miraculous excuse for price-enhancement, until she'd stopped him with, 'Look, it's a bloody hole but I'll have it.'

Mistake. He'd looked at her with clear admiration. She'd waited for the inevitable 'I like a woman with spirit' or whatever it was his generation said, because she viewed him as a whole one below her. Now here he was, giving her what doubtless he had composed as a 'special' look. He'd do well to keep clear, she thought, considering the emotional mayhem that had brought her to today's situation.

Jane had already whipped out a tape measure before Gregory had asked whether she'd packed all the glasses. Jane was close to being a bimbo, Gregory too carefully dressed and conscious of his pronunciation. They were actually quite pleasant in their own unashamedly thrusting way, but Angel loathed them for buying her house, for talking about festoon blinds and Christopher Wray lighting. She ached for the silent communion of thought that would be passing between her and Jeremy as this charade proceeded.

Gregory and Jane were in insurance, where they had made a great deal of money. They were buying the farmhouse with cash. Part of Angel was glad Jeremy did not have to witness this disposal to such people, while another part of her resented his staying away, leaving it all to her, even though she had told him not to come.

'You know you'll be welcome to pop by any time and see what we've done to the place,' Jane was saying, as Gregory let off the first bottle and the cork bulleted into the ceiling. 'Careful,' said Jane, as if she'd already taken possession.

The afternoon progressed, and Angel, concentrating on hiding her irritation, because that was the way she'd been brought up, began to feel almost glad that these frightful people were here, diluting the sadness of the occasion because they made it all seem like a farce. Towards six o'clock Jane and Gregory said they had to pop back to feed the dogs, leaving her alone with Terry. It occurred to Angel that this might have been pre-arranged, but Terry just went on packing books in crates.

'This is kind of you,' she said at one point, beginning to find the silence between them awkward.

'I was going to say, I've got tomorrow off. I could help you with the actual move, that's if you haven't got anyone else lined up.'

'But there's no reason why you should,' she said, ungraciously.

'That's up to me, isn't it?'

'Not entirely.'

He didn't answer, but carried on with what he was doing, head down.

'You're wasting your time, you know,' she said next.

'Thanks a bunch.'

'I thought it only fair to tell you.'

'Listen, babe. . .' Angel winced. 'It's my funeral, OK? You need a hand, I'm giving it to you. End of story.'

After an hour or so Gregory and Jane returned. Jane directed an unsubtle enquiring look at her brother and then saw that Angel had observed this unspoken exchange. She looked momentarily thrown then said, 'Oh, well,' and hurried off after her husband.

Angel now began to wish that they would leave, even more so when she saw a car draw up outside and Jeremy getting out of it. For a mad, exhilarating moment she imagined that he had come to stop it all, to tell these people to leave, that it had all been a stupid mistake. She hurried out of the house to meet him, then felt foolish for displaying this eager greeting and turned the 'Hello' into 'Why have you come?'

'There are some things I'll need. It will be more difficult to get them out of storage,' he said, then, 'How are you, Angel?' She felt sure he must know, that he had seen how it was with her when she'd come out of the house, before any words had been spoken; it was impossible that he couldn't know but he'd chosen to ignore it.

'I'm fine,' she said, coldly.

She went and sat in the garden, on the rustic seat, out of view from the house. She did not want to have to make introductions; they'd have to muddle through without her. Jeremy had said he would need only a few minutes. Darkness was beginning to creep into the trees. The light evenings were nearly over.

She lost track of time, and when she saw the figure coming towards her from the direction of the house, she thought at first it was Jeremy.

'He's gone,' said Terry. 'He said to say goodbye. He couldn't find you. Didn't try very hard, though, did he?'

'There's no reason why he should. We're getting divorced.' She hadn't actually considered this before, as if selling the house had nothing to do with it. Ridiculous. What other course was there now but divorce.

'I'll see you tomorrow, then,' Terry said. 'Bright and early.'

'All right,' said Angel, defeated.

The sudden silence that descended on the house seemed to rob her of any further energy. She sat down on one of the packing cases in the drawing room and gazed into the dead black hole of the fireplace. Could there be anything more sad than an abandoned grate? She considered whether or not to indulge this maudlin thought. She could have a good wallow in misery tonight if she had a mind to.

'Oh, fuck it!' she said out loud. Jeremy hated it when she used rude words.

The light was fading fast, and she allowed the room to slip into gloom. Then the moon was up, and its watery white light making an effort.

'This is your last chance, your very last chance,' she said, after what seemed like a time slip because she must have been sitting there in the dark on the packing case for an interminable period. Who was she talking to? Not Jeremy. The house?

'Speak to me,' she urged. 'Come on, be manifestful.' Sylvia was the only one who admitted to seeing the ghost. 'No more than a sliver,' she said. 'Usually while I'm dusting. You know, my back turned. They're crafty things.' Sylvia's council house had had a poltergeist in the kitchen, pots and pans flying round the place, although Cliff always maintained it was one of Sylvia's ploys to get him off the sofa. He'd just carried on watching television, the bang and clatter from the kitchen eliciting no greater response that a notch up on the volume control.

'It was Denise,' Sylvia had told Angel, as if propounding the most mundane of explanations. 'Her age, you know. You only get poltys in houses where there's a young teenage girl. It was all right soon as she'd had Chaucer, although we had the vicar in.'

The farmhouse sliver, she assured Angel, was a benign presence. 'You can tell by the atmosphere of the house. It's not threatening, is it? I mean, you can chat away about nothing in particular but you feel someone's listening.'

Angel had always felt that it was the house itself that listened.

The next morning Terry arrived very early, so early she felt sure the removal men would think he'd been there all night. He was wearing blue jeans, very tight, so you could see the exact shape of his legs. On the top half he had a rugby shirt, but somehow she didn't see him as a player, more a fashion victim.

His hair was now shaved up the back then abruptly thick as a bush, a style she'd seen on tiny children, boys, whose equally tiny sisters had pierced ears and white nylon lace on their socks. Angel could be very noticing when she was unhappy.

The house had remained silent during the night, as if sulking; Angel was such a snob she couldn't believe it would accept Jane and Gregory, who turned up with their van not long after Angel's. J & G, as they called themselves, were wearing identical shell suits, navy with emerald panels. Angel wanted to sing. The two dogs, Alsatians, peered warily from the back of the car.

'Let them out for a run in the garden, G,' Jane instructed. They were called Lord and Lady. Angel watched from the window as Lord made a beeline for the rustic seat, now awaiting loading in the drive, and cocked his leg. That dog had the right idea.

Angel wanted to leave now, as quickly as possible. She heard herself becoming bossy with the removal men, who took no notice, proceeding at their own measured pace. Sylvia arrived mid-morning, looking surprised to see the new owners and their furniture creating a traffic jam in the hallway. Angel, in the main being well brought up, had asked her to come and clear up so Jane and Gregory would have a clean start.

'I only paid £3.50 an hour before,' she overheard Jane telling Sylvia in the kitchen, 'and I'm very fussy.'

Terry's helping didn't amount to much. He found it difficult to bend very far in his jeans. Somehow, everything was loaded by mid-day, and, the dogs chasing the van down the drive, barking their heads off, Angel, restraining herself from a last look, left the home where she had been happy with Jeremy but also where it had all fallen apart.

She had hardly spoken to Terry all morning and half wondered whether he would appear at the flat, but he did, hung about while the removal men puffed and blew her furniture into the narrow confines of her new home. It all looked out of place. How could it not? It was like seeing a stranger wearing the clothes you had taken to the Oxfam shop.

Angel knew she was sighing a lot. She hated this flat, its stark white walls and cheap carpet that clicked with electricity as you walked over it. The view was a roundabout, already baked with hot, angry traffic. Terry spotted a Ferrari and drooled for a moment or two. Angel watched him and briefly wondered what he would be like in bed. Ferrari-like, thrusting and very quick?

He stayed and stayed, and she couldn't be bothered to get rid of him, perhaps didn't want him to leave, didn't want to be alone in this horrid pokey place with the world outside going round in circles.

She was wrong about him. He was a Morris Minor, hesitant at first, then a good runner, nothing spectacular, but he got her there.

'I've been wanting to do that for a long time,' he said.

'But you've only known me a few weeks,' she said, wishing he didn't feel the need to speak. She felt mildly grateful to him, nothing more; even her snobbish distastes were dulled into mildness.

He was proud of her, the way she'd seen Paul had been of Marsha. He'd pulled a mature woman who spoke with a plum in her voice. She was a bit different compared with the women, well, they were girls really, his friends had in tow.

The friends were fairly indistinguishable from one another. Mick, Chas, Dave and Theo, uniformly chinoed and polo-shirted for the Friday night pub sessions in Cambridge. She drank with them and half listened to their talk about nothing in particular. It was more nudge and guffaw than talk. The thing was, it was undemanding. Then Terry would switch to quiet and considerate as soon as they were alone back at the flat, his eyes hungry to get motoring.

'I love you,' he said, too soon. 'I love you, Angel. Love you. Love you. Love you.' He made it sound ecstatic, like a revelation from the gods.

'You don't,' she said. 'Believe me, you don't.'

'Shut up,' he said, smothering her again. 'I'll love you if I want. You don't have to love me back, not yet.' He was confident, she'd say that for him, but then it went with the job, selling homes and dreams.

Jane and Gregory were to have a house-warming. Angel tore up the invitation, which came from 'Lord & Lady' and had a colourful picture of Alsatians in party hats on the front of the card.

'I'd really prefer not to go,' she told Terry.

'Come on. Lay the ghost,' he said.

'Are your parents going to be there?'

'Naturament.'

'Won't they think I'm a bit old for you?'

'Look, I don't give a sod what they think.'

Angel's mind wandered to Grace, then Jeremy, who'd always given a jolly good sod what she thought.

'I'm sure Jane and Gregory are only being polite. They won't want me there. It's their house now.'

'They're not like that, polite, I mean. They probably want you to see all the improvements they've made, plus they want their friends to see they bought the house off a nob.'

'I'm glad you're not my brother.'

'But you will come?'

'If that's what you really want, and I'm not a nob.'

'You are, you know.'

'Is that why you fancy me?'

'Fuckin' hell, Angel, it's your body I'm after.'

He wore his tight jeans and the rugby shirt for the party. Angel had on a little black dress and her grandmother's pearl necklace.

'Wow,' said Terry, smudging her lipstick.

It felt odd, going back to the farmhouse now that it was no longer hers, yet she didn't feel proprietorial, the way she had thought she might. The driveway was lit with garden flares, those huge candles stuck in the ground. Barry Manilow sang from within. The guests were unexpectedly subdued, standing around in small clumps, searching for conversation. Sylvia was there, also in black, but with the addition of a white, lace-trimmed pinny. She was holding a tray of Buck's Fizz.

'Nice to see a friendly face,' she said to Angel, then rather rudely inspected Terry, making the connection, which wasn't difficult – Terry had his arm round Angel's waist.

'Hey, you two lovebirds,' called Jane, emerging from the kitchen, licking something off her fingers. 'Angel, you must let me show you round. You'll be surprised what we've managed to do already.'

Terry's parents were in the drawing room, his mother sitting down, his father standing behind her, like an Edwardian photograph. 'Pleased to meet you,' his mother, a tiny woman, said, giving Angel a sly once-over. Or was she imagining it? Was she being ridiculous, too self-aware?

The festoon blinds were up, red and pink with a touch of orange. The newly acquired reproduction oak furniture placed at exact angles looked as if it needed scratching, and with two pins Angel might have done it. She didn't like herself for noticing everything and inwardly sneering; if she was a nob she wasn't very good at it. Why shouldn't these people have the furniture they liked?

'Done a good job, haven't they?' Terry murmured in her ear. 'No tat.' Angel ached for Jeremy.

Jane took her upstairs to show her the main bedroom which now had a four-poster centre stage, drapped with red velour.

'I wanted to ask you,' she said, hesitant. 'Does the house have a ghost or something? Only it's the dogs, you see, howl all night sometimes, they do, and they say dogs can sense these things, don't they?' The veneer of exuberance displayed downstairs had dropped away, and she looked anxious and drawn; sleepless nights from all that howling, Angel supposed, thinking fondly of her thin friend. Perhaps he didn't like festoon blinds either.

Angel pondered whether or not to tell Jane about the sliver in whom she had chosen to believe only when it suited her.

'I think ghosts are all in the mind,' she said. 'Don't you?'

'So there is something.' Jane sighed with relief. 'It's not just me.'

'My husband never saw anything,' Angel continued.

'But you did?' Jane encouraged.

'Well, no more than a sliver.' Angel felt strangely disloyal. 'And, of course, we didn't have any animals.'

When they went back downstairs half the guests had gone, as if taking advantage of Jane's absence to slip away from a dull party, because dull it was, even with the Rolling Stones now playing. Angel thought back to the house-warming she and Jeremy had put on. They'd ended up playing Murder in the Dark. Paul had been there with, who was it? Susan, Clare, long before Marsha. She'd found herself hiding in the cupboard on the top landing with him. 'Isn't this where we started?' he'd said. It was a dangerous moment, the smell of him strong and nostaligic. He kissed her, a hard, reclaiming kiss, then there was shouting from downstairs and the game was over. That was the only time she'd been even a fraction unfaithful to Jeremy.

It was coming up to midnight, and just the four of them were left.

'That bloody woman was meant to help with the washing up,' Jane groaned, surveying the wreckage.

'She's coming back tomorrow morning,' said Gregory, 'so we can leave everything.'

'You think I'm going to bed with this mess down here?' Jane accused him.

They were in the hallway. A sudden draft chilled the air and they looked at one another, the four of them, like trespassers. The dogs, shut up in the back passageway at their own party, howled in unison. Angel smiled.

# CHAPTER FIFTEEN

'You make me feel like I'm not actually here, like some sort of ghost,' said Sybil.

Jeremy glanced over the top of his specs at Sybil's white make-up and now green hair. 'Hum,' he uttered, and turned back to the piece he was writing on her PC.

*Murder from an unexpected quarter can be peculiarly unsettling. We don't expect it from this writer, and its sudden intrusion on the page is as shocking as a dose of pornography from Anita Brookner or the grasping of an abstract concept by one of Jilly Cooper's characters. But murder is what we have and a thoroughly nasty one, too.*

*Daniel, still a chartered accountant, still living in East Sheen, develops an obsession for the Avon lady who sells lipsticks to his wife. He's transfixed as she demonstrates the ease with which the pink points swivel up out of their cases, exposing themselves, glistening columns, hard and erect.*

*'Long lasting,' she says. 'A nice feel and just right for sensitive lips.' Never has lipstick tasted so good.*

*The murder, without giving away the denouement, is a bit more than skin deep, but the writing*

> *retains a cosmetic feel, the cover-up as blemish-free*
> *as you get; but it's still a bit hard to believe a char-*
> *tered accountant living in East Sheen would have*
> *such an imagination. There again, who knows*
> *what any of us is capable of doing in extremis?*

'Jez,' Sybil whined. 'Lend us your brain.'

Marsha was beginning to feel menaced. Sometimes she thought it might be just in her head – and her belly, swelling by the day, even by the hour it seemed when she lay in the bath and watched the taut flesh move from within, like the surface of a gently simmering cauldron, tiny hillocks rising then flattening again.

The phone rang constantly but she felt so alone. Sod's Law, every television company there was wanted her now, right now. Channel Four wanted to give her her own programme, 'This is Your Life' had been rumoured; but there were no calls from America.

Four months and not a word from Paul. Jeremy kept pestering her, offering money and nannies when he'd already given her more than he should. The fact that the baby was not Paul's no longer mattered – if it ever had. Oh, she didn't mean it like that, but it did feel like hers and hers alone, perhaps because Paul had absented himself, silly man. Silly, silly man, boy. She still loved him, and it had nothing to do with the size of her stomach. That was another compartment, quite separate now, a different life.

The strange thing was she loved the baby, unborn, in much the same way she loved Paul, with a blind love that took in all the bad as well as the good, unquestioning, inevitable. He, she thought of the child as a boy, although she'd refused the tests that would tell her the sex, only glimpsed something that looked like a penis on the scan, would take over her life, already had, just as she had allowed Paul to do. She knew she had awakened something in him

114

that had taken him by surprise, and this power had intoxi-cated her as much as it had him. But there was a price to pay. With Douglas she'd got off scot-free in comparison. Thus the sense of menace. Paul would be back, she was quite certain, but how he might be she couldn't even guess. Penitent? Con-ciliatory? Loving? Murderous? Yes, she was frightened. Too quiet for too long. He'd been half mad when he left. At what-ever point he came back, the evidence would be there to con-front him, and while she feared the other half of madness, the scenario of his turning away from her waistless shape, from her child, was more fearsome to contemplate.

The whole world now knew she was pregnant. Gerald and Pauline had made the announcement last week, live on air. 'Well, folks, I've been waiting ever since she first appeared on the programme to say this one. Marsha has got a bun in the oven.'

'Really, Gerald!' Pauline exclaimed in mock horror. 'That one deserves the wooden spoon.'

'Seriously, though, when's it due, Marsha?' (camera 4 switch to the kitchen set, Marsha, quick change of facial expression from about-to-throw-up to modest, pregnant-woman's smile).

'And what's on the menu today?' asked Pauline to camera 3.

'Strawberry soup. Roes on toast and marmalade. And liquorice pipes with custard.' There was a stunned silence in the control room.

'Stupid bitch,' hissed Pauline after the programme had finished.

Marsha went to Harrods and bought a very small white Babygro. She took it home and added it to the collection of booties, mits and bibs she had already been unable to resist. Buying anything more substantial at this stage would have felt like tempting fate. 'For sale. Baby's shoes. Never used.' She remembered hearing on the radio, a winning minisaga.

She opened another drawer which contained two dozen liquorice pipes. She stuck one in her mouth and turned,

115

perhaps rather too quickly. Momentarily dizzy, she then blacked out, cascading on to the floor.


'Look! Look! There I am.'

'Where?'

'That's the back of my head. Oh, you've missed me.' Wilfred collapsed back in Jeremy's father's chair, a childlike disappointment twitching at the corners of his mouth.

'I think I glimpsed your bald patch,' said Jeremy.

'Oh, did you?' Wilfred was eager again.

'Wilfred's got more hair than you, dear,' Grace said.

'A newborn baby has more hair than me,' said Jeremy.

'Not so, dear. When you were born I thought I'd given birth to a gorilla.'

Grace was knitting, something small and custard-coloured. Jeremy had decided not to ask what it was.

'As I was saying,' said Wilfred, 'I know this producer, well, I know a lot of producers of course, but I know this chappie whose involved with "The Late Review" on BBC2. I thought I might put in a word for you, that's if you'd like me to.'

'That's very kind of you,' said Jeremy, without interest, opening the newspaper.

'You might show a little more interest,' said Grace, click, click, clicking with her needles. 'Wilfred is very well connected, you know.'

'I'm sure he is, Mother.' Jeremy turned over a page and found himself staring at a picture of Marsha. *'Strawberry soup, fish roe and liquorice pipes on the menu for Marsha'* read the caption. He scanned the rest of the piece. *'. . . expecting a baby . . . perhaps a new recipe book for cravings . . . not available for further comment.'*

Wilfred's hand had crept up to the top of his head. 'Shall I make us all a nice cup of tea?' he said.

'As opposed to a nasty one,' Jeremy might have said, would have said any other time, but his attention remained on the mother of his child. His child. He gently brushed his thumb across Marsha's face, and thought of Angel.

He'd called her last week, at the new flat in Cambridge. A man had answered the phone. He'd thought they might talk, he and Angel, just talk, see where it went. She was in the bath, the man informed him. He didn't leave a message. He took Sybil to the Groucho for one of their nouvelle school dinners. Melvyn Bragg and Barry Norman were there. Neither could fail to notice Sybil, even in the Groucho. Back at her loft he fucked her silly. 'Stupid question, but do you love me?' she asked him.

'Yes. It is a stupid question,' he said, and she started to weep, then couldn't stop.

'Sorry,' he muttered, hating what he was doing.

'Here we are, just the way you like it,' said Wilfred, setting down the tea tray. 'Oh, isn't that Marsha Miller? I met her once, you know. Lovely woman.'

'Jeremy knows that,' interjected Grace, 'don't you, dear? She's married to his friend Paul, or was.'

'You never said.' Wilfred was aghast with once-removed admiration. Nothing impressed him more than a famous name. 'My goodness, you mean she's the Marsha you visit in London.'

'The very same.'

'Yes, Jeremy knows her very well,' Grace continued, then stopped when she saw his expression, although he was relieved to know this meant Grace had not already told Wilfred what was going on.

'Of course, I wouldn't tell him something like that,' she said later when Wilfred was doing the washing up. Her needles started to click again, then stopped. 'Have you thought what you're going to do, dear?' She sounded tentative, cautious he might tell her to mind her own business.

'Do about what, Mother?'

'If you don't want to talk about it.' Clicking again.

'The answer is, I don't know.'

'But surely you'll have some sort of right. A grandchild.'
She sighed, as if savouring a kind word.

'No rights at all.'

'I can't believe that.' She sounded indignant now.

'Believe it. Don't you think I've done all the research?'

'But you see her, don't you? Stay with her some nights. I
thought perhaps . . . well, with Paul away all this time. I
mean, perhaps he won't come back.'

'It's not that simple.'

'Oh dear, these things never are, but they can be, you know.
Life doesn't have to be all complications. Look at Wilfred and
me. Perfectly straightforward. We're fond of one another and
we share a house. Nothing more.'

'He's your lodger, Mother.'

'I know, I know. It's just fortunate that we get on so well.
He is a dear, you know, Jeremy. I wish you'd make more of
an effort to like him. You're not jealous are you, dear?'

Jeremy gave her a withering look. But he was jealous, terribly so. Of his mother's cosy relationship with Wilfred, of
Angel's apparent ability to walk straight into a new life, of
Marsha's total ownership of the baby. He'd never had cause
to recognise this fiercely jealous side to his nature until recent
events. Grace had always been an adoring mother in her own
slightly fey, occasionally cruel way; there had never been any
competition before, not even with his father, who had been a
generation removed from his mother and therefore seemed
more like a father to both of them. There may have been a
touch of envy with Paul, when they were teenagers and he
had all the outward attributes, the sporting prowess, the
looks, the girls, but Jeremy had always recognised them as
outward, quietly, patiently biding his time, aware from an
early age that his own reserves were far deeper than those of
his friend. And, of course, he had won Angel, who had never
given him cause for jealousy throughout the years of their
marriage. She might have got stuck in the occasional clinch at
the early parties when they still had rock music and dancing,

118

husbands and wives drifting apart for the evening. He'd had his fair share of clinches, suddenly attractive as he entered his thirties. Two or three of them had wanted to have affairs but he wasn't interested. Nobody matched up to the prize that was Angel.

Poor Sybil was the first one he'd slept with more than once, and he was making her as unhappy as he would have the others.

Grace had resumed her knitting. The small yellow garment grew relentlessly. He looked away, a catch in his throat. He'd have to see Angel soon. It was intolerable not to, but he dreaded her new setting, her day-to-day living about which he knew nothing and was no longer any part of.

# CHAPTER SIXTEEN

Sasha Parrish had taken pity on Paul. A no-hoper if ever she'd seen one, but that made him all the more attractive for her current endeavours.

She'd moved him into her apartment after he'd been thrown out of the hotel, paid off his bill and given him a small allowance on top of the housekeeping for which she demanded strict accounting. She'd heard that men made better housekeepers these days, now that the macho stuff had gone out the window. She had a male secretary at Bracken, the best yet. He could do amazing things with the computer, stayed late exploring its labyrinth of facilities; no female secretary would do that. For herself, computers were just about as boring as it got, but she like the power of them.

Paul seemed to have settled in well to his new way of life. He'd stopped whingeing about his wife and the other guy's baby, and there was no longer the embarrassing pretence of his role as PR man extraordinaire. She'd fired him, then been surprised to discover him on the sidewalk, almost shuffling, hobo-fashion. She stopped the car, called him over. He stank. Booze, sweat, feet.

'Jogging,' he said, by way of explanation.

'In a suit?'

'Well, I don't have much kit here.'

'I can see that. What are you still doing here, Paul?'

He wouldn't go back to London, he told her. There was nothing left for him to go back to.

'Hi, sweetie. What's cooking?' she called, throwing down her bag of files, the Armani jacket. She bypassed the kitchen where he was rinsing alfalfa shoots and went into her bedroom to change for the beginning of the weekend, pulling on blue jeans, non-designer, and an old sweater.

In the kitchen, Paul, similarly dressed in jeans and sweatshirt, his attention switching between recipe book and sink, hoped Sasha wouldn't notice how little he would eat of the concoction he'd had to spend half the day preparing. Roast hedgerow, he called it, although the ingredients were a long way from free picking on the roadside. They cost a fortune from the health shop, and whatever he did to them they still tasted like compost heap. He'd sneaked a whopper burger while he was downtown, but without the onions and relish in case she sniffed the pong on his breath.

He didn't know how she coped with all the pods and seeds she stuck on the shopping list; they made you fart and you never stopped dreaming of meat followed by something really solid and sweet. He'd been cheating with burgers and chocolate bars for the past month, almost as soon as he'd moved in with her. Thank God he didn't have to share her room and her bed.

Weekends weren't so easy. Sasha liked to stay home, slob out, a non-exercise that meant he had to muck out. She expected him to be there, at her beck and call Friday pm through Monday am. She was paying him, for Chris'sake. What more did he want?

Quite a bit, actually. His old life through the dewy tint of mist rising on a rugger pitch. The huff and puff of real exertion his body now craved and literally ached to achieve. It had to be a kind of regression because he'd stopped playing years ago, losing heart soon after losing Angel. There was irony in that, he'd more or less convinced himself, because if it hadn't been for the sport Angel might never have had the time and space to fall in love with Jeremy.

It was one of the many areas of his past that made him wince when he thought about it; but there were too many 'if only's' lurking about and what he needed was an escape, and the only sort he could imagine was with a ball or a bat. So much so that when his thoughts inadvertently slipped towards that last awful occasion with Angel at the farmhouse, he invariably found his arm rising over his shoulder, wrist twisting for a spin . . .

'What in hell are you doing?' Sasha stood in the doorway of the kitchen, hands on hips.

'Oh, it's my back,' Paul said, swinging the arm back over the way it had come.

'I'm not surprised if you keep doing that,' she said, laughing, her big gob open like a baseball glove ready for a catch. 'Come on, Paul. I'm starved. What yer got cookin'?'

'God, it's hot in here.' Paul, flustered, as if his thoughts were see-through and probably were to the omniscient Sasha, felt his face burn.

'You know, you oughta find some sort of outlet for all that energy,' she said later, when they were sitting over the remains of supper, Wagner threatening indigestion.

For a moment he thought she was suggesting the one piece of exercise he could not stomach, not since . . . The music rolled into another fit of Germanic purpose. He got up to clear the table.

Sometimes he got nervous, well, more nervous, to be accurate. He didn't fancy Sasha, not in the least little bit, but he worried about what sort of man he had become, of what he might be capable. He'd lost control once, so it could happen again. It would always be there, the awful possibility.

Once or twice he had watched Sasha as they sat in her opulent drawing room and she talked in that way of hers. Provocative, but not so much in the man/woman way, although there was always a touch of that, she couldn't help there being a touch of that. No, the provocation was to do with power, the implicit dominance in their situation and how far she could push it. She wanted too much of him and he was by turns frightened and grateful.

How could he not be grateful? She had rescued him from himself, provided him with some sort of a structure to each day, and most of the time was really rather nice to him, when she could have been an absolute bitch and got away with it. She was Marsha all over again, only she wasn't Marsha.

He wondered whether he could ever have applied the same frightening thoughts to Marsha, who, once or twice, had loomed into his dreams, hugely rounded and never recognising him, as if he had become the invisible man. Perhaps that was what he wanted, invisibility, to disappear even from himself.

'Paul, you're not concentrating.' Sasha had followed him out to the kitchen, was reaching round him to take the jar of coffee beans from his grasp. 'De-caff. You know by now. De-caff or I see stars all night and the earth rocks on its axis.'

'Sorry.'

'What is it with you tonight?' The penetrating look. 'I mean, you're not exactly the life and soul most nights,' 'soul' said with that strange, withering mock cockney treatment, 'but this one you're clean out of it. You're not on anything? You're not spending the house money on dope?'

Paul smiled, thinking of the Hershy bars he'd felt so guilty about.

'Let me in on the joke, won't you!' She was on the edge of temper and thought she could afford it.

Paul took a deep breath.

'Oh, don't do that on me,' she said. 'Paul.'

The door of the coffee cupboard had snapped to.

'Paul.' He heard her shout his name once more as he left the apartment, closing the door on that big mouth and Wagner, still tolling detached triumphalism. It was a bad habit, this sudden exiting, but he couldn't find another way out.

He jogged down the hill, trying to rev up a breeze on his

face, feeling his heart pound against his chest long before he was out of breath. He lost track of time and couldn't have said where he went, only the places in his mind. That other sudden exit when he'd come home and found Jeremy and Marsha; but it wasn't that little scene torturing him now. Memory of that was just the prelude to what had happened next. However fast he ran, he could not escape the image of Angel, her eyes wide and terrified, no more than a couple of inches from his own. He had to stop seeing her like that, to force his inner gaze to other times when there was no fear, but a yearning he had disregarded until it was too late. He hadn't known he loved her and might never have thought of her in so huge a way if it hadn't been for Jeremy.

He stopped, at last breathless, leaning forward, his hands on his knees, panting like a wretched dog.

He must have thought about it all much more than he'd realised, because in his mind now he pictured Angel and Jeremy reunited, Marsha out of the picture and never really there.

With a jealousy fiercer than the original, he imagined Jeremy and Angel settled back in their smug provincial life, bound to one another closer than ever by the trauma of recent events. They were probably planning their own family now. He wouldn't be surprised if Angel weren't already pregnant. Oh, Jeremy would love that, two of them cooking for him.

He snatched a lungful, straightened up and got his legs going again, but Angel was already ahead of him, her hair long, falling over his face, a subconsciously stored sensation. He hadn't known that he loved her. He hadn't known.

He registered with lack of interest that he was lost. Rarely had he been out after dusk since the day Sasha collected him off the street like so much garbage and set about recyling him. He had even begun to think what might have befallen him next if there hadn't been that chance encounter. Vaguely, he supposed he had to find something else, other than stem bowling and rugby football, at which he could be passably good. Stoopian principles, even at such a nadir, remained ingrained.

Achievement was the only answer, although hadn't he already tried that route, pushing for a success that was beyond what he could ever do, even getting away with if for a time, in the late eighties, when you could be a brain surgeon with one O level?

Whatever it took, he had no intention of living off a woman again. Marsha edged into his thoughts. Marsha, the meals, the Mercedes. Even Marsha hadn't known that was all he had left. With the office gone, he'd been down to a mobile phone and a laptop, but his life perhaps had always seemed sort of temporary, with hindsight, because he really wasn't a man to live comfortably off a woman, was he? The thought had always been there that in due course things would reverse, when he got on his business feet again, when he achieved the same level of success as Jeremy. Always Jeremy. Sometimes he wondered how he might have reacted to Marsha's pregnancy if the father of her child had been anyone else but Jeremy.

Stiff upper something or other. Buggeration, he'd got cramp.

'Mind yourself, Pogo!' A grey-powered jogger in a minimalist vest steamed past leaving a wake of aggression.

'Sorry,' Paul called after him, lamely.

He looked around him. It wasn't that different from his own Home Counties, this leafy Californian suburb, except the air was warm and didn't smell of damp greenery. It was the smell that was un-English. It was balmy and dry, heavy and alien. If he had not been what Stoop had made him, he might have wept with the strangeness of it all.

'Feeling better?' Sasha called out when he got back. He'd been out barely twenty minutes. Everything was just as he'd left it because she knew he'd be back, that he wasn't ready to go anywhere else, that he was no threat at all.

# CHAPTER SEVENTEEN

'Someone holding. Says it's important,' mouthed the new chap who looked no more than the same grade as Sybil. God, he suddenly felt old, really old, as if the middle bit had been completely missed; straight from bright young hopeful to has-been, and practically all his hair gone, too.

Jeremy abandoned the unanswered ringing from the call he'd repeated half a dozen times over the past week. Perhaps she'd gone away, but without telling him? He felt decidedly peeved; she had no right to go in for disappearing acts, not with the baby due in less than two months.

'Jeremy Holden,' he barked into the phone.

'It's me, Wilfred.' Jeremy experienced an unexpected draining of blood. Something must have happened to Grace; Wilfred's voice contained unmistakable urgency.

'You remember I mentioned knowing that producer?'

'Which producer, Wilfred?' The blood returned, together with the irritability.

'Mike Poole. "The Late Review". You know, Mark Lawson's programme on BBC2. He wants to meet you. Lunchtime today. Tom Paulin's had to drop out.'

'Where?'

'The Writers House in Portland Place. Twelve forty-five. I

said you'd be there. Good luck, old son. Your mum's going to be tickled pink.'

'I haven't got it yet,' Jeremy said, still sounding churlish.

'No, but you will. I've absolute confidence. You will.'

'We'll see.' The connection was cut and he hadn't even thanked Wilfred. Was there to be no end to this behaviour? He felt powerless to stop himself, like a school bully who'd tasted blood.

He looked a mess. Unironed shirt, trousers with every crease but the two they were supposed to have. Living with Sybil, which he was much of the time now, although with no commitment whatsoever on his part, did not include being looked after the way Angel and Grace, turn and turn about, had provided fresh-smelling laundry, wholesome food and razor blades. He wondered how he had managed at college and then during the brief period at the flat in Shepherd's Bush before Angel had moved in. He'd never realised until now just how much he had been physically pampered all his life. The spoilt only son. The indulged husband. And yet he'd never seen it, always thought of himself, which wasn't all that often, as fairly self-sufficient, the carer rather than the cared for; but that was the fallacy of his upbringing.

It was difficult to keep his mind on track. He needed to think of the right person to review Melvyn Bragg's latest novel. Roy Hattersley? Did they really look alike? If so, Roy had the edge on him these days. Someone was still ironing his shirts.

Lawson always looked a mess, as if he'd forgotten to shave and just whipped off his tie to appear casual. Sartorial elegance was going to be the last thing the producer would be hoping to find. He wished.

The Writers House was in one of those splendid Adam terraces close to Regent's Park. The general secretary of English PEN, whom he knew, was coming down the main stairway as he went in.

'Hello, how nice to see you,' she said. She was a sexy little woman of indeterminate age and with a talent for brightening up the day. They talked for a few moments, then he asked her if she knew the producer. 'I'm meeting him for lunch, but I haven't a clue what he looks like.'

'In there,' Gilly pointed through a grand doorway. 'By the window. I saw him come in just before you arrived. Pinstripe suit.'

Jeremy did not remember lunch. He might have picked at the odd forkful. The producer wanted him that night. No time to waste. He was run through the programme's format as if on fast forward. Victoria Glendinning and Auberon Waugh were sitting at the neighbouring table. Melvyn Bragg was across the room.

'Oh, and Tony Parsons wears red socks,' was the producer's parting shot.

'How did it go?' asked the general secretary as he was leaving.

'Not bad. Not bad at all. But why did he tell me that Tony Parsons wears red socks?'

By the end of the afternoon he had been to the places suggested by the general secretary, including a hairdresser's. He felt better than he had for months as he headed for the studio, practically a whole day without thinking about Marsha, Angel, any of it. And the programme went really well. He was a natural. Just the right degree of nerves to give him that edge of bright thought. He came out into the night feeling like a conqueror. God, it felt good, really good. He'd go back to Sybil's and be nice to her. God, he'd be nice to her. Poor kid. He was soaring.

He switched on his mobile to call Wilfred and thank him, but before he could start dialling, an incoming call came through.

'Jeremy Holden?'

'Yes.'

'This is the Cromwell Road Hospital.'

Marsha looked as if she were already dead, lying so still. Only the tubes gave her a semblance of life. Jeremy took hold of her hand, soft and cold and dreadfully limp, impossible to imagine putting life into pastry. Such ridiculous little thoughts in the face of tragedy. She had been lying here for a week. Nothing in the newspapers because they'd been unable to contact the next of kin. No family at all, it seemed. How extraordinary that a person could be known to millions and yet to nobody in particular. Finally, a cursory search of the flat had found the business card Jeremy had insisted on sticking behind the telephone.

'She's had a massive brain haemorrhage,' the nurse in charge had told him. 'It's unlikely she'll recover."

'Where did it happen? How was she found?'

'A neighbour. They had a key, I suppose.'

'The baby is mine,' he heard himself saying. 'I'm the father.'

The nurse's expression chilled a few degrees.

'She should not have been left alone.'

'I didn't know.'

'No.'

'No, really. You don't understand.' And he couldn't find the words to explain.

'Marsha, I'm so sorry,' he murmured when the nurse had gone. They'd crucified the new television hospital drama. Weren't real hospitals about grapes and bedpans, not gripes and deadpans. All that emotional turmoil simmering beneath the blank expressions that were an apology for trying too hard. Clever words. Not so clever now. He began to weep, soaring down, weeping for himself, and for Marsha, for his baby, for Angel, and for the bloody awful timing of success.

He buried his face in the side of the bed on the sour-smelling hospital blanket that lay over Marsha's inert body. He sobbed a little then went quiet as a slight pressure butted against his forehead. He lifted his hand and placed the palm against the blanket. A small ripple ran like a tickle from the base of his thumb towards his fingers. The baby was still alive. Of course, the baby was still alive.

'Marsha!' he looked up at the oblivious face. Eyes closed. Tube running up through nostril.

'I'm afraid she can't hear you.' Another nurse was standing at the end of the bed. 'And shouting won't help.'

'The baby's alive.'

'Oh, yes. The baby's alive.'

After a bit they turfed him out, well, suggested he go home, the implication being that he could have sat there by the bedside for days, weeks, months, and nothing would change. The baby would be born when the time came, sooner rather than later, a Caesarean section, of course. After that they'd have to review the situation. Nothing was going to be done in a hurry. Time was neither for them nor against them. Persistant vegetative state.

He found himself catching the first train out to Amersham. Being nice to Sybil was no longer an option. He'd have been bloody awful to her without even trying. It was Angel he thought about on the train, and how he was going to find words clever enough.

# CHAPTER EIGHTEEN

'Clever bugger, isn't he,' Cliff said as the credits rolled.

Sylvia had stayed up late to watch Jeremy on the telly. She'd had her bath, then come downstairs again to give Cliff a kiss and a 'goodnight'.

'Hang on a mo, look, it's Jeremy, sitting next to the woman what says everything's "ghastly".' So Sylvia had stayed, sat down on the carpet just in front of Cliff, even held his hand for a bit, later on, when they started talking.

'Silly bugger, too. Why'd he go and leave that lovely wife of his?'

'Couldn't get on, I suppose. Other troubles, too.'

'They make life too complicated for themselves.'

'Umm.' Sylvia put Cliff's hand against her cheek. She didn't really want to talk about her former employers, not even to Cliff; she couldn't explain it, a sort of loyalty. The longer she worked for the new people, the more she remembered how good it had been working for the Holdens.

'What sort of a bloke is he, anyway?' Cliff persisted.

'Jeremy?'

'No, the Archbishop of Canterbury.'

'He always seemed, well, kind, considerate. The quiet type. I always thought she was the one with all the go.'

'A looker, too. He's not much cop, though. Looks like that

politician, you know the one.'

'He's got something about him, though.'

'Fancy him, do you?'

'Not my type. I prefer fat slobs that lie about watching telly all day and night.'

'Can't think what you're doing here, then.'

She nuzzled a little closer.

'Hang on, girl. Patrick Moore's on next.'

She got up, felt a twinge in her hip and began an awkward walk towards the door.

'Don't forget to turn that thing off, will you. I don't want to have to come down here in the middle of the night to find it hissing at me.'

'What a load of old cods.' Terry zapped the screen.

'I thought he was rather good.' Angel continued staring at the blankness.

'You're not serious!' Terry plumped up the pillow behind his head and folded his arms in a sulk.

'Don't be jealous,' Angel said. 'I'm not going to say he was no good just to make you feel secure.'

'You can be such a bitch, you know.'

'Yes.'

'If you were like that with him, I'm not surprised he did a runner.'

'But I wasn't like that with him,' Angel said, to herself now, more than with any intention of spiking Terry. She knew she had changed, and yet the way she felt now seemed more real than the person she had been with Jeremy. It was as if she'd been holding back all those years, like being on her best behaviour. No wonder she'd always been tired, even exhausted. Nothing to do with work. She was doing more of that now than ever before, yet her energy level seemed to have risen beyond anything she could have imagined. An objective observer might pinpoint it as all down to Terry, an older woman with a toy boy. That was the way she saw the relationship even though the age difference was no more than a decade.

'What were you like with him, then?'

'Compliant.' Angel snapped back to the real presence of Terry.

'Did as you were told, you mean?'

'Not exactly that. It's difficult to say. We didn't often argue, not until . . .'

'Until?'

'I don't think you really want to know.'

'How can anyone say that without making the other person want to know like crazy even if they didn't before? Only I did, want to know before,' he added. 'I want to know everything about you, babe.'

'Babe!' Angel scoffed.

'No worse than Angel, Angela. Was that his name for you, "Angel"?'

'No, I was Angel when I was at school; just one of those silly nicknames, but it stuck. I don't much like Angela, actually.'

'What do your folks call you?'

'Angel.'

'And when are you going to show me to them?'

Angel sighed in reply and slid down the bed.

'Come on, Angel. I want to meet them, be part of the family.'

'I know.'

'I love you, babe.'

'I know, and it's very sweet of you.'

'Oh, fuck off!'

They were silent for a few moments. The room had gone very quiet, only the traffic noise from the roundabout, and that had become intermittent at this hour.

Angel turned towards him and began to stroke his penis. 'I love bits of you,' she said, knowing she was being cruel and unable to stop herself.

He pushed her away.

'I want to know "until",' he said, stroppily.

'Until what?'

'You said you and him didn't argue, not until.'

'Ah, yes, until.'

'Well?'

'He got another woman pregnant.'

Terry perked up.

'Go on. Who? Some bimbo at work?'

'No. A black bimbo on telly.'

'So that's how he got on it himself. She pulled a few strings?'

'I've no idea, but I doubt it. She's a cook.' Angel wondered why she was being bitchy about Marsha, who was no more to blame than the rest of them, and whom she hadn't seen or spoken to for months.

'What happened?'

'What d'you think!'

'I mean, how did it happen? How did he meet her and everything?'

'Oh, she's an old friend, she and her husband.'

'Fuckin' hell, and what does the husband think about it?'

'He's disappeared. Working in America.'

'Sensible bloke.'

'Not especially, rather foolish, in fact, like the rest of us.'

'Don't be all cryptic.'

'Ah, cryptic.'

'Surprised, are you, that I know what that means? Who are "the rest of us", then?'

'Me and Jeremy, Marsha and Paul. Marsha's the one having Jeremy's baby.'

'Had an affair, did they?'

'No.'

'I don't understand.'

'No, I don't think I do either.'

'Angel, tell me, please.' He grabbed her hand under the duvet and clamped it back on his penis, which was getting hard and throbby.

'It only happened once, I'm sure of that. At the farmhouse. A weekend together. The four of us. We did a swap, that's all.'

'Is she a Catholic or something? I mean, why didn't she have an abortion?'

'You don't have to be Catholic not to want to have an abortion, you know. She wanted me to be pregnant, too, after she found out she was. She's a nice woman. I'm very fond of her. None of us meant it to turn out the way it did.'

'I don't understand the husband,' Terry persisted, after another moment's thought, taking it all in. 'I mean, if it'd been me I reckon I'd have gone ape.'

'He did, in a way,' Angel said.

'I thought you said he went to the States, disappeared?'

She told him what had happened then, letting it all out between sobs, but the sense of relief in having told someone was soon replaced by regret. It diminished her to have spoken of that evening. She should not have told him. It was weak, pitiful, and she felt a greater distaste for herself than for Paul.

Terry wrapped his arms about her and hugged her tightly.

'The bastard,' he said. 'Blokes like him should have their balls cut off.'


'Well, here he is, our very own celebrity,' cooed Wilfred.

Jeremy looked terrible. He sat down at the breakfast table and lit a cigarette.

'Really, dear, a bit early,' commented Grace, looking pointedly at the Silk Cut.

Jeremy ignored both of them.

'You're going to be very late for work,' Grace continued, as usual failing to pick up the vibes.

'Leave him be, ducky,' cautioned Wilfred, who was watching Jeremy and sensing a crisis.

'I'm taking the day off,' Jeremy informed them in a distracted tone.

'Such a triumph last night, I expect it's taken it out of you,' Wilfred suggested. 'Your mum and me, so proud.'

'Thanks,' Jeremy murmured, grudgingly, then, 'No, I mean it, thank you very much, Wilfred.' He made an effort to improve his temper.

'You were very late home. I suppose you went out celebrating, and who could blame you. You really were very good, dear,' Grace continued, oblivious, buttering her toast. 'And considering it was your first time.'

'Staying here or going up to town?' Wilfred butted in, but tentatively, not wanting to push Jeremy back into the black mood he had brought down to breakfast, not wanting Grace to either with her awful riders.

'London. A lot to do.'

'Well, take it easy, dear, and try not to smoke too much,' Grace went on. 'I really can't understand why you've taken up that disgusting habit, especially after the way you used to go on at me. And if you're going to sort things out with Marsha, you won't be able to smoke when the baby's arrived.'


'Where were you last night? I thought you were coming to me after the programme. You were brilliant, by the way,' Sybil said.

He lost her in a tunnel, the signal obliterated. He switched off the mobile so she couldn't ring back.

When the train got into London he grabbed a taxi and went straight to the flat off Onslow Square. He had a key, stolen, taken from a hook in the kitchen weeks ago, just in case. In case of what? Marsha collapsing with a brain haemorrhage?

The flat gushed stale air at him as he let himself in. He was feeling clear-headed, purposeful, despite having only two or three hours sleep. He knew exactly what had to be done, there was no question; old loyalties, no matter all that had happened, Paul had to be told, given the chance to get back before it was too late.

He went to the walnut bureau in the study, but its contents were minimal, Marsha's passport, her wide-eyed picture jumping out at him. Her birth certificate. Older than she'd said. Strange, that sort of vanity did not equate with the person he thought he knew. A few more bits and pieces, but culled down to nothing that wasn't official.

He tried the bedroom next, a room he had never been in before. Again there was nothing. One or two pieces of jewellery, clothing. He pulled open the last drawer. Full of baby things, all white and nestling in translucent sheets of tissue. Dear God. He pushed the drawer back in.

The kitchen seemed like the last hope. Nothing visible. Pristine surfaces. Then a drawer with a blue folder inside. He took it out and tipped the contents on to the worktop. Forms from the hospital. An information sheet about what to do when labour started. Telephone numbers to call. A list of what to pack. A letter. Sealed. He turned it over. Angel's name was written on the front.

# CHAPTER NINETEEN

'This place would fetch about three hundred and fifty K,' Terry whistled. 'How many bathrooms?'
'Three or four,' said Angel.
'Four could take it nearer four hundred.'
'They're not selling, Terry, so don't even think about it.'
'Professional curiosity, that's all.'
'You've got a mind like a tape measure.'
'So you admit I've got one. That's progress.' She liked it when he said this sort of thing. It made her feel there might be a future in him. They really got on rather well most of the time. She'd not taken it seriously at all to begin with, just let it happen, fallen in with his desires. But the more she got to know him the better she liked him. He did not make life unnecessarily complicated. He might be prone to jealousy and the occasional sulk, but could she really blame him for this? She'd been careless of his feelings, of the declarations of love.

'You sure I don't look like a wide boy?' he repeated for the second or third time, anxious for a true appraisal.
'Terry, be yourself. Just be yourself. And you look fine.'
'Not too young?'
'Why? Do I look too old?'
'You look bloody, fucking gorgeous, babe.'
'Best to leave out the fucking while we're there.'

'What, the whole weekend?'

'Just the language. It'd make me feel uncomfortable.'

Terry had stopped the car on the other side of the road, like a burglar casing the joint. He was nervous as hell but had driven sedately for someone with the suspicion of wet gel in his hair.

'Can I bring a friend?' Angel had said to her mother over the phone.

'Of course. What's his name?'

'Did I say it was a man?'

'Daughters in their mid-thirties don't bring girlfriends to spend weekends with their parents. Is he nice, darling?'

'Lovely, actually, but . . .'

'Married?'

'No. Not that. His name's Terry. He's twenty-five, Mum.' There was a pause.

'I expect he's got a big appetite. I remember your brother at that age, still eating like a horse. I'll make sure there's plenty of food.' Her mother's solution to anything perplexing was accelerated catering.

There might have been rather a lot of food over the years. The rift with her family could be traced back to the weekend she had gone home to tell them she was to marry Jeremy. She had gone alone because it had seemed easier, although as soon as she got there she wished that Jeremy had been with her.

Her parents had liked Paul and must have assumed that she would marry him. She had never got round to telling them she had switched to Jeremy, partly perhaps because of the awkwardness involved in explaining the continuing living arrangement at the flat in Shepherd's Bush; partly, too, because in the past she had spoken of Jeremy in a way that was dismissive, almost unkind.

'I feel a bit sorry for him,' she told her mother. 'He doesn't seem to have any social life. I think he's always relied too much on Paul.'

'I should think he feels a bit of a gooseberry. Why doesn't he find somewhere else to live?'

'Why should he? He was there before I moved in.'

'That's not really the point. You should be careful, Angel. He's probably in love with you.'

'Mum! I think it's Paul he loves.'

'Oh, I see.'

'No, you don't. I didn't mean it like that, at least, I don't think so.' She had wondered for a brief moment, then dismissed the notion. Jeremy was not about sex at all, or so she thought then, at the age when everything and everybody could only be defined by how she felt about them.

Her parents had met Jeremy only once, at the flat. They had come to town for the evening and had called in to deliver a belated birthday present. Jeremy was alone. He offered drinks but there had been no time, only sufficient for a quick appraisal of Paul's heavily built, and, as Angel had intimated, unattractive friend.

'I'm getting married,' Angel announced, perhaps deliberately misleading, holding on to the real surprise.

'Oh, darling! Why didn't you say? And why didn't you bring Paul with you?

'Not Paul. Jeremy.' They were having supper. Friday night. The sounds of the meal stopped. Neither her mother nor her father knew what to say, but her mother quickly took refuge in detail. 'How soon? Where will you live? The church here, of course. If it's in the summer we could have a marquee in the garden. Oh, darling, are you sure? Jeremy? We had no idea.'

'Quite sure.'

Later, in the kitchen, where the real questions always surfaced, her mother broke a glass. 'Damn thing! And it's made a hole in my rubber glove. You really are sure about this marriage? You haven't just had a quarrel with Paul?'

'No, Mum. I'm really sure. You'll understand when you get to know him. He's got a wonderful mind. I love him. I'm in love with him.'

'I've always felt the acid test is whether or not you want to have a man's children.'

'I have to admit I've not thought that far.' And she hadn't.

'Well, you should. Look at this glove!' Her mother held up the offending pink rubber. She was flustered, but not about the glove. 'You have to think what your children will look like.'

'For heaven's sake.' Angel was suddenly very cross indeed. It was intolerable, this concentration on appearance. Besides, Jeremy's looks were enthralling to her now, his slightly blubbery face and thinning hair magically transformed into an overwhelmingly appealing aspect.

That was when it started, the rift. Her parents had never warmed to Jeremy, and her mother never failed to mention Paul at least once during the increasingly rare family gatherings.

'Can we take the car into the drive now?' Angel said.

'Looks as if it will make rather a lot of noise, all that gravel,' Terry said.

'We'll leave it here, then.' Neither of them moved.

'You OK?' Angel asked, touching his denim knee.

He glanced at her, nervous. 'Don't want to let you down, babe, that's all.'

'You won't. Now, come on!'

The house sat like a desert island on a sea of carefully raked orange stones. Beyond there was a large garden backing on to woodland. The house itself was what Terry would have termed 'period manor': red brick, tall chimneys, steeply pointed gables, narrow windows as tall as doors.

The family cat waited by the open gates, as if expecting them, arching its back in a pretence at preoccupation then brushing against Angel's legs as she bent to stroke it.

Terry joined in, delaying the inevitable introductions just a little further.

Then the front door was thrown open and a tall, substantially built woman with hair the same colour as the gravel came towards them, her arms outstretched to encase her daughter.

144

'Darling. How lovely.' She kissed Angel, then turned her attention to Terry, without pause, kissing him, too. 'Come along, dears. I expect you both need a drink. Your father's in the drawing room listening to the wireless. Get him to pour you something.'

Angel's father was standing by an old-fashioned radio which was blaring out rock music. He had a pipe clamped between his teeth and a piece of paper in his hand.

'Just give me a minute,' he said, holding up the other hand. The music stopped and an announcer declared going over live to the National Lottery draw.

The three of them waited, like a tableau from the Second World War waiting for Churchill to speak to the nation.

The numbers were drawn and the piece of paper immediately crushed into a ball and tossed into the fire.

'I don't know why your mother keeps doing it,' he said. 'Hello sweetheart.'

'This is Terry,' Angel said.

Her father stretched out his hand. 'Jolly good to meet you,' he said in hearty tone, his eyes narrowing.

The room contained a number of very comfortable-looking chairs with much washed loose covers and silky cushions in beiges and pale greens. There were no strong colours, but a great sense of warmth, a room made for the family Christmases of memory, edited of the bickering and bile.

'I don't know why your mother insists on having a fire. It's barely autumn, but there we are. Look, why don't I pour some drinks and we could go out and look at the garden. What d'you say?'

They were hardly out of the French windows before her father was contriving to find out what Terry 'did'.

'Property,' Terry said.

'Really,' Father said, suddenly rather too interested.

'I'll just go and see if Mum needs a hand,' Angel said, departing before Terry could issue a visual plea.

'Dad's showing him the garden,' she told her mother.

145

'He seems a nice chap.'

'Yes, he is,' agreed Angel, as if only just realising it.

'I've invited Robert and Daphne to eat with us.'

'Oh, Mum.'

'Darling, it's so long since we had a family get-together. I thought you'd be pleased.'

'Mum, I don't want us to overwhelm Terry.'

'I don't know what you mean, Angel. You always did worry too much about bringing boyfriends home. I remember the first time Jeremy . . .' It was like mentioning the recently dead. 'We saw him on television the other night. Hardly any hair left at all.'

'Don't, Mum.'

'If you'd rather not talk about it.'

'There's really nothing to talk about.'

'But I haven't seen you since . . .'

'I just don't want us to gang up on him, OK.'

'It was only an observation. The hair.'

'Yes, but if we'd still been together you wouldn't have mentioned it.'

'Perhaps not. You know, I always did find him a bit intimidating.'

'Intimidating?'

'Yes. So clever. I always felt he could see my thoughts. Was there someone else?'

'No. It wasn't that. We just. Something happened. We were both to blame.'

'And you're not going to tell me what it was?'

At which point Angel's sister-in-law burst into the kitchen, two bottles of wine under one arm, a large bunch of flowers in the other hand and an envelope of photos between her teeth.

Angel soon became grateful that Robert and Daphne were there. They dominated the evening with their stories about cute things the children had said, potentially catastrophic episodes rescued by comedy. They were in overdrive, scripting happy families, putting on a show for the new, not quite suitable boy.

At the end of the meal the three men drifted off back to the drawing room. Angel, her mother and Daphne stayed at the table, the time for real talking now due.

'He's lovely,' said Daphne. 'Where did you find him?'

'He sold the farmhouse.'

'D'you really like him?' Angel said to her mother.

'As a matter of fact, I do. I think he's kind, and that's important in a man.'

'I don't know how you can tell, on one meeting.'

'Instinct. And he's very fond of you, I can see that.'

'And so much lovely hair,' said Daphne.

'We're not allowed to mention hair,' said Angel's mother.

'Did neither of you like Jeremy?' Angel asked.

'Not much,' answered Daphne, glancing at her mother-in-law for confirmation. 'He always made me feel a bit stupid.'

Angel thought this both accurate and unfair and began to remember with sharper focus why she and Jeremy had seen so little of her family over the years. They were like a baked Alaska, deceptively warm and inviting to begin with, then you found their cold, critical mass inside. Even the being nice about Terry was loaded because they didn't have to take him seriously. That was understood. Toy boy. The fun, silly present you got off the Christmas tree.

'Why did you split up? What happened?' Daphne asked now, as if it were her right to know.

Angel looked at her sister-in-law with a certain amount of distaste, then at her mother, who appeared to be waiting for the answer, too.

'You might as well know. Marsha is having his baby.'

The other two women closed their mouths and widened their eyes. Angel had always felt guilty for failing to feel close to her mother. She felt guilty now. Guilty and separate.

'You poor thing,' said Daphne.

'What does Paul have to say about all this?' Her mother

had instantly connected all the salient pieces of information since this conversation had begun just before Daphne's arrival. Her tone was verging on severe.

'Not a lot. He's disappeared. Gone to the States. Indefinitely as far as I can tell.'

'I don't blame him,' said Daphne. 'How awful.'

'Nice boy, Paul. Your father and I always thought you should have married him.'

Angel felt her face begin to prickle. She would have liked to tell them the whole truth, but it would ruin the rest of the weekend. There would be an atmosphere of condemnation, and Terry wouldn't believe her when she said it had nothing to do with him, that her family liked him because he did not make them feel stupid. Her mother, though, had smelled the complicity. She always did. Perhaps they were closer than close, but not in the way she had always thought mothers and daughters ought to be, with partisan blindness.

'Let's get this lot cleared up, shall we?' she said, scraping back her chair.

'Might as well,' her mother said, watchfully calm.

'I saw her on telly only a few days ago, well, a fortnight, perhaps,' Daphne was saying.

'Who, Daf?'

'Marsha, Mum. She was pregnant.'

Now Angel and her mother looked at Daphne.

'Well it's one thing to be told, another to see with your own eyes,' Daphne said, a touch peeved. Her mother-in-law could be a bit unsupportive sometimes.

They managed to clear up without more questions, although the kitchen was thick with query. Then, just as they were putting away the last leftovers, Daphne said, 'I hope Robert doesn't get any ideas.'

'Unlikely, dear, he's already got enough children.'

In the drawing room the three men were watching heavy-weight boxing on the television and being squirm-makingly blokish.

Angel's mother kept her distance following that last unfor-
tunate remark, and Angel longed for an early knock-out, but
it was to be a fight to the finish.

'They're great, your family,' said Terry when they were in
bed. 'You sure they don't mind us sleeping together?'

'Fewer sheets to wash,' said Angel, turning her back on
him.

'Come on. They're not like that.'

She brushed away his hand on her thigh.

'No,' she said.

'My folks would have me kipping on the settee downstairs
and you in my old bedroom, and Ma awake all night listening for a creak on the stairs.'

'Yes,' thought Angel, 'only I'd never go and stay with your
parents.' A shiver of loneliness ran through her. Jeremy had
hated boxing.

'You're thinking about him, aren't you?' Terry said, quietly.

'No. No, I'm not,' she said and turned to him.


'I don't like to see her so unhappy,' said her mother to her
father in the master bedroom (with en suite). 'And I said
something awful when we were in the kitchen.'

Angel's father did not enquire what it was. He never did,
but his wife repeated the little incident anyway.

'I just hope she doesn't do anything silly like have a baby
herself with that boy,' she concluded.

'We'll just have to put up with it if she does. He can't be
any worse than Daphne.'

'Don't. We agreed we wouldn't say any more nasty things
about Daphne.'

'Bad pickers, our children.'

'I thought you liked Jeremy.'

'He's let her down.'

'How can you of all people say that!' She flipped out the
bedside light and slammed her red head into the pillow.

149

# CHAPTER TWENTY

*A*ny attempt to emulate Dickens has to be foolhardly in the extreme as surely no writer will ever be able to do it better. But as our current batch of contemporary writers go, Jameson is among the best, and that's not just because he's one of Malcolm Bradbury's East Anglian boys or because Bill Buford pointed him in the direction of the serialised novel.

It's a bold move, not least because the faithful reader ends up paying six times over for what amounts to one book. In the fourth episode (published this week by Media House, price £9.99), Daniel Presley has left his wife and disappeared in South America, where, hardly credible as this may seem, he's joined a monastery.

Until this point we are left in no doubt that Presley and his wife, Anne, belong together, and surely Jameson will find a convoluted plot line to reunite them before the end of the book.

But Daniel, sinner extraordinaire, discovers to his own and everyone else's astonishment that he rather likes the monkish life. There's no question of a Road to Damascus type conversion. He remains

*the detached sceptic who speaks straight out of the
book, but the monastery and the Mexican monks
seem to provide an oasis in his life just at the
moment his thirst is greatest.*

*Back in London, Anne is blunted by a grief that
is harder to deal with than the real thing. Daniel is
not dead, so there's no mourning process, but he's
gone from her life and she can't work out what to
do next. Stuck in this emotional limbo, she turns in
on herself, shutting out the circle of friends, seeing
no one, moving, almost Miss Haversham-like into
an eccentric isolation.*

Jeremy closed down Sybil's PC and shoved into his bag the
copy he'd just read through. Marsha's letter addressed to
Angel had caught at an awkward angle in a paper clip. He
pulled it straight, then took it out, turning it over, amazed and
terrified.

Amazed because he had not opened it. Terrified because he
had a sixth sense as to its contents. Why else had it not been
addressed to him?

Sybil was across the room lying on one of the sofas, watching television, boxing of all things.

'In there! In there, you fool!' she yelled.

He got up and went over to her, bending and planting an
absent-minded kiss on her forehead. She looked surprised,
immediately switching her attention away from the telly.

'That was nice,' she said.

'What?'

'You kissing me like that.'

'Fancy making some coffee, Bill?' he said, flopping down
on another of the sofas.

'Bill!' she scoffed. 'Better that "Jail", I suppose, but it
makes me feel a bit androgynous.'

'I'm not sure you can be a bit androgynous, can you?'
Jeremy said, his mind elsewhere.

'I suppose you want it very black and strong,' she said, unfolding herself from the sofa cushions, getting up like a slave. She'd been even more horribly meek since he'd told her about Marsha.

'How awful,' she'd said. 'Will she get better?'

'I don't think so. She's all but dead. They're just keeping her alive because of the baby.'

'But who's going to look after it?'

Not you, he'd thought. You're not much more than a baby yourself.

'I shall,' he'd said.

'But will you be allowed?'

He had to know what the letter said, even considered kettle and steam, but couldn't do it. It had not escaped him that he was the only person who knew of its existence and could therefore open it and destroy it. But he wanted Angel to read it, and he wanted to be there when she opened it.

He'd telephoned several times today, but there was no reply. He did not want to call again tonight. It was bad enough when that man with the Essex twang answered the phone in the daytime. He gazed at the huge turquoise amoeba in Sybil's lava lamp, globbing its way up the glass then down again.

When Sybil came back with the coffee, setting it down on the floor, then herself, curling into his knees, he wondered again at his cruelty.

'You could bring it here. I wouldn't mind,' she'd said. 'I'd make sure there was no more dope. I'd throw out all the plants, even the cannabis.'

'I don't think so,' he'd said, picturing a miraculous reconciliation with Angel, a new home together, this time in London, a large, airy flat, big enough for the three of them.

'Why not? There's plenty of room.'

He didn't answer.

'It's me, isn't it? You don't think I'm fit.'

Again, he did not answer.

He should not have remained another minute. He should have cut it with Sybil; it was the only decent thing to do. But she had pleaded with him to stay, and he'd wanted the warmth of a shared night.

'There's no future in this,' he'd whispered to her. 'You know that, don't you? I'm sorry if I've made you miserable.'

'What's the old cliché – no living with you and no living without you – you bald bastard.'

'I wouldn't even attempt to compete with you in that department,' he said, stroking her luminous hair, then holding her in the way he naturally held a woman and which was one of those singular things that had made her fall in love with him.

In the office there was a new respect. Sniffing success, those around him were a little more careful in the way they spoke to him, edging towards deferential. They were all after the same thing, and anyone who looked as if they were about to make it had a slipstream. Hold on in there and you might get carried along.

The producer rang sooner rather than later, inviting him to take part in this week's programme. Mid-morning he rang the hospital. No change. At the end of the day he went to visit, sat by the body for fifteen minutes, surreptitiously holding her hand. He doubted she'd have let him if she'd been there. His other hand crept towards the encased baby.

'No word from any of the relatives?' the nurse enquired. 'We can't say anything to the press until they know.'

He hated the smell of the place, or perhaps it was the lack of scent. You didn't realise how perfumed and scented the everyday world was until you stepped out of it. And Marsha had always had a special pong, something vaguely orangey.

He gazed at her face for a while. So immobile, the big eyes hidden. Just a vessel now. Paul had to be found. He'd been thinking about this for a day or two, how he could use the mechanism of the newspaper to trace him. The only problem was doing so without giving them the story. Marsha was a nationally known celebrity, and this tragedy would become a tabloid treat as soon as the news got out. Sybil alone knew and she wouldn't say anything; her intelligence and news sense came to an abrupt halt at the garden gate.

'Talk to her.' He was startled, pulling his hands away from the bed as if caught in the act. 'You never know,' the nurse added. She glanced at the chart hanging above Marsha's head and went on to the next bed.

The night porter was used to him turning up late at the office.

'Nights drawing in,' he observed.

Jeremy agreed as he waited for the lift.

He rang the New York office first. Baby food. Paul had talked about baby food. Manna from heaven, he'd called it in a brief moment of the old honesty that had cemented the friendship, such as it was, when they were at school. 'Actually, I don't understand a fucking word,' he'd confided in Jeremy as they'd walked home. What was it? Latin? Economics? Jeremy didn't remember the subject, only that there had been hockey that day, too, and Paul scoring three goals. That's what you remembered.

New York ran through the company names. Bracken hit the nail. The main plant was on the West Coast. It was that easy.


They were watching 'Newsnight', another Jeremy. The baby lay between them, fast asleep. Terry was brilliant with him, and Angel enjoyed watching this brilliance. Terry, her very own yob, being clever and patient, talking to Chaucer as if he were a mate. And the baby, when he was awake, couldn't keep his eyes off Terry. Transfixed. Following his every move, absent-minded dribble running over his chins.

She was beginning to believe she could love Terry, in an easy, uncomplicated way. He was a straightforward human being. Her family had seen that. He didn't have any 'side', he just fitted in without being difficult or critical. Maybe it would rub off on her, the start of a new era with her family. She lived in hope, but spasmodically and only at a distance, the reality always dashing the dream. She wondered whether Jeremy would be on television again this week and if she'd bother to watch.

Terry found 'Newsnight' boring, but not Chaucer, even when he was asleep. The thought had crossed her mind that if she had a baby herself Terry would be rather good at looking after it. She knew herself well enough to accept that she'd be pretty hopeless if it were left to her, even though Sylvia seemed to see her as the ideal babysitter.

Denise and Kev dropped off Chaucer at the flat once or twice a week when they came into town for a night out. Sometimes Kev seemed a little the worse for wear when they came to collect the baby, and Angel worried about the trip home. 'Newsnight' was nearly over. It was getting late.

'I'll put the coffee on,' she said to Terry. 'If Kev's been drinking he ought to have some before he drives home.'

Five minutes later they arrived. They'd been to a film, not the pub, but said they'd have coffee. Denise was quite chatty these days. She'd treated Angel more like an equal since the advent of Terry.

Kev lit a cigarette and informed them there was football on the other side.

'Been good, has he?' Denise asked, bending over her baby.

'Just like an angel,' said Angel, and the four of them laughed.

The doorbell buzzed.

'I'll get it,' Terry said.

When Jeremy came into the room the easiness went, sucked away as if gobbled up by a huge, invisible vacuum pump.

Jeremy nodded to the room in general then spoke to Angel.

'Would it be possible to speak to you alone?' he said.

She bristled. Who the hell did he think he was?

'It's rather important,' he added. 'I wouldn't have come . . .'

'It's all right, babe, I'll make myself scarce,' said Terry, putting up a hand. Angel made a determined effort not to catch Jeremy's critical eye, as critical she knew it would be. Denise was already collecting together Chaucer's baby paraphernalia. Kev stuck his cigarette behind his ear and picked up his sleeping son.

'Thanks a lot, Angel,' Denise said, hurrying, scurrying, anxious to be gone, outside in air that could be breathed. And Angel was suddenly alone with Jeremy. She heard the front door bang downstairs. Her ears buzzed with fury.

'It is important, Angel.' Jeremy was looking at her very hard, overwhelming her anger.

'It must be,' she said, hating herself now for wishing he had not found her in such company, then resenting him for causing her to have this qualm.

'You'd better sit down. Would you like coffee?'

He followed her into the small kitchen, as if he had a right. She felt his gaze on her back as she did the coffee business. She felt his presence too much.

'It's Marsha.'

'Oh.' She made it sound like a disappointment when it should not have sounded like anything at all.

'She's in a coma.'

Angel swung round to face him.

'They say she won't recover. But the baby is still alive.'

A rush of confused emotions swelled and shrivelled.

'Oh, Jeremy.'

He was reaching into his pocket, pulling out the letter.

'I went to her flat. I found this.' He held out the letter to her.

'Paul. Does Paul know?'

Jeremy shook his head.

The letter stood between them like a time bomb.

'Open it, Angel. For God's sake, open it.'

A single, typed page.

*My dear Angel,*

*I hope you will never read this, but if you do I hope you will have forgiven me for what has happened.*

*I'm writing this in case anything happens to me when the baby is born. More and more I feel that this child belongs to the four of us, but my greatest fear is that he or she will continue to be the focus of despair. But he will be as innocent as the four of us are guilty.*

*What I feel is that it could just as easily have been you and not me, and I've tried to imagine how I would feel, what I would do. What I would want.*

*Angel, I want you to take the baby and bring him up. You and Jeremy. And if Paul ever comes back into your lives, be his friend again. Be kind to him. Tell him that I've never stopped loving him.*
*Marsha*

Angel handed the single sheet to Jeremy. She watched him scan the words, too quickly.

'My God, you wrote it, didn't you?' she accused him, the notion leaping forth with utter conviction.

He gazed at her steadily, the practice of a lifetime disguising surprise, dislike, then something little short of hatred.

# CHAPTER TWENTY-ONE

This had to be the most over-stated thing he had ever done. The eight-hour flight didn't help, and he'd found himself seated next to a woman in a mauve shell-suit who wanted to know the story of his life. He had made up a family and career that bore a close resemblance to that of Daniel Presley, but there had been an awkward moment when the woman exclaimed with delight that she knew East Sheen. He had been saved by the film, although it also served to remind him that he would not now be providing the nation with erudite comment on the latest Woody Allen. Instead, he was cramped up in 'economy', the only seat he could get, and winging his way across the Atlantic to deliver bad news.

Tracing Paul had been a piece of cake. Bracken Foods. Sasha Parrish.

'I'm trying to make contact with Paul Lewis.'

'Paul. Why, yes. He's staying at my place. Can I give him a message?'

'No, thank you. I'll write or something.'

'Can I say who called?'

'It's OK, thank you.' You couldn't just leave a message for someone you'd known all your life telling him his wife was effectively dead, although Marsha's condition was only part of it – the most immediate and pressing part, but possibly not enough in itself to warrant what he was doing.

The impetus to find Paul and let him know about Marsha had begun out of a sense of what was right. Paul's right to know. Absurdly, it was to do with what was decent and proper, but over the intervening days had become tarnished by Jeremy's own need to know.

He had not believed Angel. More to the point, and as she had accused him herself, he had chosen not to believe her. Even now it seemed impossible that Paul, whom he sometimes thought he knew better than himself, could have done such a thing. It had been a clumsy attempt at a pass, just about excusable given the events that had led up to it. Angel had overreacted. Nothing more than that. He'd almost managed to convince himself that this was what had happened. Almost.

The air was hot and sticky as they emerged from the plane and into another whole night to get through. Jeremy decided to find a hotel and sleep, if he could, for the next few hours. He did not want to be at a disadvantage when he met Paul, although perhaps he was more concerned that the jet-lag might allow him to put Paul at the disadvantage and he didn't want that either. Their meeting needed to be calm and controlled, no recriminations.

He didn't sleep, not until the small hours, by which time the vivid dreams came on like a sequence of video trailers: the best bits, the worst bits. Angel's pale face that night at the farmhouse when he'd come home and thought they'd been burgled. He was attacking her, trying to rape her but never quite getting there. The interruptions were Paul, wearing stained cricket whites, looking on as if he's just been bowled out and wasn't even questioning the umpire's decision. And when he turned back to the face beneath him, the eyes were closed, and suddenly it wasn't Angel any more but Marsha. He leapt from her, turned again, this time to beseech Paul, who was walking back to the crease, bat trailing through grass too long for play.

In the far distance he saw the tiny figure of Sybil pushing a lawn mower in the wrong direction, heading towards a cliff edge. He started to run towards her, but he didn't seem to be making any ground. Another figure in a mauve shell-suit was talking to Grace, and when they turned it was Wilfred. But none of them saw him. Nobody shouted out or warned him as he started to fall.

He woke in a sweat, palpitations, the emptiness of the hotel room a momentary disappointment that seemed to confirm the loss of all those people who had made up his life until now.

He took a shower, automatically inspecting the further hair loss evidenced in the plughole. He didn't think he really cared about going bald, had long ago fixed what vanity he had in other non-physical directions to do with wit and irony, but there was strange fascination in the knot of hair that would never be replaced. It was vaguely unwholesome, a kind of mutation he could do nothing about.

He realised he was inventing his own delaying tactics, even though he was anxious now to find Paul and get it over with. He wrapped himself in a huge white towel, its size, he decided, designed to make it more difficult to steal, and switched on 'CBS News'. An ice hockey player had murdered his wife. A group of Los Angeles school children had started a donkey sanctuary. It was hard to believe the presenters had legs. The man's hair didn't look real.

He had coffee and a bagel in his room, one or the other or both finding a place that brought on a pain he might have had anyway as the time drew nearer. He had Sasha Parrish's address lying flat against it on a slip of paper in his wallet.

Eight o'clock. Maybe he should leave it an hour, avoid the morning rush. Then he remembered it was Saturday. Of course it was Saturday. Paul would not be there in the day-time if it wasn't Saturday.

He took a cab across town, the driver pointing out sights because he was English on a Saturday and therefore had to be

161

rubbernecking. The biggest. The longest. The most famous. All of it passed Jeremy by. He couldn't decide whether it would be easier or more difficult if Sasha Parrish were there. The chances were she would be. On a Saturday. Perhaps if she were she'd go out. No, he could suggest they go somewhere, he and Paul. Less chance of a scene. Was that what he expected? Had Paul ever done that?

'Bugger off, Harris. Leave him alone, won't you?' But Harris had not, and there had been a fight, engendering the same pain in his gut, the very same. He'd stood by and watched Paul swinging his fists into Harris's startled face, the other boys, Harris's so-called friends, stepping back in that moment of disbelief, then one by one joining in, while he just stood there, feeling the pain that had come from nowhere, wanting to do something but somehow unable to move.

Someone had shouted that there was a master coming, and in an instant the punching and pummelling had stopped, Harris's bunch dispersing like trained commandos, Paul lying there, his cricket whites badly stained, then clambering to his feet, streaking his sleeve with blood from his nose. 'Move it, Holden. Move!'

In the relative safety of the shed where the gangmowers were kept, he'd asked why. 'You should have left it,' he said, as always regaining the upper hand. 'It's better to ignore that sort of thing.' But Paul, he could see, had enjoyed it.

'This OK?' the cab driver was saying.

Jeremy peered out at a plush apartment block. At the door he had to pass an initiative test to get by security, who had no record of his name as an expected visitor.

He took the lift. On the landing, Paul was standing outside a closed door, utterly failing any pretence at pleasure, rather looking as if he might be about to be arrested.

'Sorry to burst in on you like this,' Jeremy heard himself begin, his attention more fixed on his own swirling emotions and what now felt like almost dubious intention of his being there.

'What are you doing here?' Paul managed to say. He was frightened, Jeremy could see it straightaway, and in that moment knew beyond any doubt.

'Can I come in?' he asked, a hard edge taking over. 'Or would it be better if we went somewhere else?'

Paul had looked at him, properly, eye to eye, only once, in that split second of surprise. Now he was looking everywhere else but, casting about like a trapped animal, shoulders raised, hands plunged in his trouser pockets.

'What do you want, Jeremy? You know, I half guessed it was you, when Sasha said someone had rung.' Briefly, he caught Jeremy's gaze. 'Come on, then. Get it over with.'

Jeremy took a breath, feeling it catch against the pain. 'It's not what you think,' he said. 'Look, we can't just stand here in the hallway. You'd better let me come in.'

Paul hesitated for a moment, but he was long-trained in complying with Jeremy's wishes. He turned and pushed against the door.

'This way,' he said, close to a whisper, leading Jeremy along a hallway heavily hung with pictures that gave off an aura of the real thing. 'She sleeps in at the weekends,' he murmured.

The room they ended up in had a wall of glass as opposed to a window, a huge view on urban development.

'D'you want some coffee?'

'Yes.' It would exacerbate the pain, but the process might ease the situation a little.

The room had three vast sofas, a cabinet that probably disguised a television set, more pictures Jeremy was too preoccupied to decipher, a couple of pieces of sculpture, an acre of white carpet. New World Onslow Square. He assumed Paul was sleeping with Sasha Parrish. It crossed his mind that she might be black.

'I take it you still drink high octane,' Paul was saying as he came back. He appeared to have composed himself, his hand almost steady as he handed Jeremy the coffee.

'This must be serious stuff,' he said next, making it sound close to conversational. 'Or were you just passing by?'

Jeremy couldn't stand this a moment longer.

'It's Marsha,' he said.

'She sent you?' Paul's surprise had a sudden eagerness.

Poor bastard, thought Jeremy. Poor bastard.

'She's in hospital.'

Paul seemed to deflate.

'You haven't come all this way . . .'

'No. Not that. It would be too soon. Something happened. They're not quite sure what. She's in what they call a persistent vegetative state.' Saying it made it sound worse, if that were possible. It might have been easier, better, just to say she was dead.

'Oh, my God!' A woman in a pale green satin dressing gown was standing in the doorway staring at the dark stain journeying into the carpet.

'Quick, Paul. Do something. Cold water. Towels.' Then. 'Hey, I'm sorry. So rude of me. You are?'

'Jeremy Holden.' He looked at the women, who was not black, and felt sorry for her. His being there had ruined more than her carpet and in a few minutes she would know it, and whatever the relationship with Paul she would feel wretched for making a fuss.

He'd put her at about the same age as Marsha, maybe a bit more. She had a hard face, flinty eyes, but she was vulnerable in her dressing gown, and her face had the same puffy undercoat look he had observed about Sybil in between make-up coming off and going on.

Her attention had reset on the coffee stain, growing like an afternoon shadow. It was the first time Jeremy had seen Paul drop anything, although it had been more of a slow topple.

'You'll excuse me if I just go and put something on,' she said, already retreating.

Jeremy headed in the direction Paul had taken and found him at the sink, cold tap running.

'She's not really like that,' he said, wringing the cloth.

'You understand what I said about Marsha?'

'Look, I'd better sort out this mess.'

It wasn't as serious as it looked. No body language between the two of them. Paul, it seemed, was some kind of servant in this set-up, Sasha Parrish one of those women who liked testicles scrambled on toast as an appetiser. Jeremy was sitting opposite her at the dining table when this notion dropped on him. He smiled at her thinly. The reason for him being here seemed to have changed. She reminded him a little of Harris.

'I don't understand,' Paul was saying. 'How can it happen, just like that?'

'I think it's some kind of blood clot,' Jeremy said.

'It's very sad,' Sasha said, pushing her chair back, standing and moving away from them.

'Paul, of course, will have to come back to London,' he said, with an edge that made her give him a quick, fierce glance.

'Of course,' she said.

'I suppose I will,' Paul said, his thoughts seemingly elsewhere.

'I take it you want to?' Jeremy asked, adopting slight incredulity. It had not occurred to him until now that Paul might hesitate. Just what sort of a hold did this woman have over him? Although maybe it had nothing to do with her. Even so, he couldn't believe Paul would not come home, that he could go on harbouring the bitterness and resentment that had already kept him here too long. The other business, Jeremy's own preoccupation until less than an hour ago, could surely not be a deciding factor. Paul knew, had to know, that neither he nor Angel would let that prevent a home-coming in the circumstances. They had to work it out together now, just as they should have from the beginning. It was bad enough that they had left Marsha to get on with it alone, and he had even wondered, in the darkest moments, whether the strain on her might have contributed to what had happened. His own particular portion of guilt weighed heavy. He might have encouraged her to have an abortion instead of doing everything he could to make sure she didn't. An abortion could have resolved everything, and in time the four of them might have carried on as before, but he knew, even as this scenario or supposed solution ran through his thoughts, he could not have stood it.

'I've heard of people who come round,' Sasha was saying. 'Sometimes after years.'

Jeremy wished he could silence her. This had been one of the first questions he had asked at the hospital. Anyone, with the slightest awareness, would ask, and anyone with the slightest awareness would know that he had.

'They wouldn't,' Sasha continued, as if inspiration had struck, 'have kept her alive if there was no hope.'

Jeremy did not want to say it. 'There's the baby.'

'Oh, I'd forgotten about the baby,' Sasha said with the insensitivity of a boardroom.

Paul now stood up. Perhaps none of it had sunk in until this moment.

'I don't know what to do,' he said. 'I just don't know what to do.'

'Hey, I've just realised,' Sasha said. 'You're the other guy, aren't you?' She was assessing Jeremy with a new perspective, a little too much surprise to be in the least flattering. He couldn't help registering this and disliking both her and himself somewhat more.

'This is a bad deal,' she said, coming back across the room, adopting a manner that suggested she was about to retake charge even though the situation was not hers. For a moment she made Jeremy think of his mother, the way Grace might have been given a switch of generation and continent.

'Paul,' she commanded, 'you have to go to your wife.' She looked at Jeremy. 'That's right, isn't it, Mr Holden?' There was icy decisiveness in her voice, a total dislike. Jeremy wondered how much Paul had told her and was rather surprised that he cared; it couldn't be that he was the slightest bit bothered what this ghastly woman thought of him. He preferred to think it was a natural instinct towards privacy. He felt desperate to get out of this place where prior knowledge hung in the air.

But a swift exit was not to be. It was going to take until Monday to get Paul on a plane back to England, and the intervening forty-eight hours would pass slowly and painfully because there was nowhere else to go. Jeremy felt like a cross between a bounty hunter and a minder. He didn't dare let Paul out of sight, even though another disappearing act might have suited him better. A part of him wished he might never see or hear of Paul again, and perhaps he had seen this as the solution until Marsha's embolism, had even hoped for it. But another part, even now, mourned the loss of an oddly enduring friendship that had already survived more than it should, abuse and betrayal. The balance, for some years, had given Paul the right to take more licence than he had until the night at the farmhouse; and for a while Jeremy had, he now realised, actually weighed this balance in his tortured thinking. He had known, that night, Angel was telling the truth. Everything he knew of both Angel and Paul informed him that it had to be, and it was only himself he no longer knew.

Sasha Parrish went out during the middle part of the first day. Perhaps she, too, found the hothouse pressure of the situation too much to bear, but she, unlike the other two, could walk away.

Almost as soon as she had left, Paul again began defending her, or perhaps his own position in her life, hers in his, as if further adultery could have any real bearing at this stage.

'I'm not sleeping with her, if that's what you think,' he said. 'She lets me stay here and in return I cook for her, look after the place. If it hadn't been for her, well . . .'

'How much have you told her?' Jeremy heard himself asking.

'She knows most of it. I owed her that.'

'Owed her? Christ, Paul, she's a ball-breaker if ever I saw one.'

Paul hesitated, taken aback by a frankness that had been long absent between them. 'It's not always the ones that seem that way who do the most damage,' he said.

If there was self-pity in there it didn't resonate. It was an observation that seemed to put them in the same camp again, the sort of exchange that wiped out a couple of decades of complicated adulthood and drew on the simple bond that had formed pre-women. They were standing beside one another, and suddenly Jeremy put his arm across Paul's shoulders.

'Come on,' he said. 'Let's go out and get drunk.'

# CHAPTER TWENTY-TWO

It was like Christmas out of the trenches. A brief, intense truce. They got hugely drunk and had a bit of bother in one of the downtown bars. Trouble followed them into the lavatory, but by now Paul was back in another world, hearing different voices, seeing smaller faces blurred in memory and Budweiser chased by rye.

'Here come the Mummy's Boys.' Titter, titter. 'DBs. Dirty buggers. Day boys.'

'Ignore them.'

'Grow up.'

'How'd you like your hair washed, Fat DB?' There were five of them, or was it six? One had gone into the Church. Paul heard him once on 'Thought for the Day', a pious prig whose thought had been forgiveness. Paul had felt like ringing up or faxing the 'Today' programme and saying he wasn't sure he'd forgiven him for pushing his friend's head down the lavatory at Stoop. Three of them had held him against the urinals while the others tipped Jeremy upside down. He'd almost wanted it to be done to him, too, but he'd known it would only be Jeremy, guilty of obesity and spec-wearing. The following term he'd knocked out the front tooth of the chief titterer during a single wicket competition, found it in the grass, nearly across the boundary, given it to Jeremy on the way home, allowed him to think he'd done it on purpose. It seemed possible Jeremy had almost thought well of him that day.

No chance that he thought in the least well of him now. It had all been bad, yet the worst, by far the worst in his tortured conscience was the last incident with Angel. All the rest had been the result of a hideous mistake, the proverbial moment of madness, but what he'd done to Angel had been criminal.

He'd half expected Jeremy to pursue him, for all four of them to behave out of character, even Jeremy, whose legendary cool-headedness . . . he let out a small, involuntary titter himself as he gazed into the white porcelain of the down town bar urinal.

'D'you remember Harris?' he said, slurrily. 'Heard him on the radio. The bugger's a bishop. Can you believe it?"

'I don't know who you mean,' Jeremy said. Drunk as he was, he didn't want to hark back to Harris and humiliation, the episodes that came unbidden, rising on the taste of bile; and if Paul wanted to handle them down memory lane as the good times, he wasn't going to get any help with the map reading. Jeremy thought he was about to be sick.

'I think we ought to be getting back,' he said.

'Back? There is no "back",' Paul said. 'I'm all free spirit these days. Forward, that's the way, forward.'

'Oh, shut up,' Jeremy said, beginning to tug at Paul's arm.

They must have been drinking for hours. Out in the street it was dark. Paul, attempting to loosen Jeremy's grip, began rotating his shoulder, stem-bowling fashion.

'Why did you come?' he demanded. 'Why did you come all this way? I mean, what's the point if she's dead? What's the point?'

Jeremy lifted his free arm to flag a passing cab that slowed then carried on when the driver saw the state of his potential passengers.

'It's Angel,' Paul continued, oblivious. 'That's why you've come. All this way to hit me. Well, come on,' he swayed, suddenly freeing himself, or perhaps Jeremy had let go. 'Hit me then. I'll let you. Hit me.' The swaying turned into a stagger, and Jeremy watched him buckle on to the pavement.

'Get up,' he said, coldly.

He watched as Paul struggled, seemingly without strength or coordination, to get to this feet. He had a sudden urge to kick him and might almost have done so had it not been for a group of people on the other side of the street who appeared to be taking an interest.

'Get up,' he repeated, leaning closer to Paul, then grabbing him and yanking him into a semi-standing position. 'I didn't come all this way to get myself arrested.'

Paul had gone limp, and Jeremy now had to bear his full weight. The next cab stopped, a woman driver who demanded to know whether either of them was about to throw up and for some inexplicable reason believed Jeremy when he assured her that neither of them was.

Sasha was less generous, and in the early hours, by which time Jeremy was feeling thoroughly awake in London time, he finally managed to deposit Paul in the spare bed in his hotel room.

In his own bed he lay awake, but unable to think any more about Angel or Marsha and his own guilt, which now seemed greater than Paul's. Instead he found himself picturing Harris at prayer and wondering what it might be like to meet him again after all these years.

At some point during the night Paul's breathing became strange, short, shallow gasps. Jeremy got up and went over to the other bed, peering through the darkness until the face took shape. He didn't hate him. Never had and never would. It wasn't possible to hate Paul.

'Bloody prat,' he murmured, moving away as Paul turned in his sleep and the breathing eased into a deeper level.

He went over to the window and, pushing back the curtain a little, looked out at the traffic that went on all night, a row of assorted neon colours flashing and pulsating across the way. He let the curtain fall into place again and went back to bed. How would he have felt if he had hit Paul, he wondered? He'd never hit anyone in his life. He'd probably have missed. He missed Paul, he realised. He'd really missed him, but he was still a bloody prat.

They both slept through much of Sunday. Sasha came to the hotel and they managed a fairly civilised meal in the restaurant, due largely to Sasha's obsessional interest in what she ate, although this moved on to an appetite-suppressing monologue on the benefits of colonic irrigation. Neither of the men tried to stop her, grateful for any conversation that avoided reference to the trauma that awaited them in London.

She had brought Paul's few possessions with her to the hotel, making it clear she did not expect him to return.

In the lobby she kissed Paul as if he were a blood relative. Jeremy went with her to her car.

'Take care of him,' she said, 'whatever's happened between the four of you.'

Jeremy held the door for her, catching another draught of the powerful scent.

'He always used to take care of me, you know,' he said, surprising himself, Harris peeping round the corner.

'So maybe it's your turn,' Sasha said.

Jeremy waited until the car was out of sight before he went back into the hotel. It made a change, he thought, to meet a grown up.

Paul's gaze had not left Marsha's face for well over an hour. He watched for the tiny twitches of nerves that promised life. He imagined setting up a camera, the way they did for flowers, over a day, over a week, the shots then run together to create a stream of fluid movement. He vaguely wondered whether the hospital would allow it.

He no longer knew what he felt. He looked at Marsha and still felt angry, his mind teeming with might-have-been. She was the woman who had almost replaced Angel, the closest he had ever expected to come to that.

'Paul.' He started. He'd not heard them approaching. Angel and Jeremy. Angel, her hand now lightly on his shoulder.

None of them knew what to say. It was as if they were all waiting for Marsha to begin the conversation.

There had been very little of that between the two men on the journey back to London from the States. There was plenty to be said, none of it appropriate as they got closer to the reality of Marsha's condition. All that had been established, beyond further discussion, was the impossibility of Marsha's recovery and the fact of the baby's continuing survival.

'No change, I suppose?' said Jeremy, moving round to the other side of the bed, brushing his fingers over Marsha's cold hand.

'She looks so serene,' said Angel, whispering, as if Marsha might be woken.

'When did she have her hair cut?' Paul asked suddenly.

'I think the hospital did it,' replied Jeremy.

'It suits her,' observed Angel, her voice still very quiet.

'Don't be so bloody silly,' murmured Jeremy.

'Don't be so bloody rude,' murmured Angel.

'Don't be so bloody,' said Paul.

'Sorry,' chorused Angel and Jeremy, both looking ashamed.

'Oh, be as bloody as you like. She can't hear you.'

'All the same,' said Angel, shooting a look of distaste at Jeremy.

The three of them were silent until it became deafening.

'What are we going to do?' broke in Angel.

'What do you mean, what are "we" going to do?' said Paul, now looking at Angel, then Jeremy.

'Didn't you tell him?' Angel addressed Jeremy.

'Oh, so you believe it now?'

'Believe what?' said Paul.

'Marsha wrote a letter,' Angel began, after a pause that

173

couldn't last. 'But this doesn't really seem right, talking about it here.'

'Please,' pleaded Paul.

'She said that if anything happened to her . . . God, d'you think she had some sort of premonition?'

'If anything happened to her?' urged Paul.

'She wanted me to bring up the baby,' said Angel. Another pause. 'And Jeremy.'

'Well, you don't have to worry about that now, do you?' said Paul. 'I'm back.'

'But we thought you didn't . . .'

'Want to know?'

'Well . . .'

'Things change.'

'One thing doesn't,' said Jeremy.


'I thought those two were going to come to blows,' said the nurse, wiping a cold flannel over Marsha's face, then lifting her head a little to smooth out the pillow.

'Not long now,' she continued, moving her hands down to Marsha's belly, feeling its solid mass, a drum-like tension. 'Then you'll be able to rest in peace, dearie.' The nurse sighed, as if suddenly overwhelmed by the sadness of the situation. 'Fancy them arguing like that, at the bedside.'

'Fancy,' thought Marsha.

# Chapter Twenty-Three

She could hear everything.

At first she'd thought she was dreaming, except there were no images, just sounds.

It had started with the words jumbled, then they'd begun to fall into place. She wasn't that interested for a while. Too much effort. Then it became enthalling. She had thought she might die when she had the baby, but now she felt certain the birth would bring her back to life. So certain as to sustain her through each dreary, frustrating day. Only the activity around her informed her when it was day and when it was night; the activity and the chat. Thank God the nurses talked to her, probably in much the same way they spoke to their houseplants, but beggars could not be choosers, as Nanny used to say.

She occupied the long spells in between by dwelling in the past, bringing into mind so much she had thought lost or, more to the point, not thought about at all since the day each episode had been filed away in those far recesses nobody really understood.

The triggers were small, in every other respect inconsequential. The house off Regent's Park where she had lived as a child, its completeness arrived at through the sharp memory of the brass door handles, the inky smell of whatever the stuff used to clean them pungent in her nostrils, which reached almost the exact same height.

The brass handles opened doors into rooms of elegant splendour. Gilded Regency-style chairs were sat upon by men in serious suits who spoke in loud, commanding tones until their attention was drawn to her. 'Well, hello, and what's your name?' It had been years before she'd found out about her father's own brand of diplomacy, the buzzer surreptitiously pressed to sound corridors away, signalling the moment for Nanny or her mother to bring her into the proceedings, breaking into an empasse, giving her father breathing space to realign his argument.

The years had actually been a little under five, but an eternity when you were that age yourself.

She was ten when she was sent to boarding school and the family removed itself from the house in Regent's Park. Did the two happen simultaneously? They must have. She went off to school and never saw the house or her parents again.

'Marsha. Sit down, dear. I've something very serious to tell you.' It was the endearment that frightened her. Miss Ghent never called any of them 'dear'. She knew the name of every girl in her school and how to pronouce even the softest collection of vowels and consonants with rasping sharpness.

After that the girls in her class, and especially those with whom she shared a dormitory, had been nice to her. But the reality was that she'd already been through the grieving process when her parents had sent her away to school, so that their death was less of a blow than she allowed the other girls to think. The manner of their death added further to the new approbation in which she was held. Killed in an isolated piece of terrorism back home, although a home to which she would never return.

She went to stay with Nanny in Brixton during the holidays in a house that sounded and smelled of linoleum. Clickety pad-padding along the dark hallway with streaks of colour filtering through squares of stained glass in the front door, holding on to billions of frantic dust mots. How could there be so much going on in such a quiet, still place? Nanny was suddenly old. She hadn't seemed so when she wore a uniform, but in her own home the starched blue dress was never worn, making Marsha feel vaguely cheated, as if Nanny no long belonged exclusively to her.

They did a lot of baking in the holidays, even when the summers were hot. Everything they ate had served time in the oven. Nanny said she was a natural, that her fingers were made for pastry.

'Fancy education,' Nanny scoffed. 'Don't suppose they teach you how to cook.' Only how to be a snob. She wished more than anything that Nanny would get out the blue dress, just when she escorted her back to school the evening before the first day of term. It was bad enough arriving in a taxi from the station.

It was just her and Nanny and a brown dog at the house in Brixton. The dog was old, too, as if to match the house. It was called Lep and it had terrible breath and milky eyes. Occasionally it roused itself to bark at the postman or someone else they didn't invite in. Skidding over the linoleum, its claws too long through lack of exercise on pavements. Apart from these rare demonstrations of canine aggression, its only concern was Nanny, whom it adored with limpet-like devotion, never missing a chance to flop down on her slippered feet or press itself against her legs.

Marsha had offered to take it for walks, but it wouldn't go. There'd been one or two donkey-like tugging sessions, Lep's head twisted in defiance as the lead pulled him along the hallway on his bottom until Marsha gave up and went out alone.

She was approaching thirteen when the boy who lived next door to Nanny suddenly came into focus. Until then he had been merely a disappointment, the wrong sex for a holiday friendship.

They seemed to manage to meet in the park. Well, it was just a patch of grass really, swings and a slide in the far corner.

They skirted around one another as Lep might have with another dog, each bristlingly aware of the other but managing to sustain an air of indifference.

They were careful to be careless in the way they communicated. Both had become tall and gangling, although Douglas had an extra foot in height. They lolled agains the frame of the swings, kicking dust, squinting at the dazzling whiteness of a hot London sky.

That must have been the first summer of Douglas, when she wanted him to kiss her and was terrified that he might.

'Have you got a boyfriend, Marsha?' they asked her the first night back in the dormatory. It seemed that everyone had discovered a Douglas during that holiday. Jessica had found one in Spain. Laurel in Italy. Janice and Roberta in West Germany. Pauline had met an English boy in France.

'Douglas is from Jamaica,' said Marsha.

Lips were pursed. Distance added enchantment. No one else had foraged outside Europe. Marsha had never (and never would) mentioned Brixton.

On the last day of the last term at school Miss Leather showed then how to fold napkins to look like swans, the closest they were ever expected to come to a domestic chore. In many ways the school was more out of date than Nanny's linoleum.

Marsha now had time and pause to marvel at how she and all the other girls had managed to live in such close proximity for these formative years and yet hide so much, because she assumed that all the others had snobbery-ridden secrets. There was the suspicion that Janice lived in a semi in Barnet.

She had not seen much of Douglas in the two summers following that first. He'd spent the school holidays in Jamaica with his uncles and aunts. It was boring in Brixton without him, knowing that he was no longer just a breath or two away the other side of the long hallway with the dust mots and the coloured light, the lingering sweetness of baking, the linoleum, but no longer Lep who really had been very old.

Then the fourth summer he was there again. Huge. The gangly aspect replaced by solid muscle, glistening like newly released horse chestnuts. A face chiselled into manhood. Brown eyes drinking in the potential of Marsha's new-found chest. She was verging on plump that summer. The baking had to stop.

Contrary to appearances, Douglas' strength was now channelled into writing poetry with a Jamaican rap to it. He also talked about becoming a minister in the Pentecostal Church, this second revelation, more than the first, adding a spin to the heady sense of desire Marsha experienced when the chestnut biceps flexed in the sun.

Nanny was not fooled by the sudden interest in attending Sunday evening worship. 'Nothing changes,' she said obliquely.

The jarring contrast between the loud and swinging Pentecostal service and those tedious interludes in the school chapel where the girl in front's footwear took on attention-fixing fascination brought Marsha to the brink of belief; besides, she fancied herself in love with Douglas and began to dream of a life in the sun, the wife of a missionary. At school they had prayed daily for the old girls serving overseas in Borneo. As a 'first-year' Marsha had pictured some sort of grand hotel, the old girls in tight black uniforms with small white pinnies. Then, one day, an old girl had been wheeled in, really old, her face as if moulded from a crumpled paper bag baked to a crisp beneath the Borneo sun. There had been a sense of disappointment. Perhaps there were no hotels at all in Borneo after all.

Douglas went away again the in between A level year. Marsha couldn't possibly go to the park any more. She watched television with Nanny, dramas about men whose wives did not understand them. 'Don't fancy them any more, more like,' said Nanny, as if she knew. And she did. Her husband had gone back to Jamaica just as Douglas would one day.

The religious phase was short-lived, for both of them. Douglas became a tube train driver and Nanny encouraged the romance, as if reaping some sort of revenge on Marsha's dead parents. 'No good having ideas above our station,' she said, and for a moment Marsha thought she had cracked a joke, but Nanny's face was still stoney, eyes as hard as pellets, lips downtrodden.

She did not do well in her exams. She was bored by school, ready for the world and Douglas, whatever his station. She married him when she was still eighteen and for the next few years was allowed so little sleep she was too tired to consider her own future. But at twenty-five the money came, huge amounts of it, more than she had ever admitted to Paul. She couldn't hide the wealth that resulted from her own success, but that was somehow different. The inherited stuff had seemed to make Douglas despise her and lose interest, or maybe it was her inability to become pregnant. He had left her long before he had actually gone, stubbornly continuing on the underground long after she took only taxis. Once he had told her it was the rhythm of the train that enabled him to write his best pieces of rap.

She thought she had never stopped loving him until she met Paul and discovered the fierce, jealous, pain-inducing love that Douglas had never inspired. She had mistaken affection for love, but then lots of people did that with their first marriages. And she still felt fond when she thought of Douglas, perhaps because they had shared those formative years; so that when she'd seen him again, only this year, back in London . . .

Now, when she heard Paul's voice she also heard her own. She heard and saw without seeing his bitterness still there. 'You must keep the baby,' she was telling him. 'Keep it for me, for when I'm alive again. Everything will be all right then, you'll see.' She drifted away, back on to the plane of memory; right back to Nanny in her blue uniform days, bumping the pram down deep hard steps. Another face veering towards her but not coming properly into focus. 'Mum, mum, mum. Can you say it, sweetheart?' 'Hallaluha, my faith is in Jesus!'

Swing, sway, feeling a bit sick. Lep's filmy eyes with a don't-you-dare look, brown furry body pressed against legs the exact same colour. Cinnamon, toasting in the oven. A dusty swing, heat-soaked metal slide too hot for bare flesh.

'We'll switch her off after the baby's born.'

# CHAPTER TWENTY-FOUR

'Switch it on. Switch it on!' Grace came flapping into the room.

'It's all right. Another five minutes before it starts,' said Wilfred.

'I suppose Mark Lawson's not actually that fat,' said Grace, seven or eight minutes later.

'Television adds at least a stone,' said Wilfred, with his in-the-know tone. 'That's why I'm always so careful,' he added, not shifting his gaze from the screen.

'Funny though, I've never thought of Jeremy as tubby before,' Grace continued, ignoring Wilfred's veiled aspiration.

'Jeremy,' said Mark, 'do you feel there's any hope for these four characters?'

'I'm beginning to doubt it. Each of them is much more conventional than they would like to think. The two men are hopelessly conditioned by their public school upbringing, and the women, well, as long as they go on seeing themselves as subsidiary to the plot . . .'

'What do you know about the way these women feel?' demanded the woman called Allison who was sitting in Germaine's chair this week.

'I don't. I'm just telling you the way I see it as a man.'

'You can't really do otherwise,' chipped in Mark, with his

controller's laugh. He didn't want a feminist row this early in the programme.

'I suppose the thing is, their troubles are never going to be resolved via a conventional solution,' he added. 'Tony, do you think they'll get it right or they'll get it wrong?'

'Oh, they'll get it wrong. Be a bit boring if they sewed it all up neat and tidy. These people are never going to be comfortable with themselves or each other; it's not in their natures. Born to screw up, all four of them, Allison.'

'Well, we'll await the final episode next week. Now, cookery as entertainment and art form. A new exhibition opens on Friday featuring recipes and food as exhibits . . .'

'I thought I might go and see her,' said Grace, thoughts transcending the programme, even though, perhaps because, her son was part of it.

'Who, dearie?' said Wilfred.

'Marsha, poor soul. After all, she is the mother of my grandchild.'

'I'll come with you,' he said.

'That's kind.'

Grace began to pull at the skin on the sides of her fingers, creating a small bleed. It was a wretched little habit she'd never been able to stop and always worse when she was agitated about something.

'Wilfred?'

'Yes, dearie?'

'Have you thought any more about what we discussed?'

'What we discussed?'

'Oh, you know.' She sounded impatient now, so quickly losing her attempt at cajolery because didn't she always get her own way in the end.

'The baby?'

'Yes, the baby.'

'Well, I suppose you have got the room.'

'The house is enormous, far too big for just two people.' It had not escaped her that Wilfed had distanced himself by saying that she had the room rather than they had the room, but she chose to disregard the implication. In any other discussion she might not have liked it if he'd said they had the room. She knew exactly the hesitancy in his complicity at this moment, but ploughed on regardless because she thought him a fool, albeit one to manipulate for her own purposes.

'Shall we just watch the end of Jeremy's programme?'

Grace sucked her finger like a vampire.

'I'm sorry, but I'm not interested in Marmite sandwiches in glass cases.'

'How d'you suppose they stop the edges curling?'

'Wilfred!'

'The baby. Yes. The only, well, I was just wondering which one of us would be doing the looking after?'

'Who's going to look after it?' asked Terry, sulkily. 'Don't tell me you're going to chuck in your job and stay at home all day.'

'I thought perhaps Sylvia . . .' Angel said, with a guilty edge.

'Sylvia, in case you'd forgotten, works for my sister these days.'

'Yes.'

'What d'you mean by "yes"?'

Angel had not told Terry that she had already spoken to Sylvia about the possibility and that Sylvia had flung her arms round her and said she'd rather do anything than carry on working for Jane, who'd given her hell last week for using Mr Sheen instead of unadulterated beeswax.

'Uh, she rubs me up the wrong way, that woman. If it was a proper job, I could look after Chaucer for Denise at the same time, and she could earn a bit of money herself.'

'I should imagine your sister is not the easiest person to work for,' Angel ventured.

'Don't let's start on my family.'

'Don't let's start at all,' Angel placated. 'And don't be cross. I think I'm trying to do the right thing.'

'I don't see why, now her husband has come back on the scene.'

'Why I don't just tear up the letter and forget about it?'

Terry lolled against the sink in the tiny kitchen, watching Angel chop up lettuce and tomatoes for a late supper.

'Vicious with the knife, aren't you?' he observed.

Angel stopped what she was doing.

'Can you sell this place for me? Really quickly. I must have a proper house again, with a garden, and within walking distance of Sylvia's.'

'Is that all I'm good for?'

She advanced on him with a degree of mock menace and forced him into a clinch that disguised her own misgivings.

'What do you think?'

'To tell you the truth, babe, I don't know what to think right now. You've got me well confused.'

'Well that makes two of us.'


'I meant what I said, Jeremy.' Sybil, no make-up, Jeremy's striped towelling dressing gown clutched round her, for once looked her age. Her elfin face, the skin slightly doughy, held an underlying sadness that now pushed at the flesh, as if she had already played her last card but resolutely remained at the table.

'I know,' said Jeremy, reaching for her.

She collapsed into his arms, resting her head against his chest, waiting for the inevitable rebuff.

Jeremy tightened his embrace.

'Do you really think you could cope with a baby in the flat?' he said.

Sybil's head shot up.

'Oh God, I love you,' she said in a rush, shooting kisses on to his face.

'Steady on. Don't get too excited. Don't forget Paul's back. It's not going to be that straightforward.'

'It'll be all right. It'll be all right,' she insisted, unstoppable joy flooding from her.

Later, Jeremy, awake, thoughts teeming, gazed at the again childlike face of the thirty-year-old woman who lay beside him. Had he really convinced himself that the other two would capitulate and allow him to bring Marsha's baby to Sybil's loft, to Sybil? He was seized by a sudden desire to protect her from the critical view of Angel and Paul, and then saw that he was merely masking his own critical eye.

He was not all that certain what form the coming battle might take, how bound by Marsha's letter Angel would feel, and whether or not Paul wanted the child at all. Staying power had never been Paul forté, and while he had begun to restake a claim, Jeremy suspected it to be no more than a piece of petulance mixed with confused emotions at seeing Marsha all but dead.

His mind rolled back to a singular afternoon in the days just into long trousers; he'd almost forgotten that he'd known Paul for that far back. Something had happened in Paul's family, a dead grandparent, something quite big and sombre. Paul had come home with him, a rare occurrence. Grace had neither the patience nor sense of duty for such motherly activities, but Paul's mother must have asked, and even Grace could hardly refuse in the circumstances.

Far from being sad and subdued, Paul had switched on the charm and succeeded in captivating Grace, who had laughed and smiled her way through the afternoon, delighted and surprised at this entertainment from such an unexpected source.

Jeremy had watched, charmed by Paul himself at first, proud to have this sort of friend; but after a while he had begun to hate Paul and for reasons he couldn't properly fathom. He had become quiet and sulky and, of course, Grace had noticed and told him to remember that Paul needed cheering up, although Jeremy could not see any evidence of this need.

Later on, when Paul had gone home and Jeremy, still uneasy and baffled, had taken himself to bed, Grace had come into his room and touched his face.

'You're not to be jealous, darling boy,' she said, lightly. 'Paul's a lovely butterfly, but he won't last.'

Jeremy had understood and taken the lesson. He had made that huge leap in self-acceptance, providing him with the calm and observing manner that had got him through those ugly teen years and out the other side hardly scathed. It had sown the patience that would enable him to get his timing just right with Angel, and it should be giving him the edge even now as he moved into the critical stage of the fight for custody of his child.

Sybil's face came into focus again. He was fond of her and perhaps that would be enough. Love, he knew, was not even a consideration, but then he did not expect to find that again. He felt more calm than he had in months, as if the course was now set and he no longer had to thrash about trying to work out what was the right thing to do, set against what he wanted. The two had now converged. The child was his, and of the three of them only he could provide it with the blood bond that every child deserved.

His fondness for Sybil swelled a little as he saw her aligned with him in this worthy and proper cause. They would be all right. Angel had never really wanted Marsha's baby; and Paul, he would remain a butterfly.

It was now past three in the morning, and he saw no prospect of sleep. He eased himself out of bed, burglar-like, so as not to disturb Sybil; he had to concentrate on treating her with consideration and respect from now on, otherwise the arrangement wouldn't stand a chance. Feeling a little light-headed from lack of sleep, but light, too, in the sense of a burden lifted, he moved across the loft to the far corner where he switched on Sybil's PC.

# CHAPTER TWENTY-FIVE

Marsha had a good view. She was on the ceiling gazing down with angelic calm at the proceedings around her bed.

Paul stood one side, Jeremy the other, recognisable only by the tops of their heads, although, of course she could see a great deal more than this.

There were others in green gowns, their mouths and noses covered, too, working feverishly over her belly, hands plunging in like car mechanics.

She didn't feel a thing. Why should she? The black body was inert except for the rummaging activity; and then, like a prize from the lucky dip, there he was, a baby boy, wonderfully black, glistening like a distant memory. For a moment Marsha lost her view. The room went dark and in another life she thought she gasped. Then she was in the light again, that bright, brilliant light.

# CHAPTER TWENTY-SIX

*. . . the television adaptation of the novel has over-taken publication of the final instalment due out at the end of the month, although, with acknowl-edgement to John Fowles's device in* The French Lieutenant's Woman, *rumour has it we are to be given a choice of endings.*

*All I can say is, please don't. Life isn't like that, is it? I mean, do we really have a choice in these matters?*

*We've followed Daniel Presley from London to South America, been taken in by the extraordinary, almost unbelievable twists and turns of fate that have transformed him from chartered accountant to monk, from family man to man alone, and now, back in England, facing a choice between the latter two. There, I've answered my question. Maybe we do have a choice after all.*

*The problem for Daniel is that the man who counted beans in East Sheen can no longer be counted in the scheme of things. Life has moved on without him and choices made by other people.*

*Daniel himself has changed. It would be equally extraordinary if he had not. A touch of*

> *monkishness has remained in him. He has seen an inner light, lingered too long in the Mexican monastery, wondered whether he is better off with his wings clipped.*
>
> *Poor Daniel. We feel for him, suffer his injustices with him and, like him or despise him, wonder how he is to resolve this final dilemma.*

'What are we going to call him?' said Angel with a simplicity and wonder that defied any questioning of the assumed joint decision.

The three of them were standing by the baby's hospital crib that had been wheeled out into a vacant side ward for the visit.

'Did Marsha mention any names?' Angel continued, easing a finger into the baby's fist.

'I don't think so,' said Paul.

'No,' said Jeremy, biting back. 'How would you know, anyway?'

'I'd like to suggest Harold,' said Grace, who was sitting a few feet away. 'Then at least he'd have one name from his father's family.'

'Not now, Mother,' murmured Jeremy, glancing at Paul, who appeared to have ignored Grace's stake-claiming comment.

'I don't see why not now,' Grace persisted. 'Paul, I have a suggestion to make. Wilfred and I are prepared, would like to give the child a home.'

The other three turned their attention to her in unison.

'Mother,' sighed Jeremy under his breath.

'I don't understand,' began Paul.

'How could you!' said Angel, looking at Jeremy.

'I know this may not seem like the appropriate time, but if you all think about it, well, it has to be the best solution, at least for the time being,' Grace added.

Wilfred appeared, his hands reaching round a cluster of plastic cups issuing steam.

'Here we are. I think I've got it right. Two sugars in this one . . .' He stopped short, taking in the tension. 'Ah, she's told you.'

'I was just saying that if they all give it some thought,' Grace restarted, but her expression gave the impression the matter was already decided.

Further discussion was saved by the arrival of a nurse who bestowed a businesslike smile on the little assembly, then briskly wheeled the baby away for his feed.

'All I'm saying is, consider it,' Grace continued as soon as the nurse was gone. 'Think of the child. The only place he's going to get a, well, settled home is with us, isn't it?' And a few days later little Harold travelled to Amersham with his putative grandmother at the wheel of the old Rover (thoroughly vacuumed and polished by Wilfred the previous day) and with Wilfred in the back, like a duchess, the baby strapped into a bucket-like contraption beside him.

Grace had started humming as they turned on to the dual carriageway, and as they went past the Little Chef she erupted with a 'We've done it, Wilfred. We've pulled it off.'

The thing was, she had prepared her ground, made enquiries with the hospital, established that healthy babies, even those whose mothers remained in a coma, were not expected to stay in hospital if there was a willing family member anxious to take them home.

Wilfred had warmed a little to the plan; besides, he liked babies, always had, ever since his sister, born eighteen years after him. He had been unable to resist telling Grace about her, about the surrogacy he had assumed during the growing up years. The only trouble was that, like his mother, he didn't really want to have to go through it all again. But Grace could be very persuasive, the sort of person it really was better not to defy.

Angel, Jeremy and Paul were left to smoulder, the ball snatched from them in a game for which they had been remarkably ill-prepared. But the real match had not yet begun.

193

A few days after Grace's coup Angel wrote to Jeremy with the first strike. She tried to keep the tone of the letter objective and businesslike, knowing that it might be used as evidence at a later date. She had spent the intervening days pouring through legal tomes, checking case law, searching for precedent. The letter informed him that Marsha's letter to her amounted to legal guardianship and that she intended to seek formal custody.

Jeremy, who had already spent months attempting to establish his own legal position, received the letter with a certain amount of relief. The way was now clear for a proper legal battle and one that would avoid his having to take his own mother to court.

Paul, who perhaps was the only one with an obvious and immediate right to custody, remained disturbingly silent. Every day he now spent several hours hunched beside Marsha's bed, stroking her hand, telling her about what was happening in the world. The rest of the time he kept himself holed up in the flat off Onslow Square, watching television, listening to the radio, even 'The Archers', Marsha's addiction and a rare area of mild conflict during their marriage. Sunday mornings he liked to read the paper and he liked to read it at the breakfast table with his wife sitting opposite, but Marsha wanted to listen to 'The Archers'. Resolved by the purchase of pair of earphones.

'Eddie Grundy is in some sort of trouble. And Jennifer, I expect you know who she is, she's got this daughter, Kate . . .'

'Tell her about Shula,' whispered the nurse, over his shoulder.

'Shula? Oh yes, Shula. She's not a lesbian, is she?'

The nurse looked shocked. 'It'd be headline news if she was.'

'The doctor's going to have to speak to him soon,' the nurse said to her colleague when she got back to the desk at the other end of the ward.

'Yes, tell me about Shula,' thought Marsha.

194

'You know, I think he has Jeremy's chin,' said Wilfred, the baby snug in his arms, the tiny mouth gently pulsating in a dream that appeared to be about milk.

'I thought perhaps the ears, too,' said Grace. 'Not much else, though. He is very dark, isn't he?'

'Ooh, he's lovely. Lovely, lovely, lovely.'

'Yes,' said Grace, with her old disdain. She had not reckoned on this abject devotion on Wilfred's part. She was beginning to find it a little tedious, especially as she'd had to cajole him into the idea initially. She had started to feel mildly excluded.

If Angel was incensed by Grace's, and also what she took to be Jeremy's, peremptory move, Terry appeared more so.

'It's well out of order,' he repeated, again and again, and Angel, while grateful for his support, found herself increasingly irritated by this singular phrase of his. Everything, it seemed, was 'out of order': stiff-necked people who drove old Vauxhalls at 25mph, football referees on TV who blew their whistles to the wrong tune, elderly neighbours to the farmhouse who had complained to the police about Lord and Lady's noctural barking; the list increased by the day, as did Terry's sulleness in the face of her own growing preoccupation with the legal battle to come.

And he seemed to be making little progress in finding her the house she now wanted and a buyer for the flat.

'There's not much demand for one-beds, and the traffic noise is a problem,' he told her.

'You didn't say that when you sold it to me,' she remarked.

He told her he was going to be away for a week, some sort of property consultancy course in the West Country. He had started using condoms, too. She could feel the drift and couldn't find the spare energy to do anything about it. The traffic on the roundabout kept her awake at night, and in those raw, chilling hours before dawn, Jeremy kept intruding, as persistent as a hangover. She would not have believed herself capable of such hatred. It was well out of order.

*Jennifer Chapman*

In the week that Terry was away she went to visit Sylvia, the scene in the living room unchanged apart from Chaucer's growth. He was on his feet now, pork sausage legs stabbing at the carpet, arms akimbo. He stared at her hard with his solemn toddler expression, then smiled so suddenly that she felt tears pricking at her eyes.

Sylvia saw it all and handed her a cup of tea.

'You keep fighting, girl,' she said.

'Yeh,' piped up Kev, with unusual animation.

'How's it going, Angel?' asked Denise. They all knew what was happening.

'Oh,' Angel sighed, wiping the corners of her eyes with the back of her hand, 'I just hope I'm doing the right thing.'

'Course you are,' said Denise. 'It's what the mother wants that counts, isn't it, Mum?'

'I should say so,' said Sylvia. 'Want that freshening up?' she addressed Cliff, reaching for his mug.

'I was watching this programme the other day,' he began.

'That makes a change,' Sylvia interjected.

'As I was saying. It was about this couple who couldn't have children of their own and they got this other woman, through an ad in the local paper, to have one for them. Denise, watch Chaucer with that gear box. Anyway, this woman, she didn't want to keep the child or anything, but the socials stuck their snouts in and said the child would have to be put up for adoption and the couple that wanted the baby in the first place couldn't have it because they was too old.'

'What are you saying?' Sylvia demanded, hovering by the kitchen door. 'I'm not sure Angel wants to hear this.'

'What I'm saying, if you'll give me the chance, is that it's best to sort things out between you if you can. Soon as you gets the professionals involved – with all due respect, Angel – soon as they gets a chance to stick their oar in . . . well, I think you get my meaning. The ordinary bloke in the street just doesn't stand a chance. Believe me, I know.'

196

'You're the ordinary bloke in the street, then, are you? Couch, more like,' said Sylvia, removing herself from view.

When she came back a moment later with Cliff's refilled mug, she perched herself on the arm of his sofa and made it clear she was about to have her say.

'He's right, you know, Angel. It is better to steer clear of the authorities. They'll never let you alone once you're on the register.'

Angel was thinking that they had got it all wrong, but she did not feel inclined to say so. She wanted to drink her tea and stay there with them for a little while; Sylvia's was the only place she sensed any warmth in her life right now.

Attention soon drifted back to the huge television and Saturday afternoon sport. Kev lit a cigarette. Cliff coughed. Denise reached for Chaucer, trying to hug him. Sylvia went back to her kitchen.

Angel stayed on and began to feel uncertain about her erstwhile plan. Fond as she was of Sylvia, of all of them, could she allow Marsha's child to spend his days in this room? How did the constant television, Kev's cigarettes and gear box stack up against the nanny Grace would doubtless employ before long? She could imagine the scene in court, the social enquiry reports. Cliff and Sylvia were right. In such matters a warm and uncritical environment counted for too little; officialdom sought more tangible evidence of suitability.

Her thoughts wandered on. She had wanted Jeremy and not the child, and now she was contemplating an expensive and life-disrupting campaign to wrest the baby from him – she still had little doubt that Jeremy and Grace were in cahoots.

She disliked herself almost as much as she hated Jeremy. The cold, calculating thoughts had always been there, but in the past tempered by love, she thought. If Jeremy had asked her to have their child, she would have done so, willingly, she felt sure, but they had never even discussed it. The issue had only arisen when it was his child and not hers; and because she had seen, almost from the beginning, that he would do just about anything to secure his right, the generosity of spirit that had made the marriage happy had dissolved in the face of jealousy and then bitter resentment. The realisation that he would sacrifice her rather than Marsha's unborn child had, ironically, turned her into the person she might always have been had she not married him.

Increasingly, and hard as she tried to scuttle away from them, her thoughts dwelt on small, hitherto forgotten episodes from the marriage. She'd heard it said that when a marriage was over, even if it had lasted years and years, it could be hard to recapture even a moment of what it had been like, to recall the essence of day to day living together; but Jeremy loomed larger and larger for her. Not the Jeremy she now loathed and despised, but a quite different person, as different as herself then and now.

Unspoken sensations. The longing to be home. The sense of completeness and total absence of loneliness. The urgent desire to impart a trifle of utter insignificance to anyone else in the world. The smell of his neck. The groin-stirring, heart-thumping pleasure from just looking at a preoccupied profile on a car journey. None of it made any sense, but that was what was so delicious about it; the nonsense of being in love. How could he not have valued it as much as she had?

'Angel.'

She looked up at Sylvia, then saw that Cliff and Kev had switched to her channel, too.

'Here,' Sylvia handed her a tissue.

When she got back to the flat on the roundabout, the sound of the television could be heard in the stairwell and was quite deafening as she let herself in. Sitting in front of it were Terry, back already, and Jeremy, each with a can of lager.

Fury flooded her face. Half an hour ago she'd been making a fool of herself in Sylvia's living room over at least one of them. The 'now' Angel stomped over to the set and switched it off.

'For Christ's sake, it's nil/nil and into extra time,' Terry squealed.

'Aptly put,' said Jeremy, gazing steadily at his wife.

# CHAPTER TWENTY-SEVEN

Marsha looked vacated, as if over the past months she had been preparing herself for what was about to happen, which was ridiculous as she couldn't possibly know.

Paul, Jeremy and Angel stood around the bed. Jeremy had lain Harold beside his mother for a moment or two and now the baby was in Paul's arms, unusually quiet, his big brown eyes seemingly fixed far above the bed.

The machine that had breathed for Marsha since the birth had been switched off a few minutes earlier. In a while the doctor would return from the discreet distance she and the nurse had put between them and the small gathering by the bed. In a while the baby's gaze would drop.

But Angel could not take her eyes off Marsha. Her heart began to thud in the way it had years ago when she'd first had to speak in court, the enormity of what she did and said dictating someone's fate. It had been a traffic violation with the maximum fine £250, but it might just as well have been a hanging offence, the outcome affecting her own future as much as her client's.

Her heart was pushing at her chest so hard and fast now she felt sure the other two must be able to hear the pounding. She glanced at them, both heads down, as if they were already at the funeral. Suddenly she wanted to do something, some-how to save Marsha, to speak to her just one last time, to reassure her that she would look after everything, bring up the baby, be nice to the men. And even if she couldn't quite believe all this would be possible, she might at least be able to say sorry.

She felt terribly sorry. Not 'I'm sorry, it's all my fault', or any-thing like that, but just so sorry because it was so very terrible to have given birth to this beautiful child and never to have seen him or touched him, or smelled that sugary freshness.

She wanted to call to the doctor or one of the nurses, any-one within shouting distance. She had to tell them to get things started again, that it had been a mistake. It was like a very bad dream, the moment for action slipping away, Mar-sha slipping away.

In her mind she began to run through the sequence of what would happen next. Calmly, she had to do it calmly, at least to begin with. She would walk away from the bedside and quietly and firmly tell them. She could do it. She had the nec-essary skills to argue just about any case, even the most hope-less and far-fetched, only Marsha wasn't far-fetched, not yet.

The urgency of the situation was bearing in on her to the point where it felt as though her chest might be about to explode. Her own breathing had become difficult, but she had to keep it under control. She didn't want to make herself the object of attention. She never had, any more than had Marsha, for all her fame and success.

She went off into a sidetrack that found Marsha, at the beginning, Paul's arm round her narrow waist, signalling ownership; the split second in which she registered that she had been there first and would therefore view Marsha from the start with a critical eye. Not nice to do that, but Marsha had been so nice without for a moment trying.

Maudlin clichés swarmed in on her, buffeting against a sob that made the other two risk a quick look. 'The good die young. Too good for this world.' She bit her lip. She mustn't weep, so very self-indulgent. Besides, she had a job to do. Time running out.

The last time they had been together, just her and Marsha. The aborted lunch. So long ago. In memory it seemed a bigger day, Marsha already distancing herself as if she had known the future was going to be impossible, beyond even her niceness.

I just want to tell you that I wish with all my heart we hadn't all left you to cope on your own, but you see we were all too caught up in trying to deal with it ourselves, each of us in our own stupid isolation. Oh, Marsha, you didn't deserve this. She let out a sigh that did not sound out of place. The words remained silent.

She glanced across at the doctor and the nurse. She had only to signal, surely that would be enough.

She imagined a miracle. The switching on again bringing about the kick-start that had eluded them all this time. Marsha's eyes opening. Her waking to the three of them, the four of them. There. It was all just fine in the end. How could it be otherwise?

'Hopefully they're over the worst,' murmured the nurse. 'After all, she effectively died months ago.'

The doctor and the nurse would maintain a respectful patience and delay before attending to the next stage of things, but the tragedy was not theirs.

'D'you recognise him?' the nurse asked the doctor in a semi-whisper.

'Which one?'

'Not the good-looking one.'

'Hum. He does look familiar.'

'He's on telly. I saw him a couple of nights ago. Can't remember the name of the programme.'

I didn't even really like her, thought Jeremy, concentrating for perhaps the first time on the person who had been the mother of his son.

The flat form that lay in front of them could no longer be

seen as a precious vessel, only the body of a woman he felt he had not known particularly well. Given different circumstances he would not have bothered to cultivate any sort of a relationship. He had found her bland and difficult to reach, but if he were to be honest, which he usually managed to be, at least with himself, it was simply that he knew he had meant nothing to her and that she had not even found him attractive, not really.

Marsha was all about physical beauty. She had it herself and looked for it in others. She sought it in food, in the place where she lived. She was one of the beautiful people, and as such devoid of the flaws and uncertainties that drew him to people like Sybil and Paul, and, of course, Angel, although that was different and separate. In Angel he had created the flaws and uncertainties.

In all the time he had known Marsha she had been Paul's wife and no more, until that one night, brought about by drink and despair before he had any right to or knew anything of the real thing, the kind of despair that had made him almost deranged.

He could not remember much of that night, and it should have been inconsequential, because he doubted they would have repeated it. The memory that had haunted him was the imagined parallel, Paul and Angel, the replay. Marsha hadn't seemed to figure.

Dislike had emerged with her sudden power over what was his, too, and after he was sure she would go ahead with the pregnancy, he had resented her evident wish to exclude him, making him feel like a predator, forcing him into a role that made him dislike himself in the same way he had despised and detested the fat schoolboy with specs and flat feet. Marsha had effectively stripped away two decades of painfully cultivated self-esteem, a crafting process that had brought him more than he had ever imagined or hoped for, only to find that he could never escape being an imposter.

Marsha, without malice or forethought, had simply

dismissed him, sending him back to the sidelines. Looking at her now, all but dead, she seemed hardly any different from the way he had known her alive. And yet he would have done just about anything he could at this moment to bring her back, to be given another chance.

He glanced at Paul, who had always had the chances and the choice of messing them up. Paul should have been the one he disliked, but he had never really managed that. Perhaps poor Marsha had been a surrogate.

Death made the living feel guilty, and if he was unable to fix on Marsha's innocence, he could sense the weight of Paul.

Angel had taken the baby, moved a little away.

Paul was trying to hear Marsha's voice, but however hard he searched through the catalogue of incidents that made up their time together, he couldn't quite catch it. In desperation he tried to imagine a phone call, you always recognised a voice over the phone, but he couldn't remember a single occasion when she had called him. The memory of her was as silent as the body that lay before him.

If only she could open her eyes, then he would find her, watching him, always watching him, while he put on a performance for her; because that, after all, was how it had been. He'd assumed that she knew him all the time he had felt like someone he didn't know himself. He'd relied on that, Marsha knowing what he was really like, although it made no sense because he never had shown her his true self. God, this was the kind of thinking that had been tying him up in knots for years. He didn't like what he had been in Marsha's watching and marvelled that she, seemingly, had, although there were huge swathes of Marsha he had never fathomed, never even bothered to investigate. He'd lived in terror of losing her when he'd never even found her.

Looking at her now, she might have been a stranger, except what had happened to her had somehow brought him back to himself, the seriousness of it wiping out all the posturing pretence. And he'd lost her anyway.

The baby had started to whimper and the three adults looked dangerously close.

'Come on. Let's tell them to go home,' the doctor said quietly but firmly.

It took little more than ten minutes for the taxi to take them back to the flat off Onslow Square.

Jeremy opened the front door. Angel carried Harold inside, and Paul followed with the bag that contained the few remaining pieces of equipment for life that had been with Marsha at the hospital.

The flat now held a different smell from the days of Marsha's occupation. Gone was the faint and unidentifiable aroma of cooking spice mingled with expensive scent, although when, exactly, this had been overtaken by the equally unique vapour that had inhabited the Cambridgeshire farmhouse, none of them could tell. Doubtless it had begun when selected pieces of furniture had been brought in from the roundabout flat now occupied by Denise, Kev and Chaucer and smelling one removed from the warm muddle of Sylvia's living room. It had started then, although Paul still caught fleeting drafts of the spice and scent for some weeks after. Then, as the last vestige faded, a still earlier olfactory sensation returned, the precurser to Cambridgeshire, Shepherd's Bush.

How they had arrived at this new accommodation was a wonder to all three, even though they had, of course, experienced it before, long ago when it had seemed like the starting block for whatever they were to do with their lives.

'There is only one solution,' Jeremy had told Angel and then Paul. 'We must all live together again. I don't suppose it will be easy, but I can't think of any alternative that wouldn't be impossibly difficult.' They couldn't argue. Perhaps they didn't want to.

Wresting Harold from Grace had been a piece of cake. Fond as she had become of her grandson, she had come to prefer the idea of being able to give him back at the end of a

206

day's visit; besides, she wanted Wilfred's undivided adoration, although managing to convince herself, if not Jeremy, that it was concern for what she suspected might be the onset of arthritis in Wilfred's soft, pink hands. And Jeremy, restored to his natural good self, was more than prepared to encourage her in this belief.

Restored to his natural good self? Well, it felt that way.

'You're a bastard really, aren't you?' Angel had whispered into the yummy smell of his neck the first night they slept at their new home off Onslow Square.

'Could be,' he said, in his Jeremy way.

'Do you think Paul will be able to cope with it, this arrangement?' she continued.

'He did before.'

'That was different, and I'm not sure he did.'

'We'll just have to see.'

A little later Angel said, 'We must look after him, Paul, I mean. It's what Marsha wanted.'

Silence. The old, uncomfortable silence. Then thoughts diverging.

Terry had told her she was a cow and then insisted, for reasons that were his own, that they still attend Jane's dinner party at the farmhouse that evening.

Silence on the way there. A different sort of uncomfortable.

And no other guests. 'They couldn't come,' declared Jane, looking decidedly put out.

'We're selling this place,' she announced during the Russian eggs.

'You didn't say,' jumped in Terry.

'I am now, aren't I?' she glared at her brother. She was glaring at everyone this evening.

'Don't you want to know why?' she continued, the glare now directed at Angel.

'Come on, then,' said Terry.

'In the words of the Princess of Wales, there are three of us in this farmhouse.'

'You're kidding.' Terry glanced at Gregory in unflattering disbelief.

'Not, actually, and I think Angel knows who the third party is.'

'I do?'

'Banging and clattering. Horrid smells. Doors slamming. The dogs howling their heads off. I've had it here. We're moving, Tel. How quickly d'you reckon you can shift it for us?'

'Oh,' murmured Angel, a gentle warmth at the back of her neck.

'Who is it, then?' Terry persisted.

'Who d'you think! The fucking ghost, that's who.'

'You're kidding,' Terry repeated.

'I'm not, am I, G?'

'I suppose not,' muttered Gregory.

'What d'you mean "suppose not"!'

A malicious look of inspiration sprang into Terry's expression. 'If you're serious I might be able to find a buyer quicker than you think.' His eyes narrowed as he looked at Angel.

'Why don't you go and see the vicar?' was all she said. She wished the evening over and knew she would never set foot in the farmhouse again.

By nature Terry was generally more nice than nasty. On the way home she asked him why he had insisted on this evening.

'Seemed like the right place.'

'For what?'

'To say goodbye, I suppose.'

'I'm sorry.'

He sighed, stretching his arms on the steering wheel. 'It's all right, babe. I never thought it would last.'

'Didn't you?'

'Did you?'

Then a little further on, almost up to the roundabout: 'I don't suppose you do want to buy the place back?'

'No. Too many ghosts.'

Jeremy's mind's eye was seeing a close approximation: Sybil, her hair bleached of all colour, her skin porcelain white.

'I'll never love anyone the way I've loved you,' she told him.

He noted the past tense and felt relief.

They made love one more time and for once he did not think of Angel.

'We can be friends still?' she asked as dawn broke.

'Of course,' he said. 'Why should that change?'

'I might need a bit of help, you see, technique, that sort of thing.'

Jeremy's imagination drifted, alarmed and flattered, in the wrong direction.

'What I mean is, I've been offered a television programme.'

A strange sense of disappointment, even territorial resentment.

'Designer vegetables. What do you think?'

Angel and Jeremy fell asleep side by side and perhaps sidled into the same dream.

For Paul it was more difficult. He was not getting a happy ending. When Jeremy had broached his outrageous idea, that the three of them should live together and bring up Harry between them, all he could feel was loss, not gain. He was also aware of a sense of being manipulated. The legal position had never been in doubt: custody of Harry would automatically go to him.

In earlier days he might have protested, although he hadn't, not really, when Jeremy had taken Angel from him, and somehow he had agreed to the hideous arrangement that had kept the three of them together. He might have objected now, if Marsha had still been there, tending his ego, allowing him to be outrageous himself, but Marsha, of course, was not there, and if she had been none of it would be happening.

Often, during the long vigils by her hospital bed, he told her, or perhaps just himself, that he would have come home before long, that he had never really contemplated staying away for ever. Once or twice, when he'd been with her for hours, he felt convinced she had somehow absorbed what was in his mind. He had never felt this close to her when she had really been there.

His difficulty was that while he could have imagined coming to terms with bringing up the baby with Marsha, the idea of doing so without her was something else. Yet he had sufficient spirit left not to feel able to give in to Jeremy, not again.

He saw the temporary arrangment with Grace and Wilfred for what he believed it to be, another piece of Jeremy's plan, although at the same time he was grateful not to have to look after the baby himself, not until . . . until what? They wanted to switch off Marsha's life support. To let her die. Was it no more than selfishness on his part to want to keep her alive? Besides, what about stories of people who'd been diagnosed as brain dead, who had slept for years and then astounded the world?

During the weeks of his vigil he began to see how Jeremy's idea might become tolerable; he even felt a secret pity for Jeremy, who would never have the certainty of custody. He was quite sure that Jeremy and Angel were pitying him, but really, he had the edge this time.

He had allowed the arrangement to go ahead. It was worth it if only to banish the lonely isolation of returning to Marsha's empty flat night after night. They were all very careful of one another, the other two playing down the delight of their reconciliation in the face of his bereavement, not that he saw it like that. And when all three went to Amersham to collect Harry – arguing about the name had seemed unimportant, although he didn't much like it – Angel had asked him if he wanted to carry the baby out to the car.

One evening, soon after, when Jeremy was doing his television programme, Angel said, 'Are we doing this for Marsha or are we each doing it for ourselves?'

'I don't know,' he said.

'I'm still not sure it's going to work,' she said.

'It did before. For a while.'

'That was different.'

'Not really. I seem to remember that I had something Jeremy wanted then, too.'

It was not Angel's way to pursue such a comment. Besides, most of her was happy again, and she felt that in time she would be as fond of Harry as it was possible to be. Jeremy, of course, would look after him, now that he worked from home most of the time, but she was beginning to find nappy changing almost tolerable and she quite enjoyed feeding him. She had arranged a few weeks off before she began her new job in the London office of her Cambridge firm. In some ways she wished she had not, but had she ever expected this time to be easy? She thought she had learnt that there could be no happiness without Jeremy and therefore she had to compromise and finally accept that Jeremy now meant Harry, too. And Harry meant Paul and so it went on. Alternative living. People did it all over the world. Her mother had told her over the phone that she had to be mad. Probably. Madness was not a matter of choice.

Two police officers came to the flat. Paul was not there. The WPC sat beside Angel on the sofa in the drawing room in an encouraging, sisterly manner designed to elicit information.

Angel sat there in disbelief as the purpose of the visit was revealed. Instinct and training fought with anger and the inevitable sense of guilt until she had to ask, 'How did you hear this? Who told you?'

'We are not at liberty to say,' the male officer said. His manner was that of a cardboard cut-out.

'I'm sure you must appreciate that we have to investigate a report of this nature,' the WPC said, adopting a gentle, soothing tone. 'Rape is a very serious allegation.'

'Yes, it is, and I'm not making it,' Angel exploded, too angry, she knew, further rousing their suspicion.

The interview lasted no more than twenty minutes. The officers left, seemingly satisfied, but with an edge of irritation. Wasting police time. Angel could hear the phrase trotted out back at the police station.

Perhaps if Paul had returned to the flat before Jeremy everything might have been different.

'How could you? How could you!' she screamed at him.

'What now?' Jeremy, she thought, looked exactly the cold, calculating person he really was.

'I had a visit from the police. You told them, didn't you? What do you want, Jeremy? To see the poor bugger in prison just to leave the way clear for you, for you and Harry?' She was so beside herself with anger she failed to see the bewilderment in Jeremy's expression, disregarded the 'I haven't a clue what you're talking about.'

'After all he has been through. I just don't understand how you could do it.' The flare of anger began to fade and Angel, too, felt bewildered. She had believed Jeremy capable of going to great lengths in order to achieve what he wanted; she had seen enough evidence over the past few months, but she had never, until now, thought he could play this dirty. The betrayal, not so much of herself, but of Paul, quite took her breath away.

Thoughts and accusations rushed on. 'I mean, why did you bother to go and find him in America if all you wanted to do was this? Did you just want to make certain he'd never be in any sort of position to challenge you for Harry? And what made you think I'd ever agree to press charges? God, you didn't really think it out at all, did you?'

He had become a stranger to her again. Looking at him now, every aspect seemed loathsome. There was not even that small reserve maintained by married couples in the fiercest row.

When he saw that she had run out of steam he sat down at the kitchen table. 'Angel, did you tell anyone else that story about Paul?' His voice was very calm.

'Of course not,' she replied, but with too much haste. She was not a liar, and after a brief pause she groaned.

'You did then?'

'Terry. I told Terry. Oh, God.'

Jeremy said no more. He got up, quite slowly, and went through to their bedroom to take a look at the sleeping baby.

# CHAPTER TWENTY-EIGHT

Harry was asleep and Jeremy was writing a piece about the latest Martin Amis. He was not quite sure how he felt about it, whether it was brilliant or just missed the mark, whether the ending worked; it was so hard to tell with writers like Amis, who'd already received all the accolades. He was writing his own novel now and hadn't a clue how it might end. Books he read, and there were a lot of them, especially now he'd been asked to join this year's panel of judges for the Whitbread, were more satisfying on the whole if you felt that the characters walked off the final page to continue their lives. The test was whether you felt they were still breathing.

He tried to focus on Daniel, eponymous hero of the year's big saga.

> *Do people really change as a result of experience? This has to be the central question of the story, surely the underlying theme.*
>
> *Daniel has returned to England after his extraordinary adventures and discovered that nothing has changed in East Sheen. He returns to his old way of life, the same people sharing it with him. He has changed and yet he is the same. They have*

*changed and yet they are the same. So it has to be*
*a story about growth rather than change, although*
*you might argue that the two are synonymous . . .*

Jeremy's fingers went limp on the keyboard, then he zapped what he had just written.

'*Daniel Presley is the story of a man who wants to be someone else,*' he began again. '*He has been on a voyage of discovery that has at last brought him back to the point at which he began and from which he can never truly escape.*'

An amplified gurgle emitted from the radio intercom Jeremy had placed on the table beside the PC.

'*. . . a final instalment could have him returning to the Mexican monastery, but he would go there knowing that it was no longer a matter of escape, not from himself . . .*' The gurgles continued. He could not resist going to have a look.

The baby smiled at him, although the health visitor had insisted it could be no more than wind at this early age. He gazed steadily at the small brown face and again searched for likeness.

'I thought I could see it, but I'm not sure I can now,' Grace had said.

'What are you saying?' he had enquired in a carefully controlled tone.

'Oh, nothing.'

'Yes, you are. Come on, out with it.'

'Oh, darling boy,' Grace sighed. 'You are quite certain?'

'Quite.'

'Hmm.'

A prickling sensation came into his chest. In a minute he'd say something unkind and then feel guilty, the way he always did with his mother.

'Wilfred can't see it either.'

'Wilfred sees what you tell him to see.'

'That's silly'

'What's the point in saying this, Mother?'

'There doesn't have to be a point, does there, dear? It's just an observation.'

But she had sewn the seed of doubt that, oddly perhaps, had never been there before. Others could have said it, although of course no one else would, and he'd have pushed the idea aside without consideration, but Grace had always held the capacity to spoil his dreams and aspirations. 'Darling boy, you'll never be any good at games, so why bother? You can't turn a donkey into a racehorse. Darling boy, girls like that will only break your heart. Look at yourself in the mirror. Darling boy, I'm being cruel to be kind. Why go through life wanting what you can't have?'

It had been a process that had bound him to her, the almost indiscernible fissure between hatred and love fused in the perpetuality of a mother/son relationship that was as inescapable as the image in the mirror. He had inherited the same destructive persuasive streak; he could see that now, with a horrible clarity that suddenly explained the hitherto inexplicable behaviour of the past months.

He had never really felt the same sense of possession over Angel, perhaps because she had chosen him. The old Groucho Marx thing. He had loved her though, almost as intensely as he had his mother, and might have his son. He loved Paul, too, in a curiously protective way that had re-emerged from their schooldays these last few weeks. He had been desperate to hold the whole thing together and now all he could think about was how to pull it apart.

The weeks went by at the flat off Onslow Square, surprising only in their lack of surprises. Harry absorbed any lulls. He was not an especially demanding baby, but none of them had done it before so the learning curve was steep and intense, for Jeremy and Angel if less so for Paul, who remained with Marsha even when he was at the flat.

Angel's new job was not particularly enthralling, but she had more pressing concerns: Harry, whom she now adored and could not imagine being without, and Jeremy, or rather the entity that had been the two of them and now seemed lost. Both pretended, and what else could they do?

She began to think that perhaps they could recapture something of the past even though the circumstances were so altered. What she had in mind was the easy companionship and the vitality of the early days at Shepherd's Bush. What she saw as being back within their grasp was the period when she had still been with Paul but was discovering Jeremy: the kitchen conversations steaming with abstract concept, the creeping joy of soul mate recognition before the physical intrusion.

The impossibility of realising any of this again was kept at bay by the constant demands of a baby's routine and by Paul's preoccupation with Marsha. Paul had been out much of the time when they'd all lived at Shepherd's Bush, somehow on the periphery of what was going on but at the same time an essential component. He was out most of the time now, but again essential to the scheme of things, the delicate network of interdependency orchestrated by Jeremy even if the other two hadn't known it the first time round.

Then the day came for Marsha to be switched off. There had been surprisingly little discussion about it, and what there was, cloaked in euphemism. Horrifyingly, the real debate began the day after.

'We shouldn't have done it!' Paul cried out while they were attempting breakfast.

'Paul, we had to let her go,' Jeremy said, his voice straining to maintain calm.

'Not that,' Paul moaned, dropping his head into his hands.

Jeremy and Angel could say nothing. It was done.

'That was when we started killing her, that weekend,' Paul continued.

'Paul,' Jeremy began.

'No,' Paul shouted before he could go on. 'We killed her. The three of us. We were in it from the start. She was just an innocent addition to us. Can't you see that?'

'Paul, you're just upset. It's grief,' Angel said quietly.

218

'Of course I'm bloody upset. What did we think we were doing? Did we think we could just go on cheating the system, behaving as if we were somehow different and above all the rules? It started at Shepherd's Bush, didn't it? Going on living together like that. God, we thought we were so bloody civilised. So bloody clever.'

'I don't see . . .' Angel began, but Jeremy had now placed his hand on her arm, silencing her.

'Paul, it is tragic, what's happened, but we have to look to the future. There's just no point in agonising over the past, in trying to apportion blame. Marsha wouldn't have wanted that.'

'You don't know what Marsha would have wanted. All you know is what you want. Her child. My child.'

Harry began to cry, loudly and insistently, so that Paul had shouted this final blow.

Angel got up and picked the baby out of his Moses basket. Jeremy, too, had stood up and moved towards his son. Paul stared at the three of them, his expression very much as one might imagine that of a mad axeman.

'You don't seriously think I'm going to let this go on,' he shouted.

'You're not taking him,' Jeremy said. 'You're in no state.'

'Just don't think you can go on stealing my life.' He was up and coming towards them, then into a swerve and out into the hallway.

'Where are you going?' Angel cried.

'To the hospital. To talk to Marsha.'

'But she's. . .'

The front door slammed. The baby, startled into silence, stared wide-eyed at his uncontrollable fingers and became instantly transfixed.

'This is hopeless,' murmured Angel.

'It's just grief, that's all. We only switched her off yesterday. What did you expect?'

'I didn't expect anything; well, I didn't expect nothing, but I didn't know that it would be like this. He's so angry.'

219

'He'll get over it. Paul always gets over things,' Jeremy had begun to clear the breakfast stuff in an attempt at moving on from the scene that had just happened.

'I'm not so sure,' Angel said, still standing with the baby in her arms.

Later, seated in front of her computer at her new job, she heard a replay of Jeremy's 'We only switched her off yesterday.' It went into a loop and by the end of the day she'd heard it so many times and with so many different inflexions the words themselves no longer seemed to make any coherent or recognisable sense.

If it had not been for Harry she would have delayed her return to the flat that evening. As it was, neither the baby nor Jeremy were there when she got in. A note informed both her and Paul that they were at the television studios.

Angel kicked off her shoes in the bedroom she now shared with Jeremy and where perhaps he had slept with Marsha and Marsha with Paul and before that Douglas, or whatever his name was. The saliva in her mouth went sour and she turned away, back into the hall just as the front door opened and Paul came in. He looked utterly exhausted, his face oddly grey even though his skin tended towards olive.

Neither of them said anything, but she went towards him and with great gentleness laid her hand on his arm. He didn't flinch away but allowed her to go with him into the drawing room.

The silence continued, but it didn't feel like waiting; it was a necessary interlude, thick with Marsha claiming their time and undivided attention as she never had when flesh and blood.

How long they sat there neither could have said, but they missed Jeremy's programme. When at last they did speak it was Paul who began.

'She's really is gone,' he said.

'Yes.' Angel hesitated. 'I think it might get, well, easier to believe it after the funeral.'

'What I mean is that I've accepted it.'

'Yes.'

'She was a beautiful woman in every way and I loved her, but the strange thing is there's no surprise in what's happened.'

'How do you mean?'

'I suppose I always felt I would lose her.'

'Oh, Paul.'

'She already seems unreal. I don't think I can remember or feel what it was like to be with her. Does that make any sense?'

'Oh yes, I think so.'

'I thought you would understand. You always did, didn't you?'

# CHAPTER TWENTY-NINE

'This is turning into a hospital drama,' thought Jeremy, who only that day had watched a video recording of the latest blood-dripper, 'False Hope', due to be discussed on this week's programme. Breaking up the 'dream team' again, or perhaps becoming a part of it, there weren't many weeks when he was absent. Mark Lawson had a new novel coming out; he'd have to be careful over the review, although the book would be good, he had no doubt, but that didn't make it any easier.

He picked up a magazine that had rejected at least a dozen articles from him not so many years ago and now wanted anything he could give them. He'd considered a new twist on one of those close up and shockingly personal pieces, 'On Becoming a New Father', but he was still not sure of the ending. He chucked the magazine aside and the receptionist called his name.

The doctor, whom he knew from several encounters at literary events (his own book on alternative alternatives had been a mild bestseller), stood up and shook his hand. He had the manner of someone who had achieved greater things but was still prepared to bestow the odd favour here and there. Jeremy sat down and wondered why he always had to précis everyone he met.

'What can I do for you?' The doctor, Keith, gathered together a professional smile and latticed his fingers.

'Oh, feeling tired, that sort of thing.' Jeremy felt his face grow hot. He wanted the low-down on blood tests but didn't know where to start; and why the hell had he come to this doctor of all doctors? Perhaps he was more of a fashion victim than he'd noticed. Right now he felt like a fool.

Keith was asking him if he smoked, how much he drank. Shoes were coming off, sleeves rolling up. The scales spoke in a foreign language, accusing him of a meaningless tonnage. Blood pressure wasn't much better, with no translation in the first place.

How did he sleep? Regular meals? Any pains? Any worries?

His answers were as unsatisfactory as the deception, but Keith had moved beyond asking why he was really there, what was really bothering him, because he was indeed a physical wreck. A list of do's and don'ts were filtering through, but anyone with the slightest awareness knew them all already.

'Don't put all that on me,' Jeremy groaned.

'I'm not saying you have to take up jogging, or stop drinking altogether. You just need to change your lifestyle a bit if you want to stay in shape, feel better in yourself, more alert, physically and mentally.'

'Reading the latest Martin Amis doesn't count, then?' He wished he hadn't said that. It sounded like clever Dick crap, but Keith laughed, new boy conspiratorial. He liked that, but, thank God, Keith had not read the book, or they would have been in for a session, and who knows where that might have led? He'd probably have ended up asking about the blood tests.

Planning the day, thinking this was really what he would manage to do, he'd booked a table at Kensington Place for this evening. He knew he had to tell Angel what was in his mind, but she was so easily hostile these days he wanted it to be in a public place where she'd be unlikely to make a scene, but more to the point, away from Paul, who had already agreed to babysit. Not that he had put it to Paul like that. You babysat for other people's children, that was implicit. With Paul he had merely told the truth, albeit loaded with deception. He wanted to talk things over with Angel, away from the flat. And Paul had said fine, he wasn't going anywhere. 'Fine,' he'd repeated, after that sharp unguarded look that questioned the content of talking things over. Poor bugger, he'd be as anxious as hell, but Jeremy felt he had to speak to Angel first.

Angel herself had agreed to the meal out with surprising lack of curiosity and easy acceptance of the arrangement he had made with Paul. It would be the first time, since they had taken Harry away from Grace, that one or the other had not been with the baby. Jeremy's own sudden willingness to trust Paul had, he feared, more to do with the train of thought that took in blood tests than with growing trust in Paul's state of mind. It was a notion too appalling to allow close scutiny and one he fervently hoped Angel would not hit upon, although a part of him might have welcomed the evidence that she still knew him better than anyone else.

He left Keith's consulting rooms without progress on the blood tests front, but with a mean-minded diet sheet. He used the back of it to jot down some thoughts on 'False Hope' when the taxi got stuck in traffic. They'd had about-to-be-transplanted hearts dropped and kicked about like a football, Hard Rock beating instead. He could see 'False Hope' working towards accidental decapitation; how shocking could shocking get? Nothing, right now, seemed much worse than not being over-worried about leaving Harry with Paul.

He turned away from the piece of paper and tried to find distraction from activity on the pavement. The taxi made a spurt forward, and it crossed his mind to tell the driver to take him to Onslow Square, but he remained silent. He had arranged to meet Angel at the restaurant and he didn't want to be late, for her to think for a moment that he might have changed his mind and gone home instead; although perhaps what concerned him more was that she might have the same change of mind and the talking things over never take place.

He got there first and took a seat at the bar to wait. The soon to be famous owner, Rowley Leigh, bought him a drink and introduced him to his ex-wife who had just delivered a new novel. Talking books he could do on autopilot, his gaze flicking back and forth from the door.

When Angel arrived she was still in the black suit she wore for work. He saw her first, and in that moment it was in the same way he had watched her years and years ago when she still belonged to Paul, a curious, involuntary trick of memory that made him wonder just what it was he hoped to achieve from this evening and why it had seemed so important to meet away from the flat. He knew, even before she saw him and started towards where he was sitting, that there was an inexorable hopelessness about the whole enterprise, except that he still loved her.

'Mystery surrounds,' she said, lightly kissing him, then easing herself on to the neighbouring bar stool.

'I just thought we could do with a night out,' he said, hearing how disingenuous this sounded and already seeing that she would soon despise him for his manipulative motives. Again, he felt the ghost of Shepherd's Bush, as if he were right back at the beginning with her, only he couldn't delude himself that she might be there, too. Her manner was almost Keith-like, semi-professional, the polite, well-intentioned, even open-minded lawyer meeting a client she had dealt with before. He could add to this that the client was difficult and tricky, a proven source of grief and as likely as not ready to repeat the process.

'Only, I don't think we should be too late,' she said, sounding like a mother.

'No. No, of course not. Sara, this is Angel,' he said, as the novelist, who had slipped away for a moment, returned to the bar. 'My wife,' he added, tasting the words like chocolate after Lent. Perhaps it had been a stroke of genius coming out like this. He felt suddenly hopeful.

'Hello, and congratulations,' Sara said.

Angel smiled but looked unmistakably puzzled.

'I understand you've recently had a baby,' Sara went on. Jeremy felt his scalp tingle. It was like being complimented on getting a prize you had won by default.

'I don't know where she heard it,' he murmured over Angel's shoulder as they moved away from the bar and across the restaurant to their table. Angel had maintained her smile and thanked Sara, even gone on to 'A boy. Harry.'

'I suppose we have to come up with a story,' she said as they settled into their seats. 'About Harry.'

'We don't have to,' he said.

'I think we do. It's going to be awkward if people are starting to know. I think the three of us should agree on the same story, don't you?'

'How about the simple truth?'

Angel gave him a lawyerish look, but she was still on his side at this stage. He wondered how long before she switched. They might get through to the pudding.

'I think Harry being black will help,' she said. 'We can just say that we're helping Paul.'

'Sounds a bit thin. How many similar situations do you know of, or have even heard of? People don't live like that.'

'People live in all sorts of ways these days. Haven't you heard? The family as we knew it has passed into legend. Can we order? I'm starving.'

Jeremy tried to concentrate on the menu, but failed. Someone across the room was staring at him, as if they knew what was in his heart. It was a rude, intrusive stare that took him back to that Sunday in Aldeburgh when Marsha'd had the same treatment. That's what you got for being on telly, but she was unperturbed, accepting the inevitable. They never talked about her now, even though each of them must have her in their thoughts. Three different Marshas. His version had long ago ceased to be the amiable and compliant woman that made up the foursome. His Marsha was insular and cruel, and in all probability duplicitous.

He stopped himself from this train of thought, knowing it

was now part of the disengaging process he had set upon. He did not want to think badly of Marsha and felt he diminished himself by doing so. Whatever she had done, she had paid too high a price.

Angel was gazing at him.

'You were miles away,' she said. 'Have you decided?'

'I can't decide,' he said, then, 'I'll have the same as you.'

'But you don't like fish.'

They looked at one another. The room was getting noisy as neighbouring tables began to fill up with early evening diners.

'A decision has to be made, you know,' Angel said. They held one another's gaze, and Jeremy thought then that she knew. 'Whether it's the truth or some kind of variation, the three of us must agree and stick to it.'

'Surely we can leave it a bit longer,' he said, resuming an unseeing study of the menu.

'Why? The situation isn't going to change.'

'We don't know that.'

'What are you saying?'

'Ready to order?' A girl with an Australian accent had arrived at his side.

'Five more minutes,' Angel said quickly. 'Jeremy?'

'I'm not saying anything,' he said, backing off, unable, now that they were here, away from the flat, just as he'd planned, to express the awful doubt that had grown into certainty. And even if he told her, he already knew what she would say and how she would feel. Angel had made her decision and it was about the baby, nothing to do with the biological stuff. She would despise him if he told her how important it was to him, just as she had at the beginning and during the pregnancy. It wouldn't matter that there was absolute consistency in the way he felt. She wouldn't see it like that. And, of course, she'd be right, in a sense, but that still didn't alter the way he felt.

'I know you'll think this sounds pathetic,' she was saying, 'but I love it that Harry's black.'

He looked up at her.

'Well, I do. And in a way it does make it easier. I mean, it has to be obvious that he's . . .' She halted, trains of thought transparent as they crossed the table.

'You think so?'

'Well, the four of us. He has to be Marsha's child. Everyone will know that.'

One minute he thought she knew and the next he wasn't so sure.

'You're right, though. We don't have to decide on the story tonight, and we shouldn't really, not without Paul.'

This might have been his cue to steer the conversation on towards blood tests, but instead he told her he had decided on an omelette.

Fatal choice, and he hadn't meant it to be. She didn't have to say 'Do you remember?' or anything like that, because he did, they both did, straightaway.

'Can't we talk the way we used to? Just for tonight?' she pleaded.

He gazed at her steadily for a few moments, thinking how very much he loved her and wishing their life could be straightforward again. Why not? he thought. Just for tonight. What harm to pretend? If he reverted to the agenda he had planned there was every chance they would never have another evening like this.

So he let her begin, and soon he was there, too, in the inconsequentiality of new books and old books, people on television, stories in newspapers, and lawyers behaving badly out of court.

With a second bottle of wine they fine-tuned to the old shorthand, saying a lot without so many words, drawing on shared knowledge and understanding. They were high on it long before the wine took any effect. Living together again, sleeping in the same bed, making love, none of it had renewed the intimacy they'd managed to resurrect this evening, barging past mouthfuls of fish and omelette, puddings that tasted like, well, like something you remembered as fantastically good.

He could see in her eyes that she saw the whole thing continuing, that they would go back to Onslow Square and make love, and in the morning they'd recognise it all as having been a new beginning.

He called for the bill, hoping to pre-empt her reminding him that they'd said they would not be late back, not wanting the intrusion of their obligation, although she didn't see it like that, not any more. That was the trouble, the impossible conundrum; but hadn't he always known that she would come round, that she would love the baby when the time came.

Out in the street they grabbed a taxi. Angel was still talking, but he wasn't listening now, or couldn't hear. The closer they came to Onslow Square the further away he wanted to be. His chest began to feel tight. Angel was quiet now, perhaps sensing a shift, but then she reached for his hand, her fingers light and cool.

They had turned into the street, the driver asking which number, but they were already outside the flat.

Angel got out and turned to wait for him.

'Look,' he said. 'You go in. I have to go to the office for a while.'

He didn't miss the dismay, wiping out everything that during the course of the evening he had tricked her into believing, maybe even tricked himself for a bit. The taxi moved off. 'Where to, then?' the driver was asking. He turned, as if it could be in the least appropriate to wave, but she had already disappeared.

He slouched back in the seat and then gave the driver Sybil's address.

# CHAPTER THIRTY

'What are you up to, Jeremy?' Angel murmured to herself after a deep breath. She was standing inside the portico, waiting a moment or two in the darkest recess before fetching out her key and then having to face Paul. Her legs seemed to have lost their strength and she was beginning to tremble. She felt an utter fool, like a teenager who'd been stood up by some careless boy outside the cinema. How could she keep allowing Jeremy to do this to her? He must have planned the entire evening as some sort of game. It was as if he had become addicted to complication. But even as she thought this and began to let anger take over, she didn't doubt that he was playing in earnest, as he always had and always would.

She took another breath and faced the door.

There was no light in the hall and no sounds coming from any of the rooms. She went through to the bedroom she supposedly shared with Jeremy and where the baby's crib stood in a corner. She crept over to it and peered down at the small dark head, then instinctively bent closer, making sure of the breathing.

She retraced her steps, lightly, her shoes discarded by the bed, crossed the hall and opened the door to the drawing room where a table lamp in the far corner shed the only light.

Beside it, Paul was stretched out deck-chair fashion in one of the big armchairs they had brought from the farmhouse.

'Hello,' he mouthed, and Angel guessed he must have had a time of it with Harry.

'How long has he been asleep?'

'Not long. I think he wondered where you were.'

'Oh, Paul, he hardly knows whether it's day or night.' She flopped in the chair opposite and flung back her head.

'Did you have a good time?' Angel hated the humility and gratitude she heard hanging round everything Paul said now. He'd gone through the angry bit and the maudlin stage and now he was in the 'I don't deserve all this kindness' phase, which was bollocks because none of it had anything to do with kindness any more, if it ever had. They were each of them trapped, willingly or otherwise, Jeremy, it now seemed, the latter.

'The answer to that is yes, thank you, I did have a good time,' she said, with the flat sarcasm of the teenager outside the cinema.

'Doesn't sound like it.'

'Jeremy is up to his old tricks,' she said.

'Ah.'

'I don't know what game he is playing, but he is being as only Jeremy can be.'

'You're upset, aren't you?'

'Of course, I'm upset. I don't like games, not any more. I want straightforward.'

'You never used to.'

'Perhaps I've changed. The trouble is, I don't think Jeremy has and he never will.'

'I don't think you have either.'

'Thanks a lot.'

'I didn't mean it like that.'

'Like what?'

'Look, Angel, if you want to have a row I think you should wait until Jeremy gets back. Where is he, by the way?'

'He said he had to go to the office.'

'You don't believe him?'

'Yes! No. Oh, I don't know.' She was leaning forward now, rocking slightly, back and forth.

'I've been thinking,' Paul said. 'Perhaps it would be better if I moved out, let you two have some space.'

'But this is your flat, not ours. If there's any moving out to be done it ought to be me and Jeremy who go. And Harry,' she added, suddenly cautious, then alarm falling over her like a suffocating blanket.

'And Harry,' Paul echoed.

'You weren't thinking . . .'

'Angel, I've been sitting here trying to see a way.' He paused, got up, went towards the window, his back to her. A split second of déjà vu shuddered through her. She was frightened of him again, but it was different this time, worse in a way she could not have imagined then.

'I can't stand this repeat of Shepherd's Bush,' he was saying. 'Watching you two getting it together again, and Harry, I don't want to lose him any more than I wanted to lose you then, but I can see that I will. It's inevitable.'

She wanted to say 'You give up too easily. You always have,' but her training kept her quiet. She was listening to him give up the baby without a fight.

'I thought, if I moved out of here for a bit, you and Jeremy could have time to find somewhere else. I could go to a hotel.'

'It doesn't seem right,' she said. 'Besides, Marsha wanted us to, well . . .'

'Look after me,' he supplied, turning now to face her. 'Angel, I don't want to be looked after, not by you, not by Jeremy. I've had too much looking after. I don't want to sound ungrateful.' There's no danger of that, thought Angel, and then felt horribly mean. 'I just think it's time I, well, buggered off and left you two to get on with your life.'

'What will you do?' she asked, sensing a terrible fragility, as if it would take no more than a misplaced cough or a sneeze to break the moment, although now that it had all

233

been said was there anywhere else for Paul to go but out of their lives, at least for a time?

'I'll get a job,' he said. 'I should be able to bullshit my way into something. In fact, I could probably buy my way into something.'

'When will you go?'

'In the morning.'

'So soon,' she heard herself say, the reality striking home with an unexpected sense of loss.

'Well, there's no point in hanging around, is there?'

'You've already packed a bag, haven't you?'

'Yes.' He came and sat down again. 'Angel, there's something I want to say to you.' He seemed to have lost the calm, measured way he had said all the rest. 'It's about that night at the farmhouse.'

'Paul,' she began.

'I've never been able to get it out of my mind, and every time we've been alone together I've wondered. You see, I can't stand the thought that you might be afraid of me. You're not, are you?'

She looked at him and tried to fathom just what it was he needed to hear, and whether there was any vestige of fear in being with him, like tonight, because she'd realised that Jeremy would not be coming back.

'Only a little,' she said, at last.

Later in the night, after Harry had woken for his feed and she'd settled him again, she remained awake, trying to imagine the future, all of it uncertain again. At three am she got up and went to Paul's room. She didn't knock or hesitate, just slipped in quietly and sat on the edge of the bed until he stirred and opened his eyes.

'I don't want you to leave,' she said. 'Promise me you won't leave.'

He went to switch on the bedside lamp.

'No, don't. There's enough light from the moon,' she insisted.

'I don't know why I said that nonsense about being afraid, a little afraid of you. I'm very afraid of you, and of Jeremy and of myself. None of us can do this alone. Even Jeremy could see that. You can't just walk away from it, none of us can.'

As if to contradict her, he said, 'Jeremy's not back?'

'No.' She shivered.

'Come on, get in,' he said, lifting the cover beside him.

She rolled into the bed. She was indeed very cold.

'Where d'you think he's gone?' she said, still trembling.

'Probably kipping down at the office. He's done it before.'

'You two are both inclined to disappear when you're most needed. I don't trust either of you?'

'I'm not going to try anything.'

'I never thought you were. Just give me a hug, will you.'

'Is that better?'

'D'you think you could bear to stay?'

'God, Angel, you don't want much, do you?'

At some point in the night, dreaming about Jeremy, one of those awful, frightening dreams where she had become invisible to him, Angel registered the male body beside her and in semi-conscious relief linked her legs into his and began to move against him.

He did not respond at first, just held her. Then she felt his arousal beginning to match hers, and with a delicate precision she hardly remembered, he entered her, kissing her face but not her mouth until she gasped with the realisation that it was Paul.

He didn't stop and she didn't want him to, not now. It was too late; the thing had to be played out, a friendship that had become loving again. He was as gentle as she remembered from all those years ago, wiping out that other memory when he had come to the farmhouse for a kind of revenge. It was like two different people, the Paul who was inside her now, finding the right places, careful and considerate.

He didn't speak, not until it was over and they were lying side by side and she reached for his hand.

235

She was the first to apologise, and not just for using him in this way, but for everything that had messed up their lives.

'Don't,' he said, kissing the side of her head. 'I've got plenty to be sorry about, too.'

'Do you ever. . .?' She paused.

'. . . wonder about what would have happened if it had been us?' he said.

'Yes.'

'But it wasn't.' Then he added, 'And it isn't. You thought I was Jeremy just now, at the beginning, didn't you, and I . . .' he trailed off.

She encircled him in her arms again and they remained like that until grey light appeared.


'You don't know what you want, do you?' Sybil was sitting on the edge of his desk, as so often in the past, although there had been quite a gap. 'Poor old thing,' she added, in her knitted-cardigan voice. 'Would you like me to buy you a beer?'

She was trying not to sound triumphant. He felt bad about the previous night, but contrary to appearances Sybil was a grown up and she had just said it herself, he didn't know what he wanted. Except he did. He wanted Angel without the baby and without Paul. He wanted to rewind back a year, but with Angel as she was now. It amounted to not knowing what he wanted, the same no-man's-land.

He followed Sybil out of the office and to a rather sad bar that had fallen out of fashion. It seemed that she wanted to talk, and he really couldn't blame her, not after the way he had assumed a welcome last night. He could have talked then, but she was out of it, he hoped on the harvest from her window-sill rather than anything more sinister.

'So,' she said, setting down the two glasses of ale, 'does this mean you're coming back?'

He was surprised by this uncharacteristic directness, but even in his present confused state was able to field the question in a way that sent it straight back to her.

'Would you like me to?'

Sybil's gaze dropped, the boldness used up too soon.

'What's going on, Jez?' she asked in a small voice.

He took a long breath. He had to tell someone.

'I don't think Harry is my child,' he said.

She waited for him to go on. There had been no sign of surprise.

'He's, well, oh, God, he's too black.'

Sybil lifted her glass and swished the beer round a little, but didn't take a sip.

'I can't believe I said that,' he went on. 'It sounds positively racist.'

'Not really,' Sybil murmured, but then things were going in a direction that might suit her.

'It does, even though it isn't,' Jeremy insisted.

'Did . . .' she hesitated, again swishing the beer, a little splashing on to the table this time. 'Did Marsha every actually say that the baby was yours?'

'Not in so many words, although there were a number of occasions when it might have been easier for her if she had. That's part of the problem.'

'Perhaps she didn't know.'

'For God's sake, I don't think she was like that.'

'But you're saying that she probably was. What was she like? You've never talked about her, not once.'

'I'm not sure I knew her at all. I think she could have been one of those people everyone thinks is very nice, but if anyone had ever really got to know her they might have found there wasn't much there. I don't think she was all that interested in other people. I remember once talking with her about someone we both had a lot of contact with, but Marsha knew nothing about them, that this person had written an opera and had been married three times, the sort of stuff most of us remember about other people. But Marsha just wasn't aware. All of it passed her by.'

'What about her husband? What about Paul? Doesn't he ever say anything about her? What she was like?'

'No, but he doesn't say much at all, not now. Of the three of us I suppose he's the one that's changed the most. I've known him practically all my life, but I don't feel I know him any more either, even though we've been living in the same flat for the past weeks. I used to know what he was going to say and do before he did himself, but these days I haven't a clue. It's as if he's finally grown up.'

'Does that make you sad?'

'I hadn't really thought, but yes, I suppose it does. It's another indication that nothing is as it was.'

'And you'd like it to be?' The small voice again, flat and ready to be disappointed.

He took a gulp of beer. He felt a little better. He couldn't remember another time when he had talked so frankly to anyone. Perhaps he had changed.

'And Angel?' she said next, as if running through the cast list and finally reaching the part she wanted for herself. Did it sound like that? More beer on the table. She had not drunk any yet. She doubted she could swallow.

'Angel,' he echoed. 'Syb, am I expecting too much, loading you up with all this confessional stuff?'

'Yes, you are,' she said, because she'd never been able to be dishonest with him. 'But that doesn't mean I want you to stop.'

This little exchange could not fail to alter the way he would proceed.

'I'm being unfair, aren't I?' He looked at her with even greater unfairness, because he was fond of her and didn't want to hurt her even though he kept doing so.

'Tell me about the new TV series. How's it going?' he said.

'Oh, you can't do that,' she said, warningly. 'That's tantamount to coitus-whatsit.'

'Interruptus,' he supplied, unthinkingly.

'I'm not that daft. I was just being fey. Maybe you don't know me as well as you thought, either.'

238

Her unexpected sharpness made him recoil and wish he had not, after all, gone against the code of behaviour that had always favoured less rather than more.

An awkward silence ensued, and his thoughts drifted back to the baby. Grace would be the only person who would properly understand, but understand what? That one moment you could feel totally committed and the next hardly at all? He was ashamed of the switch but could not deny it to himself. He could not spend the next however many years, the rest of his life, pretending. He thought about the previous evening with Angel and how they had managed, so easily it had seemed, to avoid any mention of Harry, even though every conversation during the preceding days had centred on his well-being and whether they were absolutely happy with the arrangement that was now to be put in place – the nanny, Celia, who would come to the flat each morning as they left and disappear again in the evenings the moment one or the other returned. Paul they had not yet taken into the equation at a practical level, not until last night, the first time they had left him alone with the baby. Perhaps this meant neither of them considered Paul in need of looking after any more. It was possible that Paul had come through it ahead of them after all.

'Angel,' Sybil was saying. 'You haven't told me what she feels about all this, what she wants to do?'

He left it too long to answer.

'You haven't told her.'

'Angel,' he said, with complete certainty, 'will choose the baby.'

'Then so will you,' she said, with fatalistic weariness. 'Won't you?'

# CHAPTER THIRTY-ONE

A ngel never thought she would welcome a visit from her mother-in-law, especially an unexpected one.

In her now customary Afghan uniform, complete with bandanna strapped around her forehead, Grace swept into the hallway of the flat off Onslow Square, Wilfred in tow like a wire-haired lap dog tottering on its hindlegs. He had grown an Alan Yentob beard.

'I'm sorry, dear, but we really couldn't wait any longer for an invitation,' she said, with staggering rudeness. Only it wasn't really rude or staggering; she had every right, thought Angel, caught off guard in the backdraught as she closed the front door behind them.

'Where are the boys?' Grace demanded next. Then, 'And how are you, dear? Put on a little weight, I see. It suits you.'

'Oh,' murmured Angel, glancing down at herself in search of the weight. 'In the drawing room.'

'All right then, really?' Wilfred enquired in a conspiratorial way that had genuine kindness. Angel nodded and gave him a smile. Grace was already opening the drawing room door.

'So this is how you spend Sundays,' she exclaimed. Elaborate new kissing ensued, Paul and Jeremy shaking off the lethargy of afternoon.

'Just passing, Mother?' Jeremy said.

Grace gave him a look.

'Where's Harry?' she asked. 'Out riding his bicycle, or is he at university by now?'

'He's asleep in his crib,' Jeremy replied without inflexion, then shaking hands with Wilfred, who had emerged from behind Grace.

'Wilfred said he couldn't wait another minute, that he had to see the little chap,' Grace continued, Wilfred's eyes widening as Grace's did a sweep of the untidy room.

'Well, this all looks very cosy,' she said, finding a chair that wasn't strewn with newspapers.

'Mother, what are you doing here?' Jeremy asked.

'I told you, dear. Wilfred wanted to see . . .'

'Mother.'

The room became like a tableau, nobody quite sure of the next scene. There had been no contact with Grace since the day they'd taken Harry, and even though this had been achieved in what seemed like a civilised manner, bad feeling scratched round the civility. Grace had attempted a noble, self-sacrificing posture, but nobody was convinced. The novelty of having a baby in the house had simply worn off, but at the same time she couldn't resist indicating disapproval of the arrangement into which Harry was being transferred.

'Poor child will end up thoroughly confused,' she'd said; her parting shot, 'He won't know who his father is.'

This wasn't lost on any of them, although each, as Grace well knew, would apply a different interpretation.

'At least he won't think Wilfred is his mother,' Jeremy had murmured.

'Mother?' Jeremy repeated.

'Oh, I was feeling out of it, if you must know,' Grace said, immediately relaxing the tension in the room. 'Neglected, if you like.'

Jeremy softened, went over to her and planted a proper kiss on the bandanna.

'Sorry,' he said. 'I suppose we've all been a bit preoccupied these past weeks, finding a nanny . . .'

242

'A nanny?' Grace turned to look at Angel, who was still in the doorway.

'Yes, Mother, a nanny,' Jeremy pre-empted, seeing what was in Grace's mind. 'They are people who are properly trained to look after children.'

'And what do you think of all this, Paul?' Grace persisted, searching for an ally.

Paul smiled, but there was a shadow of concern in his expression. He moved towards Angel. 'I'll go and see if Harry is awake, shall I?' he said.

'I'll come with you,' piped up Wilfred.

'So,' Jeremy began, when it was just the three of them, 'you haven't got tired of poor old Wilf yet?'

'What's the matter, darling boy?' Grace asked. 'You're only like this when you're unhappy about something.'

'I think I'll go and make some tea,' Angel said, quietly.

In the kitchen she moved from cupboard to cupboard like a robot. Everything was about to come to a head, she could feel it, the tension of the past weeks suddenly beyond endurance. She didn't particularly blame Grace or Wilfred, or any of them; it was inevitable.

Ever since the evening she and Jeremy had been out for supper, he hadn't come back subsequent nights, two or three times a week. The fact was that she didn't ask him where he went because she had a pretty good idea. He said he worked through the night at the office so he could spend time with Harry during the day, but Paul said he was hardly ever there. She wondered whether she might have preferred it if Paul had lied, too, but then why should he?

She had replayed the evening in the restaurant, over and over, trying to fathom what it really was Jeremy had wanted to tell her that night. The inescapable conclusion had to be that he wanted to leave her, that he wanted to be with the albino stick-insect. But by now he must know there was absolutely no chance she would relinquish Harry, and he wouldn't leave without the baby. Stalemate. That's where they were. What they were, except she still loved him, felt her heart leap when he did come home.

It was probably only Paul's staying that had kept it all together, although she had seen the growing misery this was causing him. She had caught him watching them with the same look she remembered from the old Shepherd's Bush days, the last few weeks when she had moved out of his room so she could sleep with Jeremy. The cruelty of this appalled her now, and she wished that in some way she could make amends. Perhaps she should not have begged Paul to stay, but she would have felt so alone without him, even the nights Jeremy was home. It was with Paul she discussed the daily concerns over Harry's well-being, the trivial anxieties that seemed huge at the time; and, increasingly, Paul was the first to go to the baby in the evenings if he cried. 'You've been working all day,' he would say. He'd said nothing more about finding a job himself, but it was hardly a pressing need, not financially. Marsha's wealth had astounded all of them. Paul need never work again, except that he would have to find something to do with his time.

She couldn't think that far. She couldn't think beyond the end of Grace's visit. She collected all the tea things on to a tray, poured water into the pot and returned to the drawing room.

Wilfred was holding Harry. Grace and Jeremy were close by, but moved a little away as she came past them with the tray and set it down.

'He looks well,' Grace said to her, as if she had expected otherwise. 'Dear little chap, isn't he?'

'Yes,' she said, sensing ulterior ideas, starting to pour the tea.

'I was just saying to Jeremy. . .'

'Mother, please.'

'. . . how he must look like his mother,' Grace continued. The room had become airless.

'Of course he does,' Angel said, sounding prickly. Why

couldn't they just leave it alone, all this scrutiny? Harry was here and he was himself. That Jeremy was his father no longer made any difference to the way she felt about him; she loved him anyway and thought the two men did as well. It no longer seemed to matter which one of them happened to be the biological father.

'Well, I think he's just gorgeous,' cooed Wilfred, gently rocking the baby in his arms.

'So tell me about this nanny,' Grace said. 'Norland, is she? Your father once talked about getting a nanny for you, darling,' she added, glancing at Jeremy, 'but I wouldn't agree. I knew you'd be miserable with a stranger taking care of you.'

Jeremy didn't respond, but took a sip of his tea instead, then quickly put it down.

'I'm not sure she'll be a permanent fixture, actually,' Paul said, surprising all of them. 'I think Grace could be right. He has been more fretful since Celia took over.'

'Paul, you didn't say,' Angel said quietly. 'We'll have to find someone else.'

'I was thinking of taking on the job myself,' Paul said. He looked tight-chested, as if he was expecting opposition. But none came. 'I'm feeling much better now. You've all been so kind, but really, I have to accept my responsibilities.' He paused. It was like running down the pitch for a try, at any moment expecting a tackle, but the others were giving him a clear field.

Angel was stunned. Not by Paul, but by Jeremy, who wouldn't look at her. Without thinking, she went over to Wilfred and took the baby from him. She looked round the room again, at the others, and suddenly it felt as if she had stumbled across a conspiracy.

'What's going on?' she demanded of Jeremy, too alarmed now to care if they had a row in front of his mother.

'Nothing's going on,' he said, but still wouldn't look at her.

'Jeremy, please,' she insisted. Harry began to whimper.

'Give the baby to me,' Grace commanded.

'I'm not giving him to anyone,' Angel said, becoming incredulous. 'I want to know what's going on.'

'If Paul wants to look after Harry then why not?' Jeremy said, lamely, at last meeting her stare.

'But it's not just the looking after, is it?'

'I think it would be better if the three of us talked about this later,' Paul said.

'No,' Angel insisted, her stare still on Jeremy. 'We should sort it out now, whatever it is.' Harry was revving up big sobs.

'Oh, dear,' Grace sighed. 'Do give me the child.'

'Please,' Angel's anguish was painful for all of them. 'Tell me what's going on.'

'I think Jeremy may have been having a few doubts,' Paul began.

'About what?' Angel cried.

'About Harry,' Grace said, looking sorrowful. 'I'm right, I think?' She glanced at her son.

Jeremy moved away from the group.

'About Harry?' Angel's surprise exposed the other insecurity that had been uppermost in her mind.

'Look at him, Angel. Look at him,' Grace said. 'Can you see the slightest resemblance to my son?'

'How can you let this happen?' Angel accused Jeremy.

'I've been thinking about blood tests,' Jeremy spoke at last.

'You bastard!'

'Angel, please!' Grace sniffed.

Harry had gone quiet and still, as if he sensed the momentous nature of what was happening.

'I have to know,' Jeremy continued. 'I'm sorry, Angel, and Paul's right, this isn't the time to discuss it.'

'So you didn't plan this visitation?'

'Of course he didn't,' Grace said, huffily, but she was too alert to it all, too ready to stay.

'I think you've made up your mind already,' Angel said, Jeremy's increasing absences falling into place. 'You always do, long before you consult me.'

'I think what matters is that we're talking about it now,' Paul said, sounding calm and equitable.

'You knew, didn't you?' Angel turned her accusation on him.

'No, I didn't, actually.'

Another realisation hit Angel, and she wondered how hard it must have hit Paul, too. They'd both been duped.

'I don't understand,' she murmured, her thoughts shifting to Marsha. 'Why didn't she say?'

'Perhaps she wasn't sure,' Paul said, and Angel's heart ached for him. It must have taken a lot to say that. Then her concern shifted back to the immediate crisis. She looked down at Harry, into the dark eyes fixedly gazing at her, as if waiting for a decision.

'I can't give him up,' she said quietly.

'No,' murmured Jeremy. 'Of course you can't.'

They looked at one another, and Angel thought her heart would break. The baby began to feel heavy in her arms. She sat down. She felt slightly dizzy.

The room had gone very quiet. It seemed that none of them, not even Grace, knew where to go next.

'You know, I think you must have forgotten to boil the kettle,' Wilfred spoke, adding a nervous little laugh. 'My tea's stone cold.'

# CHAPTER THIRTY-TWO

It was Angel's mother who insisted on a party for Harry's first birthday. Balloons, cake, jelly, the whole bag, even though Harry himself was still more interested in his own fingers than the social event that was in his honour.

Audrey had made a large cake in the shape of a steam train and placed the single candle on the top of its funnel. She had painted a big round face to make the train look like Thomas the Tank Engine, but part of the icing had slipped, giving him the appearance of having had a stroke.

Audrey brushed aside the rude and unkind comments from her family and plunged in the knife. Harry, now set down on the floor, was chugging towards Paul, who, with Angel's father and brother, was drinking beer and snatching moments of cricket on the telly.

The pieces of cake were put on to plates which Angel's sister-in-law then took round the room. Everyone kept insisting that Angel should do nothing, and with the heat of late summer she would not argue. She had put on barely a stone, but she felt heavy and dreamy. She glanced over at Paul, who caught her look and smiled.

She returned the smile and then followed her mother to the kitchen where the debris of the cake had been taken.

'Are you sure you're getting enough rest?' her mother

asked almost as soon as she appeared in the doorway. 'You're no chicken, you know, for the first time. You must take it easy, darling, not work too hard, especially with Harry to contend with when you get in at night.'

'I'm all right,' Angel said. 'Really.'

She went back into dreamy as her mother set about the kitchen. The sequence began with Jeremy and the night they had been to the restaurant, just the two of them. There had been so much she wanted to say that night, things that had been said since, and things that had not. She had always taken it for granted that Jeremy was the clever one of the three of them and would somehow manage to sort everything out. She had even believed this, somewhere in the back of her mind, when everything was at its worst – the horrid pokey flat in Cambridge and poor pokey Terry, who she had worn like a hair shirt and then become one herself for him.

And Jeremy had sorted it all out in the end, of course he had. Although she'd still been angry with him when he came to Cambridge, even if it felt like rescue. Then everything that had happened after that, the awful sadness over Marsha, through all of it there had been a core of brilliant happiness, a feeling complete again. The arguments continued, but the pit was no longer bottomless because they were together again and it felt right. For a while, at least.

Then, as Paul found the beginnings of calm and Jeremy turned edgy and remote, it seemed as if the reconciliation had, after all, been no more than a false dawn. Perhaps you couldn't go back, or if you did, things could never be the same.

The day it all came to a head, when Grace and Wilfred turned up at Onslow Square, she'd felt even more estranged from Jeremy than she had during the time they were living apart. It seemed incredible she hadn't known what was in his mind, the huge mass of doubt.

When, at last, Grace and Wilfred left, Paul too went out, taking Harry with him.

'Where do we go from here?' Jeremy said, when they were alone, but neither of them could see the way forward.

They talked about blood tests and then about the evening they had spent at the restaurant. She was beyond anger. All she felt was a terrible hopelessness that it mattered so much to Jeremy whether or not Harry was his son; that it seemed he would never be able to love him as she did, regardless of blood tests.

They were in bed when Paul and Harry returned. Making love had seemed the only thing they could do, the only comfort they could offer one another. They lay listening to the sounds of Paul moving about the flat, running water for Harry's bath.

'When will you go?' she said.

'Can you get me some clingfilm from the cupboard over there,' her mother was saying, 'the one next to the washing machine.'

Angel obliged and then continued her reverie, gazing without much attention through the window and to the garden where Jeremy, Grace and Wilfred were standing at the far end of the lawn. She sighed.

'All right, darling?' her mother asked.

'Oh, yes,' she said, 'I'm fine.'

'Only another month, six weeks to go,' Audrey added. 'And the weather will be cooler then.'

'Umm.' Angel looked out to the garden again, and as if he had felt her gaze, Jeremy turned his head towards the house.

'All I know is that it's no life without you,' he had said. 'And you can't say I haven't done my best to prove it otherwise. And I've missed Harry.' He had been gone four months, during which time they had not seen one another; he hadn't known about the baby. Perhaps he would not have come to the flat that night if he had. This was something neither of them would ever quite know for sure. Equally, was there absolute certainty that things would have resolved themselves as they had without Sybil's final push? Angel had never met

251

her, but had seen her on television sounding all poetic about tubers and brassicas, crumbs of peat dripping through her fingers. She rather liked her style, although she couldn't bear to watch for too long. Jealousy would begin to bite into her throat, despite the gratitude.

'And only another four days before Paul goes,' her mother was saying.

Jeremy had come back and Paul had surprised them both by announcing that he had been offered a job that would take him back to America. Sasha Parrish was setting up her own business and wanted his help.

'You don't think he's making it up?' she had said to Jeremy.

'Possibly.'

'But that's terrible. He's been so, well, marvellous, really, looking after Harry until he started going to the nursery, and being such a friend again to me.' She chose the words carefully, not wanting to stir more jealousy, especially as friendship was all that it had been since that one night.

'He can always come back here, back to us, can't he?' she said.

'He is, in effect, our landlord.'

'I didn't mean it like that.'

'And neither did I.'

'I'm never quite certain what you mean these days.'

'I thought we'd both learnt to live with uncertainty.'

'Have we?'

'I think so, in some things, anyway.'

They were thinking along the same track, but she had to say it: 'Jeremy, just supposing this baby . . .'

'I think we've been through that one, don't you?'

They held each others' gaze, clear eyed, and for longer than people who did not love one another could have tolerated.

# SOME OTHER READING
*from*
# BRANDON

# MARIE MCGANN
## *The Drawbridge*

"Isn't it good? Marie McGann is a real find. She writes with the exhilaration and defiance of youth and the wisdom of age. A moving and triumphant novel." Fay Weldon

Brid Finucane lives in a state of ordered chaos in both her head and her house. When her husband disappears, she is forced to confront her past and its sad consequence, together with lone motherhood, alcoholism and a Polish war hero as a suitor. Her swirls of emotion are compounded by her position as an expatriate Irishwoman living in a North London suburb.

Set amongst the Polish community in Crouch End, this exceptional novel explores both Irish and Polish experiences of alienation, while at its core it is a story about the hard choices in a woman's life: choices about love and independence, loyalty and dependence.

Marie McGann was born in a village in County Galway in the west of Ireland; she trained as a nurse before entering university to study dentistry. While at Galway university she met and soon married a Polish Battle of Britain pilot, moving to Crouch End in London. There she worked as a dentist for the Haringey Health Authority and became part of the Polish community, learning their language and singing their songs. After twenty-three years of marriage, she was amicably divorced and now still lives in Crouch End with her two cats and her wild garden.

ISBN 0 86322 271 4; Paperback £9.99

# Barbara Rees
## Oscar's Tale

A Latin-American dictatorship; an emigré in London; echoes of Pinochet in a family's hidden history of complicity in torture.

At the age of thirty Oscar somehow finds the courage to take off from Costa Negra to London to make a new life for himself. With some difficulty he comes to terms with the city and manages to find himself a wife, a family and a job. He is very happy but for the thought that one day real life, in the form of his formidable mother, will undoubtedly catch up with him.

She duly descends upon London, and her arrival brings Oscar face to face, for the first time in his life, with the facts he has tried desperately to ignore – the basis for the family fortune, and his mother's part as an ally of the dictatorship in Costa Negra. In a dramatic climax Oscar uses his newly found strength to force his mother, in her turn, to confront her past.

Barbara Rees is the author of six previous books: *Try Another Country*, *Diminishing Circles*, *Prophet of the Wind*, *George and Anna*, *The Victorian Lady* and *Harriet Dark*, and she was Arts Council Creative Writing Fellow at the North London Polytechnic. She has worked for the United Nations in Rome and New York, and in 1981 she gave up writing for a time to work for an international charity. She lives in Hampstead in London.

ISBN 0 86322 268 4; Paperback £8.99

# KITTY FITZGERALD
## *Snapdragons*

"A unique and extremely engaging story of two sisters, each of whom is looking for love and salvation in their different ways." *Irish Post*

"An original, daring book." *Books Ireland*

Sometimes shocking, frequently humorous, often surreal, *Snapdragons* is a rites of passage novel about a young woman who grows up unhappily in rural Ireland after World War II. She is disliked – for reasons she cannot understand – by her parents, and has a running feud with her sister. Yet the mood of this story is strangely light-hearted, frequently comic and absolutely memorable.

She makes her escape to the English midlands, and works and lives in a pub in Digbeth, Birmingham, where her sister has settled with her husband. Her already difficult relationship with her sister is further strained when she discovers how she is living. She also learns the sad reason for her parents' hostility towards her.

A captivating story of a young girl in Birmingham and the North of England in the 1950s, its main protagonist, Bernadette, who carries on a constant angry dialogue with God, is one of the most delightfully drawn characters in recent Irish fiction.

ISBN 0 86322 258 7; Original Paperback £8.99